THE MONGOL ASCENSION

IMBRIFEX.
BOOKS

ALSO BY ANDREW VARGA

The Last Saxon King
A Jump in Time Novel, Book One

The Celtic Deception
A Jump in Time Novel, Book Two

THE MONGOL ASCENSION

A JUMP IN TIME NOVEL
BOOK THREE

ANDREW VARGA

IMBRIFEX BOOKS

IMBRIFEX BOOKS
8275 S. Eastern Avenue, Suite 200
Las Vegas, NV 89123
Imbrifex.com

IMBRIFEX.
BOOKS

THE MONGOL ASCENSION: A JUMP IN TIME NOVEL, BOOK THREE

Library of Congress Cataloging-in-Publication Data

Names: Varga, Andrew, 1969- author.
Title: The Mongol ascension / Andrew Varga.
Description: First edition. | Las Vegas, NV : Imbrifex Books, 2024. |
    Series: A jump in time ; book 3 | Audience: Ages 12-18. | Audience:
    Grades 7-9. | Summary: To stop a band of rogue time jumpers from taking
    over the world, teens Dan and Sam jump back in time to 1179 Mongolia
    where they are up against the clock to save the Mongol Empire.
Identifiers: LCCN 2023036527 (print) | LCCN 2023036528 (ebook) | ISBN
    9781955307048 (hardcover) | ISBN 9781955307079 (paperback) | ISBN
    9781955307055 (epub) | ISBN 9781955307062
Subjects: CYAC: Time travel--Fiction. | Mongolia--History--To
    1500--Fiction. | LCGFT: Historical fiction. | Novels.
Classification: LCC PZ7.1.V39635 Mo 2024 (print) | LCC PZ7.1.V39635
    (ebook) | DDC [Fic]--dc23
LC record available at https://lccn.loc.gov/2023036527
LC ebook record available at https://lccn.loc.gov/2023036528

Cover design: Jason Heuer
Book design: John Hall Design Group
Author photo: Andrew Johnson
Typeset in ITC Berkeley Oldstyle

Printed in the United States of America
Distributed by Publishers Group West
First Edition: September 2024

For my mom and dad,
who started me on my historical journey,
and to all the teachers who guided me along the way.

And, as always, for Pam, Leah, Arawn, and Calvin

Qara'atu tuk-īyan sacuba bi
Qara buqa-yin arasun-niyar büriksen bürkiren büküi dawutu kö'ürge-ben
deletbe bi
Qara qurdun-iyan unuba bi
Qatangqu de'el-iyen emüsbe bi
Qatan jida-ban bariba bi
Qatqurasutu sumun-iyan onolaba bi
Qa'at-Merkit-tür qadquldun morilaya

I have made offerings to the long spear-tipped banner
I have beaten the bellowing drum made of the black bull's hide
I have mounted my swift black horse
I have put on my strong clothing
I have grasped my iron-tipped spear
I have set my peach-bark arrow
Let us ride against the Qa'at-Merkits

Secret History of the Mongols, chapter 106
Anonymous author, thirteenth century

CHAPTER 1

My phone vibrated on the cafeteria table, its rumble barely audible over the wall of noise surrounding me. After a morning spent cooped up inside classrooms, it felt like every single kid in my high school was shouting, laughing, slamming chairs, and generally being as rowdy as freakin' possible. I glanced at the screen, expecting spam, but startled when I saw the name: J. Patenall.

No way!

I couldn't miss this call. I covered one ear with a hand, trying to block out the noise as I moved to a quieter corner.

"Hello?" I answered, my eyes sweeping the room to make sure no one was listening in. Who was I kidding, though? Seven months into the school year, and I was still the new kid. No one knew me, and no one cared what I did.

"Hello, this is Professor Patenall. Is this Dan?" He sounded fairly disinterested. He probably figured I was just another one of his students begging for an extension.

"Yes, Dan Renfrew."

"Renfrew? Are you . . . in one of my classes?"

7

Now came the hard part—keeping him from hanging up. "No, I—my dad was James Renfrew. He died a few months ago. You might have been at the funeral." Not that I could remember—Dad's funeral had been one big blur of faces and names.

"Oh, yes, of course . . ." I could hear the hesitation in his voice. "I'm so sorry about your father. I was horrified to hear of his passing. He was an esteemed colleague. How may I help you?"

"I was wondering if I could ask you about things related to his tattoo? The same tattoo that I have and . . . uh . . . I think you might have also?"

"No. No, I can't help you." A note of panic crept into his voice. "Please don't ever call me again." *Click.*

I exhaled slowly as my shoulders sagged. *What is wrong with these people?* I unfolded the worn piece of notepaper that I kept in my back pocket and found Professor Patenall's name among the countless crossed out ones. A few quick strokes of a pen and his name matched all the others. When I first started out, they had just been names in Dad's personal notebook, most of them with addresses in far-off locations. Hours of internet stalking had given me email addresses and phone numbers, but all had led to the same crappy result. Most of the people I'd connected with legitimately had no clue about my dad's tattoo and what it meant, which had led to some really awkward conversations where I tried not to sound like a weirdo. But then there had been a few like Patenall, clearly ex-time jumpers, who'd hung up as soon as I even tiptoed toward talking about time-jumping. I couldn't blame them for being scared, but why wouldn't they help me? After all, our lives had all been ruined by the same man—Congressman Victor Stahl.

Only three names remained on my list. I'd emailed them weeks ago but none of them had gotten back to me. Luckily one of them—Professor Gervers—worked at the same university my dad used to work at. Time to skip all the useless phone calls and emails and go for a face-to-face meeting.

I spun around, intent on finding a quieter spot outside the cafeteria, and ran straight into a tall, black-haired guy, knocking him to the ground. "Oh, geez! I'm really sorry," I sputtered as I offered him a hand up.

He swiped my hand aside with an irritated wave and pulled himself to his feet. Three other guys appeared instantly by his side. "Did you see what this moron just did?" he asked them, his lip curling into a sneer.

"Yeah, I saw it. He was right in your face," one of his friends replied.

Crap . . .

Of all the people to run into. Nick Fraser was a walking cliché: star varsity linebacker, rich, popular, threw the wildest parties. I didn't get invited to any of them, of course, but there was no escaping hearing about them. Nick was also the biggest bully in the school, which somehow increased his popularity, at least among the lucky ones who weren't his targets. His three sidekicks, Amir, Kyle, and Devon, were almost as obnoxious as Nick but without the rich parents. Together, they were the closest thing this school had to royalty.

"It was an accident." I tried to sound sincere even though I knew it wouldn't matter.

"I'll show you an accident," Nick growled as he dusted himself off.

Anyone else in this school would probably feel threatened. I'd seen guys actually get on their knees and beg Nick for forgiveness. But pretty much since birth my dad had trained me in martial arts and medieval weapons, so a handful of idiots with attitude didn't scare me. "Whatever. Look, I said I'm sorry. We're done."

"Who is this guy?" Nick asked, jerking his thumb in my direction.

Amir flicked his fingers dismissively. "Dan Renfrew. He's the guy whose dad died last semester. It was on the announcements."

"Oh, right." Nick stepped up to me so that our bodies were almost touching. He was taller than me, but not by much. He probably thought getting so close would be intimidating, but the only thing scary about him was his breath. "Watch your step, Renfrew, or there's going to be another funeral in your family."

I snorted and pushed past him and his friends. I had better things to do than listen to this idiot. I stepped out into the hall and the noise of the cafeteria faded behind me. Leaning against a wall of blue lockers, I found the number I'd saved in my phone. After about ten minutes of navigating the school's automated call system, I finally managed to speak to a real person who told me that the professor had open office hours today between three and four.

Perfect.

I'd drive to the university right after school. The big question was: did Professor Gervers actually know anything about time-jumping, or was he just another normal person like so many others on my list?

When the last bell finally rang, I tore off to my locker, grabbed my backpack, then raced down the steps leading outside. Little clumps of dirty snow still clung to the ground in some spots, but for the most part the grass was a muddy brown mess. The walkways were dry, though, and I dodged past the other kids on the way to the student lot across the road.

As soon as I stepped past the chain-link fence that marked the edge of school property, I knew I was in for trouble. Nick was leaning against a tree, arms crossed in front of him and an arrogant grin on his face. A crowd of kids milled around him, obviously waiting.

Not now . . .

I ignored him and continued toward the street.

Nick stepped in front of me while the crowd merged into a circle around us. I had no choice but to stop.

"You owe me, Renfrew," Nick growled, his eyes narrowing into slits.

I glanced at my phone. I had half an hour.

"Thinking of calling your dad for help?" Nick asked. "I don't think he's going to answer."

A chorus of *oooohs* came from the crowd, followed by a rush of chuckles.

Really? Dead parents are funny now?

My life had been pure hell since Dad died. The last thing I needed was attitude from some moron who thought he was king of the school. I relaxed my breathing and dropped my hands to my sides, ready for whatever this fool was going to bring. Nick thought I was one more weak target he could push around, but he'd picked the wrong guy.

Nick gave me a smirk. "You going to cry, Renfrew?"

"Look, I've got somewhere to be. Can we speed this up?" I turned around in a slow circle, scanning the crowd. As expected, spaced in even intervals were Nick's three friends. I pointed to them one by one. "I know you guys are going to jump me as soon as Nick looks even slightly in trouble, so can you at least step out front so I can see you?"

Amir, Kyle, and Devon exchanged confused glances as they stepped forward. I dropped my backpack and pulled off my hoodie. It was too baggy to fight in, and someone could yank my hood or sleeves and drag me down.

"You're pretty cocky for someone about to get his ass kicked," Nick said.

"And you talk pretty tough for a guy who needs half the football team to help him beat up one guy."

Nick's face turned red as the crowd started laughing. "That's it, Renfrew. You're dead!"

"Let's go," I said in a voice devoid of emotion.

In some primal part of Nick's brain, something must have finally clicked. His smug expression disappeared, and he looked hesitant. He was used to people cowering.

I wasn't cowering.

Although I'd only jumped through time twice, I'd already been beaten, kicked, stabbed, attacked by Norman cavalry, and enslaved by ancient Romans. Nothing Nick and his friends could dole out would amount to more than a light workout compared to all of that.

"Kick his ass, Nick," a girl yelled. I didn't recognize her, and I had no clue what I'd done to deserve her wrath. Others shouted encouragement, their phones held up, ready to capture the moment.

Nick seemed to find his courage in the crowd. He puffed his chest out and paced in front of me, performing for his audience. "You disrespected me in the cafeteria, Renfrew." He jabbed his finger in my direction. "No one disrespects me."

I glanced one more time at my phone and put it in my back pocket. "Can we skip the speeches? You're really starting to bore me."

Nick wheeled and threw a punch, trying to catch me unaware. I'd expected as much from a guy like him. I ducked and his arm sailed over my head. Before he could recover, my fist whipped out and caught him in the nose. I stepped into the punch, driving it with all my strength. Cartilage cracked, and Nick collapsed to his knees, both hands clutching his nose as blood streamed through his fingers.

One down, three to go.

If they were smart, they'd use their football skills and tackle me. I needed to take them down before they figured that out—or before any of the rest of the football team decided to jump in.

Amir closed in and threw a wild punch at me. I blocked his swing and kicked him in the groin. Dirty fighting on my part, but given the numbers, all rules were off. Amir's eyes bugged out and he crumpled forward, gripping his crotch.

Before he hit the ground, I spun to the side. I didn't want to stand still long enough to give them an easy target. A quick chop to the throat took Devon down, and he lay on the sidewalk, his face turning red as he coughed and choked.

Kyle gaped at me, all his swagger gone. His eyes darted from me to his friends on the ground, then back to me.

The crowd had grown silent. No one moved.

"We done here?" I asked.

He nodded timidly.

"Good." I picked up my hoodie and my backpack and pushed through the crowd. They parted quickly.

I started up Dad's old Audi and turned right out of the parking lot. Hopefully the traffic wouldn't be bad. More importantly, I hoped Professor Gervers actually knew something.

Pangs of guilt and sadness churned inside my chest as I drove through campus toward the Humanities building. Dad had worked at the university for as long as I could remember, but I'd hardly ever visited—I'd thought the place was old and boring, like him. Maybe if I'd shown more interest in him and his work, he might have let me in on the family secret, instead of leaving me totally clueless about time-jumping.

I parked and walked across the muddy green, past gray trees still bare from winter, until I reached a low brown building. None of the students seemed to care as I strode down the tiled hallways, scanning the nameplates on the doors.

I stood outside Professor Gervers's doorway for a minute, exhaling slowly in an attempt to get my heart rate down while wiping my sweaty palms on my pants. Once I was satisfied that I could have a conversation without looking like I was about to pass out, I knocked twice.

"Come in."

I entered a small office with a large desk in the middle of the room. Piles of books and papers covered every surface, with the clutter extending all around the room. Stacks of papers towered from the floor and every wall was covered by bookshelves. The place smelled musty, as if the window hadn't been opened in a decade.

Professor Gervers sat behind the desk, hunched over a book. He was around my dad's age, with grayish hair and glasses, and a tan cardigan over his dress shirt. He looked more like a librarian than a time jumper. But who was I to judge? I doubted anyone would look at me and imagine that "Fixer of Glitches in the Time Stream" was a line on my resume.

The professor glanced up from his book and waved me to the one empty chair. "How can I help you?" he asked, returning his attention to the book.

"Hi, Professor Gervers." I tossed my backpack on the floor and sat down, the wooden chair creaking noisily underneath me. "I hope you can give me some information."

"That is a rather general request," he said without looking up. He scribbled some notes on a notepad and then snapped his book shut.

"I'm Dan Renfrew. James Renfrew was my dad."

The pen dropped from his fingers, and he looked up sharply, his distracted expression replaced by focused fear. "You can't be here!" he said, his voice sounding near hysterical. "I can't talk to you."

"Why? Why won't anyone talk to me?"

"There's nothing to talk about. I think you should leave." He reached for the office phone on his desk.

Before he could react, I jumped up, grabbed his arm, and pulled back his sleeve, revealing a tattoo of a four-pointed star within a circle on his forearm. The mark of a time jumper.

I let go of his arm and pulled back my own sleeve, showing him the same tattoo.

Professor Gervers replaced the phone in its cradle. "I cannot help you," he said, almost pleading with me. "I just can't."

"But why? You and my father worked in the same department. You were probably friends. Why won't you help me?"

He licked his lips and glanced up at the top corner of his bookshelf, a bead of sweat now trickling down one side of his face. "I have a family . . . a wife and two daughters. Please leave," he begged.

This guy was beyond scared; he was terrified, and not just for himself, but for his family also. Victor's plot to rule the world didn't allow for any loose ends—my dad was proof of that. But for the first time, it occurred to me that those who had meekly handed over their time-travel devices to Victor, hoping that they'd be safe from his threats, still lived in fear. Victor had probably bugged this guy's office, maybe even his home. One wrong word and the professor or someone in his family would suffer. Finally, all the rejection I'd been getting over the past few weeks made sense.

"Sorry," I mumbled. "I won't bother you again."

Professor Gervers mouthed the words *thank you* and then half escorted, half pushed me toward the door. I'd barely made it out of his office before the door slammed behind me.

Another failure. I trudged down the hall, trying to figure out my next steps. My great dream of finding other time jumpers to help me fight Victor was just that—a dream. None of them were willing to talk to me. I desperately needed help. But where was I going to get it?

The double doors leading outside were just ahead when I heard someone running behind me. I turned around to see a guy only a few years older than me, wearing a university sweatshirt.

"Wait!" he said as he slowed to a stop. He handed me my backpack. "You forgot this."

"Thanks." I slung the bag over my shoulder and headed out the door.

Back at home, I tossed my backpack on the coffee table and flopped onto the couch. Unfortunately, Victor wasn't my only problem; I also had homework. Dad had homeschooled me until this year, meaning I knew more history than my history teachers and I was acing my Latin class. Math, however, was a totally different beast. Dad had made sure I could count out my change at the grocery store and do basic arithmetic, but that was it—and it worked for me. But apparently the school system believed I needed more than that.

First rule of homework: Create a good work environment.

Snack? Check.

Drink? Check.

TV? Definitely.

I pulled out my math notes, ready to begin a mind-numbing evening of homework, when a piece of paper sticking out from between the pages caught my eye. It looked like a torn sheet from a notebook.

Thursday 9 p.m. 295 Williams St. Back door. Make sure you're not followed!

My heart nearly skipped a beat. This had to be from Professor Gervers! Despite his fears, he was going to meet with me!

There was only one person I could share this news with. But not from here. Professor Gervers wasn't the only one paranoid about being watched. I knew for sure that Victor had broken into my apartment at least once. And, despite the fact that I'd never found a bug in my place, I still wasn't a hundred percent sure that he wasn't spying on me somehow.

I ran out of my condo and into the little room that held the floor's garbage chute. After a quick check down the hall to make sure no one was coming, I pulled out my phone. Sam answered after two rings. Even though I'd been on two time jumps with her, texted her constantly every day, and found every excuse to video chat with her, my heart still beat faster at seeing her again. Behind her, almost obscured by her wavy red hair, was the familiar background of her bedroom.

"Hey. Is it safe to talk?" I asked.

"Yeah, Mom's at bingo and my dumb stepdad went out with his stupid friends." Her green eyes glanced around the screen. "Where are you?"

"Garbage room. Doesn't matter," I said, keeping my voice low, but barely containing my enthusiasm. "I made contact!"

"With what?" She raised an eyebrow and looked at me quizzically. "Aliens?"

"No! Another time jumper." As I began telling her about the meeting with Professor Gervers, her eyes grew wider and wider. And when I got to the part about "Thursday night. In an alley behind a building downtown," I stopped myself. "Okay, yeah, I hear it. But I don't think it's a trap. He worked with my dad. They were probably friends."

Sam cocked her head to the side and gave me the are-you-freakin'-serious look that I knew too well. "Should I remind you again how much friendship means to these bastards? Didn't Victor say he was your dad's friend?"

I winced as the horrible memory of last summer flashed through my mind. Me coming home to find Victor and Dad fighting in the living room. Victor stabbing Dad in the chest with a sword. And Dad using his last bit of strength to toss me a strange metal rod that ended up sending me back in time. "I'll be careful," I said quietly.

"How about you meet in public? That would be a lot safer." Typical Sam, always expecting the worst. Unfortunately, she was usually right.

"He won't do it. The guy's terrified of Victor. I know it's risky; that's why I'm telling you. You're my backup if anything goes wrong."

"Backup?" She gaped at me. "What do you expect me to do from Virginia? The best I can do is call the police if you go missing. And they won't do squat until you've been gone for at least a full day. You'll probably be dead by then."

"Who else am I going to ask? I literally have no friends. You're the only person I can trust."

Sam exhaled loudly and rolled her eyes. "I think this is a terrible idea, but I know you're going to do it anyway. So just be careful, okay? If anything feels the slightest bit wrong, run like hell. And send me the exact details of where you're going to be, and live stream the whole thing."

"Don't worry. I'll be careful. So . . . how are you?" I asked, shifting to a more casual tone. Our chats were always the best part of my day.

Sam gestured behind her. "The usual. Homework piling up, and I have work in an hour. How about you?"

"The same, except double the homework and none of the real work. I did get into a fight today."

"The other guy okay?"

"Guys, plural. Four of them jumped me because I bumped into one of them during lunch. I think a broken nose was probably the worst of it."

"I still don't understand why you bother going to school. Why don't you just chill and live off the money your dad left you?"

"Because that money is going to run out at some point—and then what? Do I take my nonexistent diploma, and my education in dead languages and history, and try to find a job?" I snorted. "No matter how much I hate school, I still need to go. And the classes aren't that bad . . . except for math."

Sam grinned. "It's better than fighting Romans."

"Sometimes I'm not so sure."

"I have to go, Dan. My homework won't finish itself. Be careful, okay? Whatever you do, don't trust this guy."

I tried to think of some witty response but came up blank. "Don't worry, I won't."

She gave me a quick wave, then the screen went black. I headed back to the condo and sank into the couch. Was Sam right? Was I about to walk into a trap? Underneath the nerdy-professor clothing, was Professor Gervers really a cold-blooded killer?

In two days, I'd find out. Until then, math was waiting for me.

CHAPTER 2

The next day, as soon as I pulled into the student lot and stepped out of the car, I could feel a change in people's attitudes. Since last fall, when I'd first started at this school, I'd been pretty much invisible. But now I was the guy who had punched out Nick Fraser and his gang in less than a minute. Instead of carelessly bumping into me as they passed, people gave me a wide berth on the sidewalk. The girls who leaned against the fence, having a smoke before school, smiled at me and nodded, when before they wouldn't bother looking my way. A little spring entered my step. It felt good to be recognized.

But as the day wore on, my newfound fame grew annoying. In the halls, people whispered and pointed. Every time I looked up in class, someone was staring at me. By lunchtime, I couldn't wait to sit at my usual table for one. As I pushed through the double doors into the cafeteria, I stifled a groan. My normally empty table had become the focal point for pretty much every outcast in the school, who sat at the surrounding tables watching me with a mixture of nervousness and hope, trying to decide whether I was some sort of savior who would protect them from future bullying or just another bully waiting to turn on them.

I scowled and tossed my lunch bag on the table. Yesterday I just didn't want to be invisible—now I'd become the center of attention. I took my seat and scanned the caf. Nick was nowhere to be seen. Maybe the rumors about him taking a few days off to let his broken nose heal were true. As for Amir, Devon, and Kyle, they sat quietly at a table by themselves, bothering no one.

From the corner of my eye, I caught a glimpse of someone approaching. With every sense on edge, I spun around in my seat, expecting the entire football team to be sneaking up on me, looking for revenge.

Jenna Alvarez stopped midstep, startled by my sharp reaction. She wore a long-sleeved shirt and tight, ripped jeans. Her yellow cafeteria tray held a plate of fries. "H-hi, Dan," she said tentatively.

"Hi, Jenna," I said, my voice coming out an octave higher than usual. We'd been in the same English class last semester, and I'd definitely noticed her. With her sparkling laugh and long, glossy, black hair, she was hard to miss. We'd said hi a few times and maybe had a couple short discussions about homework, but I doubted she remembered those. Hell, I was surprised she knew my name.

She glanced back to her table of friends. They urged her on, waving their hands in a shooing motion.

A blush crept up her cheeks. "Um . . . I notice that you always eat here alone." Her eyes passed over the empty chairs. "Would it be okay if I sit with you?"

Jenna Alvarez wants to sit with me?

"I guess." With my foot, I nudged a chair away from the table for her to sit. It scraped noisily along the floor. Probably not the most chivalrous of gestures, but I'd seen the movie *Carrie*. I knew what happens to the unpopular kid when the popular kids start pretending interest.

Jenna sat down beside me, close enough that our legs were almost touching. "Would you like some fries?"

Was a bucket of pig's blood about to fall on me? Was Nick hiding somewhere, waiting to ambush me? Quickly I turned in my seat and swept the room again with my gaze, looking for anything out of place. Nothing.

"No thanks," I finally said.

Then, to make things weirder, Jenna didn't eat either. She repeatedly tapped her plastic fork against the edge of her plate, as if weighing a major decision. Abruptly she slammed her fork on to the tray. "Want to go out sometime?" she blurted. "You know . . . get a coffee? See a movie? Anything?"

"Me?" A stupid question and I knew it, but I'd never been asked out before. My brain didn't know how to deal with this situation.

"Yes, you. If . . . if you want to."

I sat there stunned. A girl was asking me out. A hot, popular girl. Should I say yes? What about Sam? "I . . . uh . . ."

Jenna stood up to go, her face flushed with embarrassment. "Sorry. You probably have a girlfriend."

"Wait!" I managed to blurt out.

Jenna paused, one foot already directed toward the safety of her friends.

What do I tell her?

Sam was the most incredible person I'd ever met. She was smart, beautiful, strong, brave, and had already saved my life countless times on our two trips into history. She was my best friend, and I'd trust her with my life. But, if I was completely honest with myself, she wasn't anywhere close to being my girlfriend. We didn't hang out, see movies, hold hands, or do anything that normal couples do. Not to mention that she'd told me countless times she wasn't interested in me.

I looked at Jenna, who was waiting expectantly. "N-no . . . ," I said slowly, the word almost struggling to get out. "No," I said again, this time more firmly. "I don't have a girlfriend."

It hurt me to say it. It was like admitting defeat—that Sam and I would never be more than friends. But I'd been hopelessly hung up on Sam for too long. I owed it to her to finally take the hint and move on.

"Yeah, I really would like to go out with you," I added before I chickened out. "How about tonight?"

Jenna's face broke out in a huge grin. "Great!" She handed me her phone. "Give me your number."

I punched in my number and handed the phone back to her.

"That's awesome!" She smiled radiantly. "I'll message you after school so we can figure things out. See you tonight!"

With a flick of her hair, she grabbed her tray and headed back to her usual table. She had a grace about her. Not like Sam, who could move through a forest without making a sound, but a certain elegance, like a movie star walking along the red carpet. As she sat down, the girls at her table crowded in, glancing my way and giggling.

My hands shook as I took a bite of my sandwich. *A date.* What would I wear? Where should I take her? With Sam I was comfortable; I'd probably take her to a movie or to a nice restaurant, but was that what people did in high school? If I took Jenna somewhere lame, would I become the laughingstock of the entire school? I tossed my sandwich aside, my appetite suddenly gone.

I spent the rest of the day's classes in misery. I needed to cancel this date before I made a fool of myself. What if she brought her friends? What if this was all some setup planned by Nick? But I couldn't even text her to cancel—I never got her number. I pulled out my phone countless times and sat there staring at it, trying to think of the least awkward way I could bail.

By the time the final bell rang, I still hadn't thought of an excuse that sounded remotely believable. The stupid phone sat in my sweaty hands, its screen blank. This looming date was stressing me out even more than my meeting with Professor Gervers. But at least with time jumpers I knew how to act. The opposite sex? No clue.

My phone vibrated in my hands.

Want to go bowling? :D

Bowling? The queasy feeling in my stomach vanished. I could handle bowling. At least, I was pretty sure I could. Jeans and a T-shirt. Dorky rented shoes. And if Jenna brought friends, it wouldn't matter.

Sure, I texted back.

We exchanged a few more messages, figuring out when to meet, and where. I left school feeling pretty damn good about myself. Surely, I thought, there had to be at least some chance this date wouldn't be a complete train wreck.

I got to the bowling alley at seven and found Jenna waiting for me inside the front doors. As always she was looking great, dressed in a simple T-shirt and black yoga pants, and with her winter coat over her arm. Sam never wore tight clothes. On time jumps or at home, Sam's clothes were always loose and bulky—a suit of armor to protect her from prying eyes or hands.

"Dan!" Jenna hugged me briefly. "You made it!"

Sam hardly ever hugged me either.

"Anyone else showing up?" I asked, expecting her to have friends somewhere close.

"No, just us." Jenna grabbed my hand. "Come on, let's get a lane."

It turned out I sucked at bowling. In the heat of battle against the Normans, I had hurled spears at charging horsemen with surprising accuracy. Why should bowling be that much different? The pins didn't move, and I just had to roll the ball down a flat alley. But for some reason I couldn't get the hang of the arm swing, or the leg movement, or whatever. Ball after ball rolled into the gutter.

"Have you bowled before?" Jenna asked, a playful smile on her face.

"Nope."

"Really? Never?"

"My dad wasn't into normal activities." I gripped another ball and tried to focus over the crashing of pins all around me. With tentative steps I approached the lane and released the ball. It rumbled down the lane, hooked to the right, and barely managed to knock over two pins.

"Oh yeah. I heard you were homeschooled. What was that like?"

"Okay, I guess. I got to go to school in my pajamas." I selected another ball. "But my dad's curriculum didn't involve hanging out with people my age."

"That must have sucked." Jenna stepped behind me. "Let me teach you the basics." Her hand closed around mine. Her skin was much softer than Sam's, whose hands were strong and calloused from years of archery.

Jenna leaned in so close I could feel her breath on my neck. She smelled like flowers. "You need to be lower when you release the ball," she said. "And aim for the arrow in the middle of the lane."

I moved slowly toward the lane and tried to remember what she'd said. My brain wasn't working too well, though. All I could think about was her warm touch and the smell of her perfume. Somehow I remembered to release the ball, and it slowly weaved down the lane and knocked over five pins. I pumped my fist in victory. I wasn't ready to quit school and go pro, but at least I'd hit something.

"Not bad," Jenna said.

"I have a great teacher."

She smiled and palmed a ball, positioning herself at the front of the lane. Except for me totally sucking at bowling, this date was going a hell of a lot better than I'd thought it would. Jenna was pretty *and* good company. We were joking, laughing, having fun. If only I could stop asking myself: *Why did she ask me out? Why now?*

We finished two games, both of which I lost by huge margins, then we grabbed a slice of pizza before I drove Jenna home and walked her to the door. On the porch, she turned to face me. "That was really fun, Dan."

"It was. I had a great time."

"Want to have lunch with me tomorrow?"

Lunch. Where this had all started. "Uh . . ."

Jenna took a step back. "What? You didn't have fun tonight?"

"No! No! Everything's great. Bowling was awesome. It's just . . ." How could I say this without sounding totally paranoid?

"What?" she demanded.

I looked directly into her deep brown eyes. "Why did you ask me out? We've barely spoken all year. Why now? Is it just because I beat up Nick?"

Jenna blushed and cast her eyes downward. "Well . . . sort of. Ever since English last semester I thought you were kind of cute. But you're so serious—not like the rest of the guys. I tried everything to get you to notice me. Nothing worked."

Huh? "You did?"

"Yes! I said hello to you every day. I'd ask about your weekend. I even asked you for help with homework once—and I get straight As!"

Geez . . . Was I that oblivious?

"Sorry," I said. "My last few months have been kind of rough."

"That's okay. I get it. I heard about your dad—I can imagine the stress you've been through. Anyway, after yesterday, I figured all the girls would be after you. My friends convinced me to ask you out before someone else did." She spread her arms wide and shrugged. "And so here we are."

No buckets of pig's blood. Just a girl who was interested in me, and had been for a while. And if I hadn't been so obsessed with Sam, I might have noticed. "Okay, okay. Which table tomorrow, yours or mine?"

"We'll figure it out." She gave me a peck on the cheek and opened her door.

The entire drive home I spent thinking about how different Jenna was from Sam. Jenna was like a princess, dainty and graceful. But Sam was a queen, strong and self-assured. They were both great, but

Jenna won out in the most important category—willingness to spend time with me. I had gone out with Jenna because I couldn't think of an excuse not to, but now that our date was over, I wanted to see more of her.

But no matter how much fun I'd had, I still needed to focus on tomorrow's meeting with Professor Gervers, and Sam was the only person who could help me there. As soon as I got home, I spent a few minutes crafting a message containing everything she needed to know: Gervers's full name and office number, the meeting location, as well as what I planned to wear. If I went missing, the police would have a trail to follow, and it would lead them right to the professor.

Lunch with Jenna the next day was better than any I'd ever had. We sat at my usual table; I wasn't ready to be the only guy at a table full of girls. The entire dating thing was new to me, so I didn't plan on rushing anything.

This slow approach seemed to be working with Jenna. We weren't one of those annoying couples that dotted the cafeteria: the ones who gazed into each other's eyes and fed each other French fries. We sat close enough to look like a couple, but far enough apart that we weren't in each other's space. Despite my initial panic, I felt comfortable with her. We ate our lunch and chatted easily.

"You doing anything tonight?" Jenna asked, the hopeful lift of her brow hinting that she wanted to go out again.

"I have a few things I need to do."

"Anything exciting?"

Entering dangerous territory. I didn't want to lie to her and then have to remember those lies in the future. Way too complicated. I'd follow the rule of telling the truth, but just enough to answer the question. "I'm meeting with a professor who used to work with my dad."

"Wow. That's cool. What do you two talk about?"

Time travel. Saving the world from the clutches of an evil madman. "Not much. I just need him to help me through some stuff."

Jenna rested her hand on mine and her face grew serious. "If you ever need to talk about things . . . you know . . . you can talk to me."

"Thanks, I will."

Great . . . So much for not lying. I couldn't see myself ever talking to her about my problems—at least not the important ones. She'd get questions like "What shirt goes better with these pants?" or "Should I try the chicken or the steak?" Sam would always be the one I'd turn to for the serious stuff—she was the only one who'd understand.

How had my dad done it? How had he met my mom, dated her, and gotten married while time-jumping? Had he ever told her? It would have been a pretty big thing to hide, his disappearing for a few days at a time. Everything was new with Jenna, so I could still deflect her questions. But how could I get close to someone and keep the truth from them? How could I ever explain that there was an entire community of people who jumped through time to fix glitches in history, and that I was one of them?

I took another bite of my sandwich and turned my attention back to Jenna. I'd worry about the truth later. Right now I planned on just enjoying her company—and making sure there *would* be a later.

CHAPTER 3

When seven o'clock rolled around, I locked my front door and took the elevator down to the parking garage. Normally the trip downtown would take only half an hour, but the note had said to make sure I wasn't followed, which meant leaving early.

The streets were dark already as I began driving to the meeting. I took the world's most convoluted path, cutting through subdivisions, doing four right turns in a row, catching lights right at the yellow. When I finally pulled into a parking spot three blocks away from the meeting place, I was certain no one could have followed me.

The address Professor Gervers had given me was a three-story brick building in a rough part of town. The upper two floors had black-and-orange For Lease signs in the windows, while the ground floor housed a women's shoe store. None of the windows were lit, giving the entire building an abandoned look. The street had the same empty feel. No people, and only a few cars parked here and there.

Why would he pick this place? I'm here, I texted Sam, and then started the live stream from my phone.

A narrow alley separated 295 Williams Street from the building standing next to it. The glow of the streetlight reached only partway into the alley, leaving the path beyond shrouded in shadows. I let my eyes adjust to the darkness and then peered into the gloom. Nothing moved.

I lowered the hood of my sweatshirt so I could hear better. The distant sound of cars speeding by on the highway created a background hum to the night, but otherwise everything was quiet. Not even a dog barking. My better judgment screamed, *Go home*, but I ignored it and slinked down the alley, every nerve on edge.

I crept into the service road behind the shoe store and its neighboring buildings. Trash littered the area, spilling over from the dumpsters at the back of each building. The acrid stench of garbage and urine made me want to gag, but I shook it off.

A man was leaning against the back door of the shoe store, his hands hidden in the pockets of his dark winter coat. He wore a baseball cap with its brim tilted down to hide his face. I couldn't tell if it was Professor Gervers or someone else. I swung my phone toward him and he raised a hand in front of his face.

"Put that thing away!" he snapped.

"Sorry." I put the phone in my pocket without shutting off the live stream. Sam would get audio, at least. "Professor Gervers?"

"Are you alone?" came his muffled voice.

"Yeah."

He pulled his hand out of his pocket, revealing a small silver handgun. He motioned with it. "Give me your phone and your wallet."

Instantly I raised my hands. "Take whatever—"

"Shut up and do what I tell you!"

With trembling hands, I took the phone and wallet from my pockets and passed them over.

"Nice try," he sneered as he shut off the live stream. "Now get on your knees and put your hands behind your back."

Crap! Crap! Crap!

I dropped to my knees, on the verge of hyperventilating, my heart pounding like it was about to explode from my rib cage. Was this Victor's doing? Was Gervers working with him?

The man walked behind me and pressed the muzzle of the handgun against my scalp. Suddenly, all I could focus on was that small cold point touching my skin.

"Please . . . I'm just a kid." *A stupid, stupid kid who is way out of his league. Why did I come here?*

"Shut up! Do as I say and you might live." A cloth bag dropped in front of me. "Put this on your head."

Without a second thought, I slipped the hood on. As soon as I did, he grabbed my wrists and duct-taped them behind my back. Despite the bleakness of my situation, the slimmest of hopes dawned within me. You don't tie people up before you kill them—which meant he was kidnapping me. I still had the two million dollars I'd inherited when Dad died. Maybe I could use it to buy my freedom.

"I got him," the man announced to someone else.

Seconds later a car drove into the alley, its tires crunching to a halt behind me. A door slid open, and a pair of hands dragged me into what had to be a minivan, dumping me on to the floor. The gunman got in behind me and slid the door shut. With a squeal of tires the van tore out of the alley, my body rocking from side to side as the driver sped around the corners. Hands patted me down, checking my pockets, my coat and my sleeves.

"He's clean."

"You get to choose where this van ends up, Dan," a voice said, deeper than the first man's. "Either back here, where you step out alive, or in a forest, where no one will ever find your body. Do you understand?"

"Y-yes," I stammered, my words muffled by the hot confines of the hood. *There's a chance I'll get out of here.*

"What's your phone password?" the gunman asked.

"3267."

Someone fiddled with my phone for a few seconds. "Who's Sam? Why are you sending him texts about this meeting?"

My slim hope grew a bit larger; they hadn't counted on me having backup. "Sam knows everything about this meeting," I replied confidently. "If I don't call back in an hour, everything I've sent him will be handed over to the police."

The gunman laughed. "He has nothing. He knows the address of a shoe store and saw a live stream of a guy in dark clothes leaning against a door."

"What about Professor Gervers?" I asked. "Sam knows I met with him. The police are going to head right to his office if I disappear. They'll find out he's in league with you."

Another laugh. "There's no record of Professor Gervers ever meeting with Dan Renfrew. You went to his office hours, remember? And even if the police do happen to question him, the professor is currently attending a university event with hundreds of his colleagues. He has an ironclad alibi."

I'd walked straight into a trap. Why hadn't I just listened to Sam? "What do you want?" I muttered, my voice barely audible.

"Why were you trying to meet the professor?" the deep-voiced guy barked.

"My dad never told me anything about time-jumping," I explained. "I've been kind of making it up as I go whenever I end up in history. I was hoping to meet other time jumpers and learn things."

"Wait! You still have your time-travel mechanism?"

The question threw me for a second. These guys couldn't be Victor's men; otherwise, they'd have known I did. So were they the good guys? "Uh . . . yeah."

"Why hasn't Victor taken it?"

The truth was, I had no clue why Victor let me keep it. At Dad's funeral Victor had confronted me and threatened to take it away. But when he found out that Sam was my time-jumping partner, it was like he had an instant lobotomy. He'd gotten all apologetic and insisted that Sam and I both keep them. Not that I was going to tell these guys any of that. "I don't know. Maybe he decided murdering my dad was enough pain to inflict on me. Or maybe he got tired of taking them since he'd already taken two others from me."

"Two? We know you had your father's. Where did you get the others?"

"A pair of Victor's guys attacked me on my first jump. I killed them and stole theirs."

The interrogation paused and I heard some muted whispering between the men in the back with me—much too quiet for me to make out the words. "What were their names?" the first man finally asked, his voice less harsh than before.

"I don't know. They never told me."

"Do you remember what they looked like?"

I'd never forget the first man I'd killed—his face was burned forever into my memory. "One guy had black hair in a buzz cut and was huge like a wrestler. The other one had light-brown hair, cut really badly. He was shorter than the other guy. Kinda reminded me of a weasel."

Again some whispering, then the hood was ripped off my head. I was in a van with heavily tinted windows. A guy in a baseball cap was driving, while the two in the back with me had their faces hidden by ski masks. The one on my right pulled out a laptop from a black travel bag. "I'm going to scroll through some pictures, and you tell me when you see the men you killed."

He started up some app I'd never seen before, logged in, and then began scrolling through pages, each with a large image of a person, as well as notes: occupation, education, birth date, current address, known associates, that kind of stuff. Some pictures had been taken from up close and looked like personal photos. Others were fuzzy, as if the photographer had taken the picture with a zoom lens. As for the notes, some men had paragraphs of details, while others only had a few words.

"Is this a list of every time jumper?"

"Most of them." He continued scrolling.

No mistaking the person on the next page. "That's him." It was the one with the bad haircut. He looked better in this photo, dressed in a suit and tie, and with his hair combed. He was probably an accountant in real life. When I'd last seen him in Anglo-Saxon England, he'd had a knife at my throat.

"Are you sure he's dead?"

"Positive. He took an ax in the back from an Anglo-Saxon warrior named Ceolwulf."

"And when did this happen?"

"Um . . . it was 1066 in history, late last June in our time."

He examined the notes at the bottom of the screen for a few seconds before turning to his partner. "The kid's telling the truth. He was reported missing in early July." He typed "Killed in 1066 by a local" in big red letters at the bottom of the screen and then began scrolling again. "Show me the other one," he said to me.

The other guy was harder to figure out; I had to go through the hundreds of profiles twice before I found it. It was one of the grainy pictures, hard to see clearly. "That's him. I stabbed him in the throat with an arrow."

The stockier man stared intently at the screen for a few seconds. "Vladimir Smirnov. Russian. Last seen in June of last year." He typed "Killed in 1066 by Dan Renfrew" at the bottom of the page in the same red letters, then snapped the laptop closed. "So what were you hoping to get from the professor?" His tone was softer, not nearly as harsh as before. I sensed a definite shift in attitude, as if I had passed some sort of initiation.

"Before he died, the guy with the bad haircut told me part of Victor's plan. I know it has something to do with time jumpers taking over the world and killing billions of people in the process, but all of that seems pretty vague . . . I want to learn more about his stupid plan so I can stop the arrogant prick."

The man laughed. "How old are you, kid?"

"Seventeen—but I'll be eighteen in a few months."

He shook his head. "Forget it. This is too big for you to handle. Victor's plan has been in the works since before you were born. And better people than you have tried to take him down and failed." He tapped the laptop. "Do yourself a favor and just run away as far as you can."

My stomach lurched. That was the same advice my dad had given me in a note I'd received after Victor attacked him. "I don't want to run. My dad was fighting this, so I want to fight it too. I'm not going to give up just because some guys in a minivan tell me to."

"I admire your spirit," the other kidnapper said, "but Victor has almost all of the time-traveling community on his side."

"Then how do I stop him? Please help me. The bastard killed my dad. I want to see him suffer!"

The two kidnappers exchanged glances, then the taller one directed his attention to me. "What's this information worth to you?"

"Wait . . . I have to *pay*? I'm talking about stopping Victor. You guys should be tripping over yourselves to help me."

"Yeah, well, nothing in life is free, kid," said the man with the laptop. "We want time-travel devices or information."

"Jump rods?" I snorted. "Are you out of your freakin' minds? Those things don't grow on trees, you know."

"And yet you're already on your third one."

"Yeah, that was a fluke. Plus it's my last one. Anyway, I already told you about the two dead jumpers. That should be worth something."

"It is. We're not going to kill you."

I ignored his implied threat. We were clearly on the same team— now we were just haggling over whether I got to actually play or sat on the bench. "Why do you even want a jump device? Is there a way to stop Victor with it? Does it have something to do with the city in the time stream?"

The man with the laptop stared at me. "What?"

"You know the big, blinding light that happens when you jump through time? Well, there's a city there. Like, floating in the darkness behind the light."

"You guys never told me about a city," the driver said. His voice sounded younger, not as deep as the voices of the other two. And there was an odd familiarity to it.

"That's because there isn't one," said the smaller kidnapper.

"It was there," I said. "I saw it. I was doing a double jump because my jump rod got stolen in Celtic times."

The stockier man snorted. "Double jumps are impossible."

"So is time-jumping," I snapped. "But I don't see anyone here arguing that point. So, tell me, how will a jump rod stop Victor and his gang from taking over the world?"

"It won't," the driver said over his shoulder. "Nothing will stop Victor. He's already won."

"Then why bother with jump devices?"

The smaller kidnapper turned to the larger one, as if expecting him to answer, but he only grunted, "I got my reasons."

I exhaled loudly and rolled my eyes. "Well, don't hold your breath. I'm sure as hell not giving you one—even if I did have an extra. If you guys have no plan to stop Victor, then no information you have is worth it."

"Suit yourself. You wanted this meeting. Not us."

I shrugged. "So what now?"

The man on my right took out a knife and sliced through the tape binding my hands. "We drop you off."

I massaged some circulation back into my wrists. "You sure you can't tell me anything?"

"Nope. Not until we get something more from you than the names of two dead jumpers."

I shook my head. "You guys really, really suck as mentors."

The van slowed down and came to a stop. "This is it, Dan—end of the line. Don't ever call Professor Gervers again."

"So what if I come across some information that might be worth your while? How do I find you?"

He scribbled on a piece of paper and tossed it to me. "That's your username and password. Memorize them, then burn it. Go to the ancient history discussion forum at that site and start a forum topic about anything. We'll find you within a day or two."

I barely had time to put the scrap of paper in my pocket before they shoved me out of the van and onto the soggy grass, my phone and wallet landing beside me on a patch of dirty snow. The van began barreling down the street even before the door was fully closed, the red taillights fading into the distance.

I pulled myself off the grass and wiped the muck off my pants. I'd managed to survive my meeting with the "good guys." Someday a job interviewer would ask me about how I'd handled a stressful event, and I'd have to make something up, because no one would ever believe the kind of crap I went through on a regular basis.

I snatched my wallet and phone from the ground. Four messages, all from Sam. I went straight to the last one. About to call 911, it read.

I'm good, I sent back.

Within seconds another message appeared. Prove it.

I smiled. There was something comforting about Sam's complete mistrust of absolutely everything. I took a selfie standing next to a tree and sent it to her. In the background was a row of houses with their lights on. Clearly I was safe.

My kidnappers had dumped me off only a few blocks from our original meeting place. I started walking back to pick up my car and video-called Sam.

"So was it a trap?" she asked.

"What happened to 'Hi, Dan. How was your evening?'"

"Fine. Hi, Dan. How was your evening?"

"Well, I walked into a trap."

"I knew it!" She shook her head.

"I'm okay, though. Thanks for asking." I proceeded to tell Sam everything.

"Were my dad and brother on the laptop?" she asked.

"I didn't see them. But I didn't see my dad either. I think it only had pictures of living jumpers."

"We *have* to get the complete set," Sam declared. "Maybe they know who murdered my dad and brother."

"Not at the price they're asking," I chuffed. "Even if we did have a spare jump rod, I'm not trading it for a glorified PowerPoint."

"Yeah," Sam sighed. "That's a pretty steep price. Do you have any other names left on your list?"

"A few, but I'm not holding my breath. Even if any of them are time jumpers, they're not going to help us. Victor has all these guys petrified."

Sam twisted a lock of her hair around a finger and began nibbling on the ends. "You know what that means, then, right? We gotta dust off the jump rods, catch the next glitch, and see if we can get lucky finding information in the past again."

"Seriously?" I groaned. "Time jumping is the best plan you can think of? There's gotta be a better option."

"You know there isn't."

I hadn't even seen my jump device since Sam and I returned from Celtic times. For the last few months, it had been locked in a safety deposit box at the bank, in case Victor changed his mind and came looking for it. The mere thought of using it again made my palms sweat. There was just so much to hate about time jumping. First, there was the complete random nature of it. While my jump device had been stored, there might have been twenty glitches—or none. Then, when we did follow a glitch, Sam and I had no clue where in history we'd land, or when, or what the actual glitch would be, or how to fix it. About the only certainty in any time jump was that someone would try to kill me.

But unfortunately Sam was right—with no time jumpers willing to help us, we had run out of options. Time jumping was the only way to get answers.

"All right," I sighed. "When the next glitch happens, we're outta here."

CHAPTER 4

I stood at my locker the next morning, listening to all the people around me talking about their spring break plans—vacations down south, hanging out with friends, parties. As for me, I was still trying to figure out if I'd forgotten anything for my own potential mystery spring break destination. After retrieving my jump device from the bank, I'd spent hours last night packing so I'd be ready whenever the next time glitch happened. I'd filled my leather backpack up with bandages, trail mix and cereal, ibuprofen, and a wool blanket. For clothing, I made sure I was obeying the first rule of time travel: don't stand out. Ignoring this only led to problems—usually involving angry people and pointy objects. I had the tunic and pants from my trip to Celtic times, plus a wool cloak and leather boots I'd bought from a medieval costume website.

After the multiple near-death experiences in each of my previous jumps, I decided to bring armor and a decent weapon on this one. My dad had brought back so much stuff from his visits to history that it took a full wall of my apartment to display them all, but that didn't make the choice easy. I had to bring something that would be available in a lot of different time periods, and in a lot of different regions. In the end, I chose a shirt of Anglo-Saxon chain mail I had picked up on my first jump and my sword from Celtic times. The blade was cheap steel, prone to bending, but it would serve its purpose. With a quick change, I could travel to almost any era and look like I belonged there.

"Whatcha thinking about?"

I jerked back, startled by the voice.

Jenna was smiling at me, leaning against the locker next to mine. She wore a light green top and jeans, her black hair pushed back by a yellow hairband.

"Still half asleep," I replied.

"How did your meeting with the professor go?"

Well, they put a gun to my head, kidnapped me, and threatened to kill me. "Pretty good. We didn't finish until late." I remembered that yesterday at lunch Jenna had hinted at going out. "You doing anything tonight?"

"Nothing special. I was just going to stay home and watch a movie and have pizza." Her eyes brightened. "Do you want to come over?"

"Yeah, cool." Movies and pizza was what I did most nights. It'd be great to finally watch a movie with someone else. And who knew what else might happen if it was just the two of us? "What time?"

"Six?"

"Great."

She glanced at the floor, suddenly becoming very interested in her shoes. "Umm . . . my parents are going to be home too. Will that be a problem? They're usually pretty cool."

Oh, yeah, parents. Forgot people had those. "Not a problem." Even with parents around, hanging out with Jenna was better than watching movies by myself.

I opened my locker to grab my notebook for my next class, and then I remembered my other potential plans. My turn to look awkwardly at the floor. "Uh, listen . . . I may have to cancel last minute. There's this thing that I was going to do, and I'm not doing it . . . at the moment. But there's a chance it might . . . suddenly happen."

Jenna's ever-present smile faded.

"This isn't about your parents," I assured her. "I honestly do have plans—they're just not definite. There's only a slim chance, practically zero, that I'll have to bail. But if I do, we can have our movie night when I get back. I promise."

"More meetings with professors?"

"Camping." That was the excuse Sam always gave her mom when she went time-jumping. To be fair, traveling to the past usually did involve a lot of roughing it in the wilderness.

Jenna's lips curled in distaste. "You mean you willingly leave a perfectly warm house and go out into the woods? No running water? No soft bed? You know it's still cold out, right?"

Looked like I didn't have to worry about her wanting to tag along. "It's fun," I said. "Sleeping under starry skies. Cooking over fires." *Getting rained on while you sleep. Running away from people trying to kill you.*

"So. Last-minute camping? Do you camp . . . alone?"

How to tell her as little of the truth as possible without lying? "I go with my friend Sam."

"Does he go here?"

"No. Sam lives kinda far away, so we don't get to hang out much. That's why the plans are last-minute. We have to figure out a time to meet up." *Now please don't ask me what Sam looks like.*

The bell rang, and before Jenna could ask me anything else, I grabbed my books and slammed my locker shut. "I can't be late," I blurted as I jogged down the hallway. "See you at lunch," I called over my shoulder. Not the bravest way to handle the situation, but if there was anything I'd learned from time-jumping, it was that sometimes running away was the best option.

As I headed to the cafeteria for lunch, I was prepared to create all sorts of diversions. If needed, I would spill my drink on myself, Jenna, or even the whole cafeteria. The rest of my lunch was fair game too. I didn't care how many dropped sandwiches or thrown pieces of fruit it took—there was no way I could answer any more questions about Sam. I sat down next to Jenna and placed my open can of soda dangerously close to the edge of the table.

"Hey," Jenna said with little enthusiasm. She leaned with one elbow on the table and poked at her sandwich with a finger. Clearly something had happened to dampen her mood.

Perfect. If Jenna was having a bad day, I could probably direct our conversation there for the rest of lunch. That would score me some major thoughtful-guy points and shift focus away from my unexplainable plans. "What's wrong?" I asked.

Jenna sighed. "I texted my mom to ask if you could come over, and she decided to turn pizza night into formal dinner night."

That's it? I'd hate to see how she'd handle a *real* problem. But I knew I should act like it was important. "That's too bad," I said. "I guess our movie night is off?"

"No, it's still on. This dinner is all about them scoping you out. My parents can be . . . overprotective." She turned to me, disappointment etched across her face. "I'll understand if you don't want to come."

Last night I'd had a gun to my head—I was pretty sure I could handle Jenna's parents. "This 'scoping' doesn't include making me eat anything weird, does it?"

The smile returned to Jenna's face. "No. I think we're having pot roast."

A home-cooked meal? I hadn't had one of those in about a year. My own lousy "cooking" consisted mainly of take-out food or whatever I could microwave. My mouth watered at the thought of pot roast, potatoes, and gravy. All for the small price of meeting some nosy parents.

I squeezed Jenna's hand. "I'll be there. But give me the rundown on your family so I know what I'm walking into."

When I'd met Sam's mom, I'd been barefoot and covered in dirt, hiding behind the shed in her backyard—quite possibly the worst first impression ever. For Jenna's family, I had turned it up a notch and wore my best jeans and a collared shirt—I was even wearing shoes. I stood on the front porch, ran my fingers one last time through my hair, and then rang the doorbell. A loud barking came from inside, followed a few seconds later by the sounds of a dog scratching at the door.

"Sit, Lilo! Sit!" a woman's voice said. The door opened partway to reveal a woman who looked a lot like Jenna: same black hair and twinkly eyes, similar face, but older. She had one hand on the edge of the door and the other on the collar of a black fluffy mutt that was aching to get outside.

"Hi, I'm Dan." I put my hand out. I wasn't really sure whether moms shook hands with teenage boys, but I was pulling out all the charm I had—which wasn't much.

Jenna's mom gave an amused smile and shook my hand. "I'm Amalia. Please come in, Dan."

"Thanks for inviting me to dinner."

"My pleasure. It's nice to finally meet the young man Jenna keeps talking about."

"*Mamá!*" Jenna yelled, followed by a rapid burst of Spanish that I had no hope of understanding without my jump device translating for me. The stomp of footsteps sounded inside the house and then the door swung completely open. Jenna stood in the foyer, her cheeks red. "Please come in before my mom embarrasses me any more." She pulled me inside, barely giving me time to kick off my shoes by the door. The aroma of pot roast and gravy wafted through the air. I'd missed that smell, and with every breath I could feel myself getting hungrier. Their house reminded me of the one I'd grown up in: two stories, nicely furnished, hardwood floors. The big difference was that family photos and personal items decorated every corner of their home. They even had Jenna's latest school test stuck to the fridge. My own house never had held this much warmth or personality—it had always been like living in a museum.

Jenna led me to the living room, where a couch and the TV waited. Unfortunately, so did her dad, who stood up from the couch and offered his hand. "You must be Daniel." He spoke with a slight accent. "You can call me Hector."

"Pleased to meet you, sir." I shook his hand firmly.

"Jenna says you're new to the school this year," he said as he sat down again.

"That's right. I was homeschooled until last June."

Jenna's mom came into the living room and sat down in a chair across from the couch. From a tactical perspective, I was now directly in between the two parents. Both were seated while I stood. This was rapidly feeling like an interrogation.

"Mom! Dad! He's just here to watch a movie," Jenna protested.

"We're only saying hello," Mr. Alvarez said. He turned to me. "Jenna told me you lost your father recently. I'm so sorry, Daniel."

"That must be terrible," Jenna's mom said gently. "How is your poor mother doing?"

"Oh, uh . . . actually, she was killed in a car accident when I was really little." I didn't want to dump a sob story on them, and I hadn't even told Jenna about my mom yet. I'd always kept that part of my life quiet, especially around school. The last thing I wanted was for jerks like Nick to start calling me Little Orphan Dannie.

"Oh, you poor boy!" Mrs. Alvarez gasped. "I can't imagine. Who do you live with now?"

"I live alone." I should have paused before answering, because my words came out flat, betraying how sad and lonely I was. Both Jenna and

Mrs. Alvarez looked at me like I was some wounded bird that needed to be wrapped in a blanket. "I have my own condo," I continued, forcing myself to sound more cheerful. "So it's not all bad. And my dad's best friend is technically my guardian, so I can ask him if I need help with anything. But most of the daily stuff like paying bills, buying groceries, and all that, I do on my own."

Neither Jenna nor her parents spoke, clearly shocked and struggling for something to say. Mrs. Alvarez was the first to recover. She grasped my hand and gave me a look full of pity. "Come, let's get you some dinner. Jenna, go get your brother."

Jenna walked to the bottom of the stairs and hollered, "Lucas!" while her mom led me to the kitchen, where the table was set for five.

Lucas, who looked about twelve, eyed me while dropping into his chair. "Are you Jenna's boyfriend?"

Jenna buried her face in one hand and shook her head.

I gave him an awkward smile and took the seat beside Jenna. As soon as I sat down, Lilo lay down at my feet and looked up at me expectantly.

"That dog. Just ignore her," Jenna's dad said as he passed the potatoes. "So, Daniel, do you play any sports?"

So much for pity putting an end to the interrogation. "I've been training in martial arts all my life," I said, leaving out the medieval-weapons part.

"Is that where you got your scar from?" Jenna's brother asked.

"Lucas Antonio Alvarez!" Jenna's mother plopped some potatoes on her plate and waved the serving spoon at Jenna's brother. "Manners."

I laughed at the question; it sounded like something I'd ask. "It's okay, Mrs. Alvarez." I turned to Lucas and traced a finger over the long horizontal scar on my forehead. It was about the length of my thumb and ran just above my eyebrows. "I got it from a hammer." *Swung by a Norman knight during the Battle of Hastings.*

"You see, Lucas?" Jenna's dad declared as he piled a few slices of meat onto his plate. "That's why you have to be careful with tools. They can be dangerous."

I took a sip of my drink before anyone saw me smirk.

"And what about your school?" Mr. Alvarez asked me. "Amalia and I are very proud of Jenna and her accomplishments. We know that she will be accepted to many good colleges and she has a great future ahead of her. What colleges have you applied to?"

Ugh. Should I have brought my taxes with me too? Was dinner going to be followed by a fun game of Guess Dan's Credit Score? "I haven't applied to any colleges," I admitted. "Since my dad died, I've been kind of unfocused. I missed all the deadlines." Not to mention that with Victor threatening the world, I didn't see the point of going to college. "But school is definitely in my future," I added, because I knew that was the sort of thing Mr. Alvarez wanted to hear.

"Good! Good!" Mr. Alvarez said. "A man needs a good education to succeed in life. And what about work?"

"Hector! Let the boy eat!" Jenna's mom said.

"We are just talking, Amalia," Mr. Alvarez said defensively. "I am getting to know the young man."

My phone pinged with a text. The scraping of cutlery across plates stopped and everyone turned toward me. "Sorry," I said sheepishly as I pulled my phone out, dreading a message from Sam telling me it was time to jump. Despite Mr. Alvarez's heavy grilling, the entirely normal world of Jenna's family was something I didn't want to miss out on.

To my relief, it was only Sam asking me what I was doing. I switched my phone to silent mode before shoving it back into my pocket.

"Was that about your camping plans?" Jenna asked.

"No. It's nothing."

"Ah? So you like camping?" Jenna's dad asked, his face lighting up. "When I was a much younger man, I used to love to camp." Before I could say anything, he launched into a story about the time he went camping and woke up to see a huge boa constrictor just outside his tent, which he followed with another story about howler monkeys that kept him up all night by throwing seed pods at his campsite. I didn't mind him prattling on—it stopped him from asking me questions, plus his stories were pretty funny. I sat and savored my food, occasionally nodding or laughing. I couldn't remember the last time I had enjoyed a sit-down dinner at the kitchen table with a family. A lot of people take something so simple for granted, but it was one of the best things I'd done in a long time.

After we had finished dessert and helped clean the table, Jenna made shooing motions to her parents, then led me to the family room. We ended up spending the rest of the evening together on the couch, watching a rom-com. At first a full cushion width separated us, but by the end of the movie, Jenna's head lay against my shoulder and I had my arm around her. Jenna's mom and dad gave us space, although they did magically appear every fifteen or twenty minutes—to see if we wanted anything to drink, asking if the movie was any good, to check if we wanted a snack.

When the movie was over, I didn't want to go, but it was past ten and Jenna's parents were starting to make less-than-subtle comments about the time. I said good night to Mr. and Mrs. Alvarez, then Jenna walked me out to the front porch.

"I had a lot of fun," I said, my breath coming out frosty in the March air.

"Sorry they hovered so much," she said, rolling her eyes. "I told you they were overprotective."

"Their excuses were pretty bad." I chuckled, but the truth was, I'd give anything to have parents hovering.

"Do you have any plans for spring break if the camping falls through?" she asked, her tone hopeful.

"Not a thing."

"Do you want to hang out this weekend then?"

"That would be awesome. Just no bowling."

She laughed. "Don't worry. We'll figure something out." She wrapped her arms tightly around herself to ward off the chill.

"I had a great night, but I don't want you freezing to death out here, so I better go." But I made no move to leave. I didn't want this night to end.

Jenna didn't seem eager to say goodbye either. Despite the cold, she remained on the porch, looking at me expectantly.

Clearly, this moment called for more than a *see ya later* or a handshake. But what?

I decided to play it safe and leaned in for a hug. Jenna must have thought I was moving in for a kiss, because she angled her head up to meet mine. Our lips collided briefly and then Jenna stepped back, her face flushed and her eyes downcast, as if she had done something she shouldn't have.

Nope. That can't be our first kiss.

I tilted her chin up and kissed her again. This time longer and deeper, with more conviction. She didn't pull away.

Much better.

"Good night, Jenna." I leaped down the porch steps, my pulse racing. As I opened the car door, I looked back to see her still standing on the porch, watching me. She smiled and waved as I pulled away.

As I drove, I couldn't stop thinking that a minor miracle had just happened. For a few brief hours, I had entered the world of normal. A place where families eat dinner together. Where the family dog begs at the table. Where a girl kisses you while you hold her close. Sam always claimed that the normal world was boring and full of ignorant people. But if this was normal, I could get used to it.

I was still basking in the warm glow of the evening as I opened the door to my apartment. I couldn't wait to hang out with Jenna again. Maybe we could—

My phone buzzed, interrupting my thoughts.

Time to go.

Damn it! So much for my weekend plans.

10 minutes, I texted Sam back, then composed a long, apologetic text to Jenna explaining that I'd be camping for the next few days after all.

In my bedroom, I quickly changed into my time-jumping gear and put on my backpack, then went over to the laundry room to retrieve the jump rod from its hiding place in a box of detergent. Even though I'd jumped into history twice, it still felt strange that this weird hexagonal rod of ancient-looking metal, slightly smaller than a baton from a relay race, was about to send me back into time. But, sure enough, its six movable sections felt cool to the touch, signifying that somewhere in time a glitch had occurred.

I plugged my phone into the charger so it wouldn't be dead when I got back, then made sure the straps of my backpack were tight and my sword securely in its sheath.

Ready, I texted Sam.

She wrote back right away: 10 sec.

Ten . . . Nine . . . I began to count down in my head. After the last jump, when me spending an extra minute hiding my phone had resulted in Sam waiting an hour alone in potentially hostile territory, we'd decided to coordinate our countdown better so we'd arrive in history at roughly the same time.

Seven . . . Six . . Five . . . Four . . . I took a deep breath as nervous anticipation filled me, as if I was on a roller coaster just before its first drop. *Three . . . Two . . . One . . .*

"Azkabaleth virros ku, Haztri valent bhidri du!"

The glyphs etched into the multiple faces of the rod glowed with a blazing intensity, bathing my kitchen in a blinding white light. I shut my eyes from the glare as the noise from the street outside vanished, and the smell of stale pizza that clung to my apartment faded into nothingness.

CHAPTER 5

The last time I traveled through the time stream, a hurricane-like wind attacked me, trying to rip me away from Sam. This time there was no wind, only a quiet sensation of floating like I was drifting down a lazy river on an inner tube. The only things I could sense were the dazzling light piercing my eyelids and the cold rod in my hand. I opened my eyes a crack, hoping to catch a glimpse of the city I'd seen before, but the brightness forced me to shut them again.

The floating sensation lasted for about thirty seconds, then the light dimmed and solid ground appeared beneath my feet. I began blinking away the purple spots, catching a momentary glimpse of green hills, before a wave of dizziness forced me to my hands and knees. With all my senses on edge, I shut my eyes again and strained to hear any sounds of people. Insects hummed in the grass, and a warm breeze, reminiscent of early summer, carried the scent of greenery and soil. But there were no footsteps, no voices. It sounded like I was alone.

After a few seconds, the dizziness passed and the purple spots disappeared. Carefully I got back to my feet and turned slowly to get my bearings. All around me stretched endless low hills covered in grass and the occasional cluster of trees. Far off in one direction the hills grew taller and forest-covered, leading eventually to mountains. I felt small and insignificant against this vast landscape. And worried—Sam was nowhere to be seen.

I crouched in a small clump of bushes and twisted the sections on the jump rod to the combination that detected other rods. Holding it out in front of me like a flashlight, I did another slow circle. The jump rod tugged, like a magnet drawn toward metal, in five separate directions.

Crap . . .

Victor's guys must have shown up. It made sense. After all, their grand homicidal scheme to rule the world wouldn't work if history collapsed and everything was rewritten, so they needed time to flow correctly just as much as I did.

Which one's Sam?

I turned in another slow circle, trying to identify the sharpest pull, which also meant the closest time jumper. The rod pulled most strongly toward a valley between two hills.

I drew my sword and began heading in that direction, my steps slow and cautious as I scanned all around me, alert for any flicker of motion, any glint of metal in the bright sunlight. If I was heading straight for one of Victor's guys, I needed to spot him early so I didn't walk into an ambush.

This empty grassland felt so alien after my first two jumps, which I'd spent mostly in forests. Here, I was only too conscious of how visible I was—a lone speck on a wide field of green. And with hardly any trees, there was no concept of movement. Minutes passed, and the hills seemed just as distant as before, as if I was walking on a treadmill.

Another sweep with the jump device, and it still pointed dead ahead, but oddly it pulled in only two other directions this time. Two of Victor's guys must have decided to head back. Meaning I now had a one-in-three chance of finding Sam.

Slowly I covered the distance to the gap between the hills, the pull of the rod growing constantly stronger. What if it wasn't Sam? Would one of Victor's guys and I just agree to both walk away and pretend we never saw each other, or would we end up fighting to the death?

I began to regret bringing just a sword. If the other guy had a bow, he could pick me off long before I got close.

Slinking lower, I entered the valley, where a quick-moving stream tumbled noisily over its rocky bed, drowning out all other sounds. My heart began to beat faster. The jump rod seemed to be pointing to about twenty paces ahead, where the stream curled around a rocky bend.

I took a few more hesitant steps, then dove to the ground as a hooded figure became visible against the backdrop of boulders—the arrow in his bow pointed straight at me.

"Dan!" Sam hissed. "It's me!" She lowered the bow and pushed back her hood, letting her mass of red hair spill over her shoulders.

I exhaled loudly as I pulled myself up off the ground. "I thought you were one of Victor's guys. There were four of them out here when I first landed."

"Yeah, I know. I've been keeping track of them." Sam tapped the archery bracer on her left arm where she kept her jump device hidden. "And right now they are"—she did a slow sweep with her arm and frowned—"gone." She shrugged. "I guess we're in charge of fixing this glitch now."

"They're gone? All of them?" Sure enough, when I swept my jump device, it only pointed to Sam, who was making her way toward me, silently as usual, her feet always finding the solid areas without any twigs or loose rocks. She wore her regular time-jumping gear: baggy gray tunic and pants, thin leather gloves, brown boots, and a drab green cloak.

She stopped only a few steps in front of me. This close, I could see that her eyes lacked their usual sparkle and her shoulders kind of drooped. "Are you okay? You look upset."

She sighed. "I am just so glad to be somewhere other than home." She sounded sadder than I'd heard her in a long time.

"What's wrong?"

"Oh, you know, the usual crap with my mom. Today she accused me of stealing cash from her, when I know for sure she lost it at bingo. But she was probably too drunk to notice. We've been fighting all day." Sam pressed her eyes shut. "I can't stand living there."

"Can I do anything?" I ventured, even though I knew the answer.

"No, thanks. I'll be okay," she said with little conviction. "Her mood will pass, like it always does, and then everything will be fine for a few days . . . until the next thing." She wiped her eyes with a sleeve. "It's almost funny that my life is such a hot mess I'd rather risk it in history than be home."

"You sure I can't do anything? You could stay with me if you want. I have plenty of room. You know I'd do anything to help you."

"I know. But I'm good . . . for now at least." She waved a hand dismissively. "Besides, in a few months I'll be leaving for college, and I'll never have to see my mom or my creepy stepdad ever again."

"Did you decide on one yet?"

"Nah. I'm still waiting for all my acceptances." She clapped her hands together. "But enough about me—let's get to the important stuff. How long have you been here?"

"Probably twenty minutes. You?"

"Same. I guess our plan worked."

I squinted into the distance, trying to pick out some landmark among the endless green hills that would help identify what part of the world we had landed in. "Any idea where we are?"

"Nope. If I had to guess, I'd say Montana. Not that I've ever been there before, but I've seen pictures."

"Ugh . . . I hope it's not Montana. If we've landed in the Wild West, we're going to look pretty stupid dressed like this."

Sam poked a finger at my chest. "What's with the chain mail?"

I shrugged. "Well . . . I was kind of getting tired of being stabbed at all the time. Do you think I should take it off?"

"No. Keep it on for now, at least until we figure out where we are. Speaking of which . . ." She spun the sections on her jump rod to a new combination and swung it in a slow circle, until it pointed to the far end of the valley. "The time glitch is that way. You ready to go find out what brought us here?"

"Might as well. History isn't going to fix itself."

After months of snow and gray skies and cold, it felt great to be walking in the sunshine, surrounded by green. Even better, I was with Sam again. It had been months since I'd seen her in person, and I could feel a bounce in my step because she was near.

"You must have been doing something fun tonight," Sam said. "You usually text me right back."

"I was at a friend's house," I said, hoping to leave it at that.

"You have a friend?" she asked, her tone a mixture of excitement and disbelief. She shook her head. "Sorry, that sounded rude. I think it's great you've got someone to hang with. What's his name?"

No way I could dodge that question. "Jenna," I mumbled.

"Oh . . ." Her measured stride faltered for a step, and some loose rocks skittered from beneath her feet.

"We've only hung out a few times."

"Cool. What's she like?"

Okay . . . The girl I had a major crush on was asking me about the girl I just started dating. Did not see this coming. "Well . . . she's nice."

"Nice?" Sam snorted. "I hope you never said that to her. 'Hey. Jenna. You nice,'" she mimicked in her best caveman voice.

"All right, she's better than nice. Sure, she's no hell-raising redhead who's saved my life tons of times, but I have fun with her."

"What can you even talk about?" Sam pressed. "Everyone who goes to my school is a complete idiot. I can't imagine the people at yours being that much different. Do you honestly care about the latest TikTok or what some lame celebrity posted five minutes ago?"

"Okay, maybe we don't talk about rocket science. But you know what? She's normal. She has a normal family. She does normal things. When I'm with her, I can lose myself in easy conversation and not have to think about saving the world all the time."

"Ooooh . . . she's nice *and* normal." Sam raised the back of her hand to her forehead and batted her eyelashes as if she was about to faint. "You should write poetry, Dan."

"You know what I mean. Sometimes I just need an escape from the drama of time-jumping."

"Is she pretty?" Sam asked hesitantly.

"Yeah."

Sam didn't say anything for a few seconds, and I hoped that would be the end of it, but then she turned toward me with an oddly pained look in her eyes. "Is she, like, your girlfriend?"

I shrugged. "We've only gone out twice, so . . . not really. We went bowling, and then tonight I had dinner at her house with her parents."

"Bowling?" Sam gave me a puzzled look.

"Yeah. You roll a heavy ball down a wooden lane and try to knock pins over."

"I know what bowling is," she snapped. "It just doesn't seem like something *you'd* do."

"It was fun. Next time you're at my place, we should go."

"Won't your new *girlfriend* mind?" She sounded almost spiteful now.

"Sam. She's not my girlfriend. And no matter what, you're still my *best* friend. If I want to go bowling with you, I'll go bowling with you."

Sam raised an eyebrow. "Does Jenna know who your best friend is?"

"Well . . . not exactly," I replied, my bravado deflating. "Honestly, she thinks you're a guy and we're on a camping trip. But what's with the inquisition here? Does it bother you that I'm dating her?"

Sam's cheeks flushed. "No! Of course not!"

I stopped and looked at her, wondering if I could be wrong, but everything about her stance and expression told me I was right. "Yes, it *does*!"

"Don't be stupid," Sam said, but the color of her cheeks only deepened.

"Uh-uh. I know you almost as well as I know myself. You're upset. But why? You must've told me a hundred times that we're never going to be more than friends. You should be happy I'm not bugging you anymore."

For a few seconds Sam said nothing; she just stared at her feet. "Maybe I was wrong," she finally said, her voice quiet.

"What?" My jaw dropped open. "Are you saying we might actually have a chance of being together?"

Sam rubbed a tired hand across her eyes. "I . . . don't . . . know."

"Come on, Sam. We wouldn't be having this conversation if you didn't feel something about me." I rested a hand on her shoulder. "Do we have a chance? Because if we do, Jenna's gone as soon as I get home. She's great and all, but she's not you."

"You don't understand. You're right—I should have been happy for you. But the first thing I felt when you told me her name was jealousy and . . . and . . . sadness. I need to figure out—"

She snapped her head up and her eyes went wide for a second, then she pushed us both to the ground. Over the babbling of the stream, I could hear the sound I dreaded the most: the low thump of hooves. *Why is it always horses?* Too many nights I would wake up in a cold sweat, dreaming of horsemen charging after me.

Sam lay flat beside me. "Where?" she mouthed.

I closed my eyes as the hoofbeats grew louder, reverberating from the valley walls. They could be coming from anywhere. Sam pulled out her jump device and swung it in a slow circle, stopping with it pointed toward the hill on the left. A second later, a man with tanned skin and almond-shaped eyes came running over the rise, his legs churning. Judging by his thin build and lack of facial hair, he couldn't be much older than me. He wore a fur-lined hat and a filthy wraparound coat that went down to his knees, with an even dirtier pair of pants underneath.

His bow was recurved like Sam's, and the quiver over his shoulder held only two arrows. His brown eyes widened when he saw us, but instead of running away, he headed straight in our direction, his left leg dragging as he ran.

My jump rod translated his panicked yell: "Merkits are coming!"

Meerkats? As in Timon from The Lion King?

Probably not. But whatever this guy was freaked out about was probably bad—and it was heading our way on horseback. Even worse, since Sam's jump device had been pointing right in his direction when he'd come over the hill, there was a good chance this guy was the source of the time glitch. His problem was now our problem.

The pounding hoofbeats turned into five horsemen galloping over the same hill. They were dressed similarly to the limping guy, in wrap-around tunics, dirty leggings, and furry caps. Over their shoulders hung short bows and quivers, and each of them carried a spear. As soon as they caught sight of us, they charged.

"I'm guessing this isn't Montana," Sam muttered as she sprang to her feet, drew her bow, nocked an arrow, and pulled the bowstring to her cheek.

I jumped up and placed myself between the charging horsemen and Sam. Five hostile horsemen with spears and bows and one runner of unknown intent. It was either five-on-three or six-on-two. No matter how I sliced it, our odds sucked.

I gripped my sword tighter. This was a new personal record for me: less than an hour into a time jump and I was already getting ready to fight for my life.

CHAPTER 6

The horsemen sped toward us, clods of earth flying from the hooves of their mounts. Sam's arrow hissed over my shoulder and sank into the chest of the lead rider, dropping him out of the saddle.

With shouts of outrage, two of the attackers leaned low over their horses and charged with their spears out, while the other two held back and drew their bows. I couldn't see the limping man anywhere. Sam fired again, but her target ducked at the last instant, and her arrow sailed harmlessly over his head. The two archers fired back, their arrows streaming toward me in a blur of white fletching. I leaped to one side but felt a sudden burning sting in my upper right arm, as if I'd been stabbed. An arrow had obviously penetrated my chain mail, and the shock of pain sent the sword flying from my hand.

"Spearmen coming!" Sam yelled.

Fear gave me speed. With a grunt I yanked the arrow out of my arm, tossed it aside, and lifted my sword off the grass. The ground trembled beneath my feet as both spearmen galloped toward me. I sprang to the left so that I was facing only one of them, his deadly point closing in on my chest. At the last moment I dodged his thrust and slashed down with my sword, snapping the end of his wooden spear. With my return swing I hacked at his midsection, cutting through his grubby tunic and into his flesh. The force of my blow knocked him out of the saddle, and he crashed to the ground at my feet.

Sam fired again, and this time her arrow sank into the neck of the other spearman's horse. The wounded animal whinnied and reared, dumping him to the ground.

Two riders down. Where are the archers?

I whipped my head around, trying to spot them before they shot me.

Both lay facedown on the ground, arrows in their backs. The limping man stood behind their riderless horses, his quiver now empty.

I exhaled slowly and turned to face our last attacker, the one who had been thrown from his horse. He rose slowly to his feet, clutching his spear in white-knuckled hands. He stood staring at Sam for a few seconds and then dropped his weapon. "O great Temujin," he called over to the limping man. "I surrender and throw myself at your mercy."

Temujin slung his bow over one shoulder and hobbled to stand just in front of the spearman. "You would swear loyalty to me?" he asked, his voice stern, as if he was used to command.

The spearman bowed his head. "Yes, noble Temujin, I would."

Temujin's eyes narrowed. "What about your own people and your khan? Have you not sworn loyalty to them? Would you so quickly forget the pledges you gave them?"

The spearman licked his lips and his eyes darted back and forth. "Yes . . . I would."

Temujin nodded and reached forward, placing his left hand on the man's head in an almost fatherly fashion. The man's nervousness vanished, and he gave a slight smile. Without warning, Temujin's right hand whipped out, jabbing something that looked like a sharpened fragment of antler into the spearman's neck. The man clutched at his throat and collapsed to his knees, blood gurgling from the wound.

"Faithless dog!" Temujin spat. "I would never trust anyone who would throw away their loyalty so easily. You are a coward. You forsake all you hold dear, just to save your own life." He gave the kneeling man a kick, sending him sprawling into the grass. "May seven wolves feast upon your treacherous bones."

Temujin wiped his weapon clean on the dying man's shirt and then turned toward me and Sam. From underneath the rim of his fur-lined cap, his eyes shifted warily between us. With slow, deliberate movements, as if not to seem threatening, he tucked the sharpened antler into the wide sash at his waist. Keeping his hands visible in front of him, he began inching forward like a boy approaching a tiger.

"What now?" Sam whispered from the corner of her mouth as she kept her bow trained on him.

"No clue," I whispered back. "Looking at these guys, I'm guessing we're somewhere in Asia. But why would the jump rods even send us here? We have no chance of passing as locals. How the hell can we possibly make up a story to explain how we got here?"

The man halted a few paces in front of us, stopping any further discussion. Without saying a word, he bowed nine times toward Sam and me, each bow so deep that his head dipped to the height of our waists. He then inched forward, taking the smallest of steps, until he stopped directly in front of Sam. Eyes wide with curiosity, he reached out with a hand and tentatively stroked her hair, sniffing a handful of it before letting the red tresses slip, a few strands at a time, between his fingers. He then held the hand next to Sam's cheek, comparing his tanned skin to her almost white complexion. "Hair of flame and eyes the color of the forest," he declared, his voice emerging in an awed hush.

He stepped in front of me. He was about a head shorter than me, and his dark-brown eyes held a feverish gleam that spoke of either fierce intensity or madness. For a few seconds he studied my face closely, a strong, musky odor of sweat and horses coming off his clothes. I stood my ground under his scrutiny, not breaking eye contact in case he took that as a sign of weakness or fear. He ran a hand over my chain mail, his fingers glancing lightly over the metal as if he was scared to touch it. "And you, with eyes the color of the sky and a shirt of iron." He bowed again. "Do you speak my tongue?" he asked, the words coming out slowly, as if to a foreigner.

"We do," I answered, the jump rod translating my thoughts so that the alien tones of his own language emerged from my mouth.

A slight smile creased his lips and he bowed again. "I am Temujin, son of Yisugei. I thank both of you for saving me from the foul Merkits. How are you called?"

There was no use in even trying to make up a name he'd recognize. "I'm Dan."

Temujin nodded enthusiastically. "Dan," he repeated.

"And I'm Sam."

"Dan and Sam, you saved my life. I owe you a debt, and I will not rest until I have repaid you."

"You can start by telling us where we are," Sam said.

Temujin pointed to a mountain in the distance that didn't look any different from the other mountains around it. "We travel in the great valley of the Keluren River, in the shadow of Burkhan Khaldun, the sacred mountain. I came here seeking guidance for my quest. It is here that Tengri speaks to me, telling me what must be done."

Well, that was a dead end. I was pretty good at geography, but I'd never heard of the Keluren River, and I'd definitely never heard of any sacred mountains.

Sam motioned to the corpses strewn across the grass. "You called them Merkits. What does that mean?"

Temujin's face twisted as if Sam had asked a question that even a child should know the answer to. "Merkits are a people from the north of my tribe's lands. They were hunting me."

"Are there any other tribes in this area?" Sam asked.

"Many." Temujin raised his arm to shoulder height and moved it in a complete circle, jabbing his finger in different directions. "Tayichi'uts, Kereyits, Onggirats, Naimans, Tatars."

Great . . . Another dead end. None of those tribes held any meaning for me. "Any Huns or Mongols?" I asked, desperately trying to get some sort of sense of where we were in history.

Temujin thumped his chest with a fist. "I am Mongol. I belong to the Borjigin clan." He said that last bit proudly, as if it should mean something to us. It didn't.

One mystery solved—we were in Mongolia. Now to figure out when. Which wasn't going to be easy. Even if the Mongols used a calendar, I doubted I'd be able to translate "fifth day of the year of the Yak" into something I'd understand. "How many years since anything important happened around here?" I asked, hoping he might mention some event I'd recognize.

"It has been seventeen years since I first drew breath," Temujin said. "And there have been eight passings of my people to the summer grazing grounds in the hills since I was promised to my wife Borte." The enthusiasm disappeared from his face and he clenched his fist. "And there have been eight long years of hardship and suffering for me and my family since my father was poisoned by the treacherous Tatars."

"Sorry to hear that," I said, deciding that a statement like that deserved some sort of response. Unfortunately, none of the events he'd mentioned helped me figure out the year. I should have known better. Temujin had probably spent his life herding animals and wasn't even remotely aware of the outside world. I went over what he said and did some quick math in my head; at least his numbers were ones I could handle. "So you're seventeen now, and you got married at nine?"

Temujin gave me the same look my math teacher gave me most days. "No, not married—promised. My father went to the Onggirat tribe and arranged my marriage when I was nine and she was ten. We were to be married once I became a man. But after my father died, enemies in my own tribe cast my family out. They were jealous of my father's power and wanted it for themselves. So I have spent years wandering through the wide steppe and the deep valleys, gaining loyal friends and growing in strength, so I can prove myself a man and take my rightful position as ruler of my people."

"Umm . . . so, where are your loyal friends now?" Sam asked. I knew that tone: she was trying to hide her skepticism but not fully succeeding.

"We were riding together through the forest when the Merkits attacked us. My horse was shot out from under me, and I was left alone on the trail. Most of the Merkits chased after my friends, but some decided to come after me. I ran like an elk chased by wolves but, in my haste, I twisted my ankle. Only my skill with the bow has kept me alive and free this long. But I was down to my last two arrows; they would have captured or even killed me if you had not shown up."

"Why were they chasing you in the first place?" I asked.

"A few moons ago, after years of being apart, Borte and I were finally married. But the foul Merkits stole her from me, and they know I will come to get her back." His eyes grew fierce with determination.

Sam placed a hand on his shoulder with a soft, compassionate look that I rarely saw in her eyes. "That's terrible," she said. "We'll help you get her back."

What? Where did the real Sam go? She'd never exactly been the sappy type. And to jump into something without even consulting me? That really wasn't her style.

Temujin bowed again toward us. "You must have been sent by Tengri himself to help me. How else could you appear in the middle of the steppe without horses, and just in time to save me? No matter how long it takes, I shall make sure that you know the depths of my gratitude." His eyes misted over, and he swiped at them with a dirty sleeve. "A man without friends is as small as this palm," he said, holding out his hand. "But a man with friends is as large as the steppe." He stretched his arms out wide. "With you by my side, I am now as large as the steppe." Temujin bowed to us once more. "The hour grows late—we must return to my camp. I will check the bodies of the Merkits and gather the horses." Without waiting for our response, he hobbled toward the first corpse and began stripping it of arrows, weapons, and anything of value.

"How's your arm?" Sam asked.

With the rush of battle and the shock of meeting Temujin, I had completely forgotten I'd been hit. I rolled up my chain-mail sleeve and the shirt underneath it to reveal a long trail of drying blood that led to a small puncture wound in my bicep. The arrow had pierced my skin but not deeply.

"It doesn't look too bad," I decided. "My chain mail stopped most of it."

"Shouldn't it have stopped *all* of it?"

"Unfortunately, chain mail isn't that great against arrows. The smaller the arrow's tip, the more likely it will punch through the links."

"Well, we better get you patched up." Sam poured some water on the small wound to clean it, and then slapped on a bandage from her backpack. "There, I think you'll live now."

"Thanks. No kiss to make it better?"

Sam ignored that suggestion and picked up one of the Merkit arrows. She eyed the white fletching, the wood, and spent considerable time examining the point. "This is weird," she said. "The tip is animal horn, not metal. And look at the horsemen: none of them have metal either. Their spear points are all animal horn also." She gestured to my armor. "No wonder our friend over there was so amazed at your chain mail."

"We must be really early in Mongol history then." I glanced down at my chain-mail shirt. "I know that the first rule of time-jumping is 'Don't stand out,' but I think both of us are way beyond that here. So I'm keeping the chain mail—even if it isn't that great at stopping arrows."

"Agreed. I'm not taking the metal tips off my arrows either—that'll leave me firing feathered sticks at people."

I rubbed a hand along my jaw. "If we so clearly don't belong here, why do you think the jump rods dumped us here?"

Sam twisted a strand of her long red hair around one finger and began chewing on the ends. "Dunno. With my hair, I kind of stand out in most places, but the jump rod has only ever dumped me in spots where I could at least pass for a local. Time jumpers from Asia should be fixing this glitch."

"Maybe they were. There *were* four others here when we first landed."

"That's what bugs me. We never should have landed in the first place. The jump rods don't send you places where you don't belong."

"Should we . . . leave?"

Sam removed her jump device from underneath the leather archery bracer on her left forearm, spun the sections to the setting that found other time jumpers, and did a quick scan. "We can't. We're still the only ones here. Unless someone else decides to show up, we're stuck fixing the glitch."

"Is that why you were so quick to help him?"

"Yeah." Sam pointed at Temujin as he looted arrows from another corpse. "The jump rod points right at him. So we either follow him or stay here with the dead guys. Seemed like an easy choice."

"Are you sure it's not because you're turning all sappy and romantic, and you felt sorry for him and his stolen bride?"

"No!" Sam punched me in the arm. My right arm. Exactly where the arrow had hit me. I winced. Sometimes being right wasn't worth it.

We both snapped our heads up at a pained whinny. Temujin had gathered the reins of all the Merkit horses except for the wounded one. It now flattened its ears and stamped its hooves, warning him off. With tentative steps Temujin crept forward, his arms spread wide and with gentle clicking noises coming from his mouth, until he was close enough to reach up and stroke the poor animal's muzzle. Slowly the horse quieted enough for the Mongol to gently withdraw Sam's arrow.

He examined the arrow closely, sighting along the shaft for warps and running his thumb along the tip's metal edges. When he finished his examination, he placed it in his own quiver, then mounted one of the other horses.

Standing on the ground, he had appeared clumsy and awkward, but in the saddle, he sat with his back straight and a commanding look, like he was born to ride. He flicked the reins of his mount and led a pair of other horses toward us.

"Please take these fine animals. They are the best of the group." He passed us the reins of the chosen horses, leaving the rest to follow him.

The horses were small, only a bit larger than ponies. If Temujin said they were the best, I'd have to believe him. Each came equipped with a sturdy leather saddle, tied with two straps around the belly, and with a bridle and stirrups. Mongol weaponry might be primitive, but their saddle-making was the best I'd seen in history so far. Sam and I mounted our horses and began trailing after Temujin as he led his horse at a casual pace.

We passed over a few rounded hills, and then into another shallow river valley. He kept his horse along this path, leading us upstream and deeper into the hills.

"So why'd the Merkits steal your wife?" Sam asked him.

"You ask many questions. Do you not know how the people of the felt-walled tents live?"

We were in way over our heads here. We didn't look like Mongols, we didn't act like Mongols, and unless Sam had some extensive knowledge about the Mongols that she'd never told me about, we knew nothing about their culture or history. "No. We don't," I replied.

Temujin waved his hand dismissively. "No matter. You helped me defeat my enemies, and now you help me find my wife. That is all that is of importance to me." He pointed past some low hills. "My tribe has always lived near the sacred mountain Burkhan Khaldun, on the shores of the Onon River. That has been the way of life for my people for as long as the storytellers can remember. We bring our herds down from the hills in the winter, to let them graze on the thick grass in the valleys. And in the summer, when the heat grows strong and the insects bite, we move our herds back to the hills to grow fat." He clenched his fist around the reins. "And, just like mixing sheep from different herds makes the blood of each herd stronger, so the tribes have always taken wives from their neighbors. It is the way of our people. We raid each other for horses, for sheep, for wives . . . or just to raid. The strong always take from those who are weaker. My own father stole his wife—my mother—from the Merkits."

He closed his eyes for a moment before opening them again. "We have long memories here. Insults that happened in the past are always remembered—and always avenged. I thought I had grown strong enough to marry Borte and to keep her safe. But three Merkits heard of my joy and came and took her from me. They punish me for the act of my father." He sighed and looked wistfully off into the distance. "I miss her. She has light in her face and fire in her eyes."

I now felt my own sappiness levels starting to rise. Everything about this guy made me feel sorry for him. Dead father. Kicked out by his tribe. Lost. Alone. Just trying to get his life back together—and then his wife gets stolen. He was like a Mongolian version of me, except even more hard-done-by.

Temujin jerked upright in the saddle and his eyes went wide. "More riders approach!" He reined in his horse and swiveled his head in all directions. "They come from in front of us."

Sam turned her horse around. "Then let's go back downriver!"

"No! We cannot run. The horses are tired and have no strength." With a grim look of determination, Temujin pulled out his bow. "We have only one path. We must fight."

"Fight?" I gulped. "But we don't know how many are coming."

"It does not matter. If we run, they will hunt us down and attack us from the back. But if we attack now, surprise can win where our small numbers fail." He pointed to a spot about twenty paces to the right. "Sam, you shoot from there." He pointed to another spot on the left. "I will be there. And Dan, you charge up the middle."

Charge up the middle?

I wanted to argue that his plan royally sucked, that there had to be a better way to handle the situation. But unfortunately, I couldn't. Everything Temujin had said made perfect sense. And with the drumming of hooves getting louder by the second, we'd run out of time.

With the blood pounding in my ears, I drew my sword.

CHAPTER 7

Four horsemen came galloping around the bend in the river, with extra horses following behind. The lead rider raced a few lengths ahead of the group, his horse splashing through the shallow water.

All the riders were armed with bows and spears, but none of them had their weapons at the ready. Like Temujin had planned, we had the element of surprise. Now we had to use it.

I kicked my horse and charged ahead, leaning low in the saddle, trying to present as small a target as possible while I closed the distance.

The lead rider saw me approaching and, with a speed I didn't think possible, he whipped out his bow and aimed an arrow right at me. His eyes bored into mine, showing no mercy.

My breath caught in my throat as I stared at the arrow's deadly point. I was too close for him to miss but still too far to get him with my sword.

"Hold, Khasar!" Temujin cried. "Put down your weapon!"

For a second, the archer glanced past me and toward Temujin. Then his eyes grew wide, and a look of relief appeared on his face. Just as quickly, he lowered his bow and reined in his horse.

What? Temujin knows this guy?

I yanked hard on the reins of my own horse so it came to a halt only paces from the other rider, and then slowly let out a huge breath. Two close calls, and the day wasn't over yet.

Temujin and Sam rode up beside the pair of us. "Dan, this is Khasar, my younger brother," Temujin announced, a huge grin spreading across his face. "And with him ride Belgutei, Jelme, and Bo'orchu."

I gave Khasar a slight nod of acknowledgment but still held my sword in hand. Just because these guys were friends of Temujin didn't mean they'd be my friends too. Beside me, Sam must have had the same thought. She had lowered her bow so the arrow pointed down, but her fingers rested on the bowstring and her eyes didn't leave the four horsemen.

The other three riders approached just as warily. They had their spears out, but held them point down. They sat stiffly in their saddles, as if ready to fight at a moment's notice.

"What kept you, Khasar?" Temujin asked. "Did you return to your ger to shear your sheep?"

Khasar pulled his horse up next to Temujin's, his brown eyes never leaving me and Sam. "Maybe the next time my *wise* older brother decides to talk to the great spirits, he will ask them for advice on how to stay seated on his horse so that he does not get left behind." He pointed at me and Sam, mistrust etched on his face. "Who are these fair-skinned ones?"

"Friends sent by the great blue heaven. They saved me from the Merkits."

Khasar guided his horse in a slow circle around mine, his mouth curling into a sneer as he looked me up and down. He and Temujin had a lot of similarities. Same hair. Same eyes. But Khasar was thinner, almost wiry-looking, and he didn't have that spark—of what? insanity? willpower?—that Temujin had. He motioned rudely toward me with his chin. "What tribe are you? You look like no man I have ever seen before."

"Enough, Khasar!" Temujin snapped. "They saved my life, and they have agreed to help me rescue Borte. It does not matter what tribe they come from—they now are part of my tribe. I name them Mongols." Temujin stared down each of the four men in turn. "Does anyone disagree?"

Khasar scowled but said nothing. The other three riders bowed their heads in silent agreement and pulled up alongside Temujin. The largest of them had a thick chest and rode with his sleeves partly rolled up, showing thick forearms. He squinted at me and Sam from under his fur-lined cap. "Do they speak our tongue?" he asked Temujin, his tone cautious. "How are they called?"

"The man is named Dan. And the woman is Sam."

"Yes, we speak your language," I added.

The big man visibly startled in the saddle, but quickly regained his composure. He brought his horse right next to mine and grasped both my wrists in his large hands in a welcoming manner. "I am Belgutei, son of Yisugei, and I thank you for saving my brother."

"Uh . . . you're welcome," I replied.

"Are you wounded, Temujin?" another of the men asked. He appeared to be the oldest, but not by much. If Khasar was about four-teen, and the rest were seventeen-ish like Temujin, then he was probably twenty. The thin beginnings of a mustache clung like a dirty smudge to his upper lip. He jumped off his horse and began patting Temujin down as if looking for injuries.

"I am fine, Jelme. Only my ankle hurts. I twisted it, nothing more."

"Let me look at it," Jelme insisted, as he began tugging at Temujin's boot. "What if it is broken? What if it bleeds?"

Temujin wrenched his leg from Jelme's grasp. "Leave me, Jelme. My ankle will be fine again in a few days."

"What of your pursuers?" Khasar asked, looking past us in the direction we had come from. "Did any escape?"

"No, we killed them all," Temujin replied. "And those who chased you?"

"They were far too many to fight, so we led them along forest paths until they lost sight of us. We then turned back to search for you."

The last of the four men led one of his spare horses over and passed the reins to Temujin. "Your horse looks tired. Take one of the fresh mounts, as we still have much riding to do today." He directed a welcoming smile toward me and Sam. "I am Bo'orchu, son of Naqu-bayan." He reached into a bag slung from his saddle and extracted a skin full of liquid. He yanked out the wooden stopper with his teeth, swallowed a mouthful, then passed the bag to me. "I bid you welcome to our group."

I took the bag from him and sniffed the contents. The horrid smell of sour milk attacked my nose and my stomach recoiled. "What is this?"

"Airag—fermented mare's milk." Bo'orchu motioned for me to drink. "It will make you strong, like a stallion."

"You can see that Khasar does not drink enough of it," Belgutei remarked.

Khasar scowled as the others laughed at him.

Although not a single part of me wanted to drink the foul-smelling stuff, I knew that it was being offered to me in the spirit of brotherhood and friendship, and if I didn't drink, I'd risk offending these guys. So I tipped the skin into my mouth and let the smallest amount of liquid drip in. Vile did not begin to describe the taste of airag. It was like drinking carbonated milk mixed with vinegar. But everyone was watching me, so I choked down the small mouthful, resisting every urge to gag, then handed the skin back to Bo'orchu.

He passed the airag around to the other riders, who all took a long gulp. None of them experienced my reaction, but instead they drank deeply, as if relishing the taste. When the skin finally reached Sam, she made no move to grab it, just stared at the bag as if it contained poison.

"Drink with us," Bo'orchu insisted. "This means you are Mongol now."

"You have to try it," I insisted. "You don't want to insult them." As the lone female in an all-male group, I really didn't believe anyone would be insulted if she passed—I just wanted her to share my misery.

She gave me a glare that could have melted my chain mail as she reached out and took a small swig. Her face contorted into a grimace as she swallowed.

"You drink well." Bo'orchu laughed and he clapped her on the back. "Tell me; are all the women in your lands like you, with fiery hair and skin so light?"

"No, not all of them," Sam wheezed as she fought back a choking cough.

Khasar nudged his horse in between Bo'orchu's and Sam's. "You do not wear braids," he observed. "Are you married? Have you been spoken for?" He stood up in his stirrups. "If you are looking for a husband, you will find no better man than me. I am strong in battle and would provide many sheep and horses for you."

"She can find no better man than you?" Belgutei laughed. "She can find four better men right here." The four Mongols laughed as Khasar's face turned red.

"Khasar," Temujin said, half chuckling and half in admonishment. "She comes from far-off lands and does not know our ways. Leave her be." He turned to the others. "Now let us ride back to our camp, before more Merkits find us."

We began heading along the valley, keeping close to the river. Khasar rode at Sam's other side, saying nothing, but his eyes never left her. As we rode, Belgutei poked at my armor with a stubby finger. "A full shirt of iron." He shook his head in admiration. "You must be a great lord in your lands."

"No, just an average guy."

This only seemed to impress him more. "And where is this land, where everyone has coats of iron?"

"Uh . . . really far to the west."

Belgutei cast his eyes west, his face full of longing.

Temujin caught his look. "One day, Belgutei, when I reach the end of the path that heaven has set me on, we will be a strong nation with shirts of iron for every man. But first we must stop fighting among ourselves. Right now the tribes are like arrows in a quiver—"

"Not this again," Khasar groaned, rolling his eyes.

Belgutei tilted his head back and stared at the sky, a totally bored look on his face, while Jelme rode closer to Temujin, intent on what he had to say. Only Bo'orchu seemed indifferent to Temujin's statement. He continued riding along, a half smile on his lips, as if he was just out enjoying a ride in the countryside.

Temujin pulled an arrow from his quiver. "Pick up one arrow and it can be broken easily." With a flick of both wrists, he snapped the arrow in half. "But bring the arrows together and bind them tightly so they do not separate"—he pulled a handful of arrows from his quiver and pressed down on them; they didn't bend—"then no man will be able to break their strength. One day the rest of the tribes will see the wisdom of this path. I will bind them together so that our backs cannot be broken. Then we will head to the lands to the west and to the south, and we too shall be wearing coats of iron."

"And how do you shoot a bundle of arrows from your bow?" Khasar scoffed. "Maybe if your stories made sense, big brother, you would have an easier time getting the other tribes to follow you."

Jelme stiffened in his saddle. "How dare you speak to Temujin like that? He is the favored son of heaven. His dream *will* come true."

Belgutei snorted. "Favored son of heaven? Is that why we have to make our way to Merkit lands and bring back Borte? Is that how Tengri treats those he favors?"

This comment set off a huge argument with Temujin and Jelme on one side and Belgutei and Khasar on the other. Bo'orchu shook his head and let his horse slowly fall away from the group, as if this was a regular occurrence among the four of them.

Sam and I held back even farther, letting a large distance grow between us and the five horsemen. Sam waited until we could barely hear them arguing, and then she motioned her head toward the group. "Do you know anything at all about the Mongols?"

"Not much. My dad barely covered them. I've seen one or two movies, but I don't know what was truth and what was just Hollywood." I slapped at a mosquito on my wrist. "From what I remember, they were the world's best horsemen and deadly with the bow. They had a leader named Genghis Khan, and under him they conquered the largest empire ever, stretching all the way from China to Europe. They weren't the nicest people—ruthless, killed millions."

"That's it?"

I shrugged. "Sorry, it's all I got. Since our first two jumps were in Europe, I figured the jump rods would only be sending us to European glitches. So all I've studied is history in that part of the world. Do you know anything?"

"Are you kidding? There are no Mongol history courses in Virginia public schools." Sam chewed thoughtfully on a strand of her hair. "I don't like not knowing. Other than Temujin, we don't know who we need to keep safe. Our goal seems to be to help him get his wife back, but why is that such a big deal to history? Do their children end up doing something monumental?" She snorted at the thought. "I find it hard to believe that a bunch of guys who can't even keep a shirt clean become that important to history. And listen to them—they sound like the morons at my high school. There's the popular kid"—she pointed at Temujin—"the guy sucking up to the popular kid"—Jelme—"the jock . . . and the guy everyone picks on"—Belgutei and Khasar—"and the stoner just going with the flow"—Bo'orchu. "These guys shouldn't matter in the slightest to history, so I don't understand why we're here. We don't know their culture, their beliefs, their history. We know *nothing*." She raised her hands skyward. "It just doesn't make sense—why would the jump devices send us here?"

"Hey, don't look at me for answers; you're the experienced time jumper. I'm just happy they haven't tried to kill us."

"That could change," Sam chuffed. "They're basically primitive sheep herders. Who knows what's going on in their minds? For all we know, they could be planning to kill us while we sleep"—her eyes took on a hunted look—"or worse." A shudder rattled her frame. "If these are the last Mongols I ever see, I'll be happy."

I sighed and pushed the hair away from my eyes. Sam was a master of taking a bad situation and figuring out how it could get worse. As much as I wanted to trust Temujin, I knew nothing about him or his friends. Everything Sam said could be right. But one of us had to be optimistic. "Temujin said three guys stole his wife, and there are seven of us. We go in, kick some ass to get his wife back, and then—poof—the time glitch is fixed, and we can go home."

"I hope you're right," Sam muttered, but the slump of her shoulders showed me she wasn't convinced.

We rode on quietly for about an hour, skirting the river, following its slow-moving course upstream as it snaked through the valleys. The rumble of our hooves and the jingling of my chain mail drowned out all other sounds. As we began rounding the edge of a low hill, Temujin and his friends slowed their horses to a walk. "We are here now," Temujin called back to me and Sam.

But there was nothing ahead of us, only more grass and rocks. What was he—

Crap . . . The blood drained from my face.

Ahead of us, thousands of horsemen filled the plain, sitting, laughing, joking, eating, wrestling with each other, and tending to horses and weapons. It was an army. A huge one. Probably over twenty thousand men. And as far as I could see, not a single woman among them.

As I sat there on my horse, numb with shock, Temujin rode calmly ahead. "We have reached camp," he said, a grin on his face.

"They're all with you?" Panic raised my voice an octave.

"Yes." He pointed to a large group of men sitting where the grass grew the longest and their horses grazed. "Those are my near-father

To'oril Khan's band of Kereyit warriors." He then pointed to a smaller group of horsemen. "And those are my own loyal Mongols."

"You brought an entire army to get your wife back?" I gasped as I tried to stop myself from hyperventilating. "You said three men stole your wife."

Temujin nodded. "Yes. Three Merkits stole my wife: Toqtoa Beki of the Uduyit Merkits, Dayirsun of the Uwas Merkits, and Qa'atai-darmala of the Qa'ad Merkits. They are the three khans of the most powerful Merkit tribes." His eyes lit up with hatred and he clenched his fist. "I will make them feel pain. I will make them suffer loss. I will crush their tribes and scatter their people, so that no Merkit will ever raid Mongol lands again."

My stomach recoiled like I'd just been kicked in the gut. Sam and I were in the middle of a Mongol army heading for war.

CHAPTER 8

Being the new kid in school sucked, but being the new guy in the Mongol army was a million times worse. Everything about me and Sam screamed *different*: our clothes, our hair color, our height, our weapons. As we rode into camp, men swarmed around our little group, crowding so close that we had to push our horses past them, nudging them out of the way. Men kept pointing at my chain-mail shirt and at Sam. And the comments I heard rippling through the crowd implied that both were ripe for the taking.

Sam edged her horse so close to mine that our feet were actually touching. Her head kept darting around, and her eyes were wide with fright. I probably didn't look too different. I gripped the reins so tightly my knuckles cracked.

Khasar leaned from the saddle and patted Sam's thigh. "Do not fear, Sam of the fiery hair. I am here to protect you."

Brave words, but it would take more than one scrawny teenager to keep us safe if things went bad. Temujin had said this was his army, but how much control did he have over them? Would he be able to stop this mob if they decided to attack us? He just kept riding ahead, oblivious to the hungry stares directed at Sam and me.

My hand drifted toward the jump device tucked into the back of my pants. If things went bad, I'd only have a few seconds to pull it out and get myself back home. "Do you remember the command to jump out?" I whispered to Sam.

"I-I-I think so," she stammered.

"Yes or no?" I hissed.

"I don't know! I can't remember anything right now."

I couldn't blame her. It was only after our Celtic time jump that we had learned the setting to return home midglitch. So neither of us had had the chance to practice it. Hell, we didn't even know for sure if it worked. "We might have to make a run for it," I whispered.

"You realize we're surrounded, right? How can we—"

"Move aside for To'oril Khan!" commanded a voice.

The crowd around us parted, and an older warrior rode through the gap. The fur lining his hat wasn't simple sheepskin, but glossy and thick like mink fur. And around his waist, a colorful silk sash held a sword in a scabbard decorated with ribbons and brass fittings.

He grasped Temujin by both shoulders and grinned like a father welcoming home a lost son. "You have returned at last." He then peered past Temujin at Sam and me. "And I see that you have discovered more than wisdom in your quest."

Temujin bowed his head. "Noble To'oril Khan, come ride with us, and I will tell you all that has passed. But first I must clear the hunger from the eyes of these men." He clapped his hands. "Hear me, brave Kereyit warriors of To'oril Khan. These are Sam and Dan, two travelers from lands far west of here. They saved my life from a band of cowardly Merkits, and for this act of bravery and friendship I name them Mongols. They are now part of my tribe. Anyone who treats them otherwise brings insult upon me—and upon the most honored To'oril Khan."

To'oril Khan pulled himself upright in the saddle and glowered at the men of his tribe, making sure they knew that Temujin's words had his authority behind them. The crowd around us began to disperse, doing their best not to pay us any further attention.

I exhaled slowly and unclenched all my muscles. "I think we're going to be okay now," I said to Sam. Although I wasn't sure if these words were for her benefit or mine.

"We'll see," she said quietly.

We followed Temujin and To'oril Khan as they led us toward the smaller group Temujin had identified as his own band of Mongol warriors. As we passed, men stared at us but kept their distance. Ahead of me, the two leaders chatted, sharing laughs, while occasionally glancing back at me and Sam.

Temujin finally stopped right in the middle of the camp and lowered himself out of the saddle, wincing as his weakened ankle twisted underneath him. Jelme leaped down from his horse, slung his arm around Temujin, and helped him find a place to sit on the grass. As the rest of the riders dismounted, boys rushed up to take their horses away. The one who came for my horse nearly tripped because he was staring so hard at Sam and me.

"Are we staying?" I whispered to Sam.

"For now. But I'm going to play it safe. Cover me." While I kept an eye on the surrounding Mongols, she nonchalantly drew her cloak around herself so it hid the view of her arms, and then began wriggling underneath it, as if she was trying to strip off her tunic or something. I realized she must have taken her jump device out from her bracer to change its settings.

"You set it for home?"

"Damn right. Your turn."

Since my jump rod was tucked into the back waistband of my pants, I probably looked like I was pulling out a wedgie, but I did the same cloak trick as Sam and quickly adjusted the jump device to the new setting. "What now?"

"Same as always. We find the glitch and figure out how to fix it."

Together we walked over to Temujin, who was sitting with To'oril Khan, Jelme, and the others in a small circle on the open grass, their saddles and gear strewn all around them.

"Come! Join us!" Temujin said cheerfully.

We sat, fully conscious of the crowd surrounding us. They kept a respectful distance, and even though many were watching me and Sam, even more were staring at Belgutei and Khasar with expectant looks on their faces.

"Do you want to hear what happened to us while we were gone?" Belgutei yelled out to them.

The crowd roared back their approval.

Khasar and Belgutei began telling the tale of their dash for safety through the forests as the Merkits chased them. The crowd laughed and shouted as the brothers tried to outdo each other with tales of their own bravery. I found myself getting wrapped up in the story, and even Sam seemed to relax a bit. She leaned over and rested her head on my shoulder.

Temujin waited until his two brothers were done, then told the tale of his encounter with the Merkits, and how Sam and I saved him. He downplayed his own part in the fight and spoke so highly of me and Sam that it sounded like we'd defeated five hundred Merkits, not five. The men cheered at the end of his story, and even Khasar gave me a nod of respect. I had thought Temujin's story might buy me and Sam a bit of breathing room, but it only made the men more eager to crowd around us, begging to touch my armor or stroke Sam's hair.

Temujin rubbed his chin thoughtfully. "Your appearance draws too much attention," he decided. "We must make you look more like Mongols." He took off his hat and offered it to me with both hands. "Please, take this. It will hide your light hair."

I shuddered just thinking about how many bugs might be crawling around in that fur. But not accepting the hat would probably be some sort of insult. So I held back my revulsion and took the hat from him with both hands. I even clasped my hands together and bowed, since that seemed to be the way to say thank you around here. I then plunked the gross, sweat-stained, stinking thing on my head, and hoped lice would be the worst of my problems.

Khasar yanked the hat off his own head and held it out to Sam. "Although hiding the radiance of your hair is like covering the brightness of the sun itself, I insist you take this."

Sam eyed the cap as if it was going to bite her. She struggled to put on a smile, and then took the hat from him and placed it on her head. "Thank you, Khasar," she said, her words sounding full of appreciation but her eyes conveying anything but.

"We need more!" Bo'orchu said. He rummaged around in a saddlebag and pulled out a knee-length tunic. "Put this over your shirt of iron," he directed to me. "Men are moved to action by what they can see. If you hide your shirt, their hearts and minds will not be led along paths they should not go."

Now that was advice I could use. I accepted his tunic, which wrapped around me like a bathrobe that I fastened with my sword belt. It had a high collar, extra-long sleeves, and was a bit on the baggy side, but it felt comfortable. And although it was splattered with dirt and food stains, it was clean compared to the rest of the clothes everyone wore. Probably cleaner than some of the things lurking at the bottom of my laundry hamper back home.

"Would you like my cloak?" I asked Bo'orchu as I unfastened it from my shoulders. Now that I had Bo'orchu's tunic, I didn't need the cloak too; it would be way too hot.

Bo'orchu fastened it around his shoulders. "Look at me," he said to the others, as he spread the cloak out around him. "Now I look like a khan."

"I would offer you my deel," Khasar said apologetically to Sam as he pointed to his tunic, "but it is my only one."

Belgutei shrugged. "I also have only the one I wear now."

Everyone's head then turned toward Jelme, who sat there snacking on something. A silence hung in the air as the four men looked at him expectantly. "I keep an extra deel in my saddlebag in case Temujin has need of it," he said. "With my lord Temujin's permission, I will give it to the woman."

"Of course, Jelme!" Temujin agreed. "She is one of us now. Treat her like you would my sisters."

Jelme retrieved the long, drab tunic and with a reluctant scowl passed it to Sam. The garment hung limply in her hands as she looked around at the sea of Mongols surrounding us. "I guess I'm going to do this the hard way," she muttered to herself.

While everyone watched, she took off her bow, quiver, and cloak and placed them on the ground. She wrapped the deel loosely over her tunic then squirmed like an escape artist in a straitjacket for a good thirty seconds. With a flourish, she removed her tunic from inside the deel, then pulled the deel tighter around her before tying the belt and slinging her bow and quiver over opposite shoulders.

Even in her usual baggy tunic and cloak, Sam looked amazing. But now, with her hair flying out from under her fur-lined cap, and the fletching of her arrows poking over her shoulder, she looked regal, like a Mongol queen.

Khasar looked her up and down and nodded. "You look like a proper Mongol now. But looking like a Mongol is different from *being* a Mongol. Have you any skill with that bow?" He pulled out his own bow and tugged on the bowstring. "I am one of the best archers of all the Mongols. I would like to see how you fare against me."

"Maybe later," Sam muttered.

"Why not now?" Khasar asked. "The sun still gives light."

"Yes!" Belgutei hoisted a skin full of airag. "Let us see your skill."

More men took up his case, until a good portion of the clearing was clamoring to see Sam's skill with the bow.

Bo'orchu rested his hand on Sam's arm. "I know our ways are different from your land's, but you should take up this challenge. Our women do not fight; they stay in the ger and tend the fires or cook food. A woman skilled in the weapons of war is something these men have not seen, and probably will never see again. Show them now—and be done with them. But if you ignore their cries, they will constantly be asking."

Sam shook her head and grumbled under her breath. "What's the target?" she asked to the cheers of the surrounding men.

Khasar snatched Belgutei's airag skin and tossed it as far as he could away from the camp, where it landed with a liquid thump in the grass. Men eagerly leaped to their feet and moved their horses out of the way to allow a clear path to the target.

"Hey!" Belgutei protested. "That was almost full."

"It will not be when we are done." Khasar pulled a red-fletched arrow from his quiver and turned his face to Sam. "Three arrows. Most hits wins." He sighted along his bow and released. His arrow pierced the skin and airag seeped out. The men watching cheered.

"Your turn." Khasar waved his arm in a flourish.

"Come on, Sam. You got this," I urged.

She took a breath, placed the tips of her middle three fingers on the bowstring, pulled it back to her chin, and with one eye shut, she sighted along the arrow. With a twang of bowstring, the arrow flew through the air, striking just next to Khasar's, and leaking more airag into the ground. The men cheered even louder now—and I cheered along with them.

"What a strange way of pulling a bow," Khasar observed. "Is that the way women are taught to use bows in your lands?"

"Um . . . no," Sam said. "Where I come from, everyone shoots like this. Why? You do something different?"

Khasar held up his thumb, revealing a thick ring made of horn.

"This is how we shoot in our lands." He grasped the bowstring with his thumb, and then wrapped his other fingers around his thumb as he pulled the string back before firing again, his second red-feathered arrow hitting right next to his first.

Sam's second shot also pierced the airag skin.

Khasar nodded in appreciation. "You are beautiful and skilled. The man who finally shares your ger will be most fortunate." He fired a third shot, which hit home next to his previous two. Three shots, three hits.

Sam's eyes narrowed on the target. A second later her third shot also pierced the skin. The clearing shook with a thunderous roar.

"Khasar shoots just as well as a woman!" Belgutei yelled, and the men around him bellowed with laughter.

Khasar's face reddened. "Can you do better, you big, dumb sheep?"

"Probably not." Belgutei shrugged. "But I hear the laughter of men bringing shame to you, not me."

Khasar scowled and then turned to Sam, his look softening. "Excellent shooting. Can you do as well from horseback?"

"Sure," Sam replied, "if the horse isn't moving."

He chuckled. "No, my pretty one. At full gallop."

"That's impossible."

"Just wait and see." Khasar grabbed one of the horses that still had a saddle on it and jumped onto its back. He then rode over to the airag bag, picked it up by one of the many arrows sticking out of it, and rode it to the far end of the meadow, where he dropped it before returning to his starting point. He then pulled out his bow and clasped three of his red-feathered arrows in his right hand.

"Yeah!" he yelled, and his horse began galloping back across the meadow. Khasar leveled his bow and fired three shots in rapid succession. Two hit their target but the third hit the ground just next to the airag bag.

I wasn't much of an archer, but I recognized good shooting, and this was beyond good. Even those men who had been laughing were now cheering him.

Khasar collected the airag bag and the arrows and trotted back to us. "Your arrows," he said to Sam as he leaned from the saddle and handed her the three gray-feathered shafts. "And your airag bag," he said to Belgutei as he dumped the now-perforated leather sack at Belgutei's feet. Then Khasar hopped out of the saddle and sauntered over to Sam.

"That was incredible," Sam said. "How do you manage to keep on target with your horse bouncing around like that?"

"I only shoot when the horse has all his feet in the air."

Sam took a step back. "But that gives you hardly any time to aim."

"I did not say it was easy." Khasar grinned smugly. "So, I have won the contest. What is my prize?" He leaned in close to her.

"What? We didn't agree on any prize."

"But we agreed to a contest. What is a contest without a prize?"

I had to hand it to the kid: he was smooth. It was clear from the cocky way he stood and the flicker in his eyes that he wanted a kiss or some other display of affection from Sam. But I knew he was going to walk away disappointed. Sam chewed her lip and her eyes darted back and forth as she tried to figure some way out of this situation.

Khasar stood with a hand on his hip and an expectant smirk on his face. "Have you decided yet how to reward me, beautiful Sam? I have some ideas."

Sam's eyes brightened, and she held out the three arrows Khasar had just handed back to her. "Here's your prize—I hope you can put them to good use."

The smirk disappeared from Khasar's face. "I had hoped for a kiss."

"And I had hoped to beat you. We don't always get what we hope for."

He smiled and pointed the three arrows playfully in her direction. "You are cold like the northern winds to me now, but just wait, Sam of the western lands. I will warm your heart and make you my wife." He grabbed the reins of his horse and led it off to the grazing area.

Sam shook her head and groaned. "Why me?"

"Pay no mind to Khasar," Bo'orchu advised. "He is like a puppy, young, eager for mischief, and always trying to prove himself a bigger dog than he really is. But if you grow tired of him and wish to douse the fires of his heart or turn aside the staring eyes of men, you must follow our customs." He pointed to Sam's hair. "Your hair, hanging free as a horse's mane, incites the hearts of men to beat faster and does not warn them that you are taken. Women of our land who are married wear two braids, while all others wear many."

"You mean that's all it will take to get him off my back?" Sam yanked the fur-lined cap off her head and with quick fingers began twisting her hair into two long, thick braids that she tied off with some gauze from her backpack.

"Khasar!" Belgutei yelled to his younger brother, who was still tending to his horse. "It appears your future bride is actually married."

Khasar tossed his saddle to the ground and raced over. "No!" he howled when he saw Sam's braids. "It cannot be so."

"Afraid so, Khasar," Sam said, with a smile.

He shook his head, a resigned expression on his face. "I should have known." He turned to me and scowled ominously. "Do not fear. If you fall in battle, I will take care of her."

"What?" I exclaimed. "You got it all wrong. I'm not—ow!"

"Sorry, honey," Sam said. "Did I jab you with my arrow?" She smiled at me sweetly, but her eyes held a pleading look.

I sucked the blood from the back of my hand. "As I was saying, I'm not dying any time soon."

Belgutei chuckled. "So, Dan of the iron shirt. How many enemies have you raided? Have you seized many herds of horses and sheep?"

"I've been in a few fights," I admitted.

"And what is war like among your people?" Temujin asked, his interest clearly piqued. "How many men fight? Do they all wear shirts of iron? How do they proceed into battle?"

"It all depends on who's fighting." Leaving out the times and places, I told them about the two battles I'd been in previously, and how thousands of men in large groups rushed at each other, usually in full armor. Temujin was full of questions: how long men could fight while running in armor, how quickly their armies could move, what sort of weapons they used, and how these armies fought on horseback. With each of my answers, Temujin nodded, as if making mental notes. Finally, he looked me in the eye. "And did you lead men?"

"Yes. In the biggest battle I commanded a group of about twenty."

"And were those men on horseback?"

"Yes."

Temujin rubbed his chin thoughtfully, as if what I had just revealed was hugely important, and I felt like I had passed some sort of test. He said nothing for a few moments, then glanced over at the sun, barely visible over the distant hills. "We should get some rest, for we leave at sunrise. Much hard riding lies ahead of us, and we are already late." He began limping toward the blanket that Jelme had laid out for him. As for the others, Khasar and Belgutei lay down back-to-back, and Bo'orchu stretched himself out on the grass with his head resting on his saddle.

No tents. No fires for warmth. And not a single complaint from anyone. These guys were hard-core. I removed the wool blanket from my backpack. "Looks like we're camping under the stars tonight," I muttered to Sam.

"Could be worse—it could be raining." She pointed to an empty patch of grass. "How about over there? It looks pretty free of horse crap."

"Fine with me." I spread my blanket out on the grass and Sam placed hers next to mine. "So we're married now, huh?" I said quietly as we both sat down.

"Yeah, sorry about that. I needed to get Khasar to back off somehow. It's okay, right?"

I shrugged. "Judging by the looks I've been getting, most of these guys would kill me just for my chain mail. So us being 'married' doesn't really change anything for me."

Sam glanced around at the thousands of men in Temujin's army, and a shudder shook her body. "I've never felt so out of place. I remember my dad telling my brother that the jump devices only send time jumpers to places where they'd fit in. So you'd never get African time jumpers sent to fix a glitch in Aztec history. Which is why I still don't understand what we're doing here."

"Maybe there are no actual Mongolian time jumpers, so the jump devices just figured to send anybody?"

"Maybe."

"And Temujin doesn't seem to care what we look like, so maybe the jump devices knew it didn't matter who was sent here?"

Sam took off her Mongol hat and dragged a hand through her hair. "He might be tolerant, but it's the thousands of other guys I'm worried about."

"You don't think Temujin will be able to protect us?"

"I'm not willing to risk my life on it."

I looked up at the rapidly darkening sky. A few faint stars glimmered beyond the insects humming on the breeze. "We could always leave," I suggested. "Let Victor's men jump in to solve the glitch and hopefully get killed in the process."

"They left already. And if we take off, there's no guarantee any of them would come back. Whether we like it or not, history depends on us."

"Not necessarily *us*. If you're too creeped out, I'd be willing to stick it out on my own."

Sam cocked her head as she looked at me, a slight smile on her lips. "You *would* do that for me, wouldn't you?"

"You know I would."

She squeezed my hand. "Thanks. But I'll stick around for now. I have the jump device set for leaving, so if things look even remotely bad, I'm outta here."

"Sounds good. Hey . . . uh . . . about earlier, just before we met Temujin. We were talking about the possibility of there being an *us*."

She glanced down. "I'm not saying no. I'm saying I don't know. I still have to figure a few things out. Can this conversation wait until we're not surrounded by thousands of Mongols?"

I squeezed her hand then let go, so she wouldn't feel me trembling with excitement. For the first time, the idea of something happening between us hadn't received a full-on smackdown. "Yeah, sure. Whatever you want."

"Thanks. I knew you'd understand." She kissed me lightly on the cheek. "Now let's get some sleep. Do you want to take first—actually, I'll take first watch." She grinned. "I don't want a repeat of the last time jump."

"Geez." I chuckled. "A guy falls asleep on *one* watch shift . . ." I lay down and drew my blanket around me.

"Good night, Dan."

"Good night, Sam. And if you change your mind about jumping out, just let me know." We were heading into a Mongol war, and I had a bad feeling that our worst fears were going to turn into a brutal reality.

CHAPTER 9

I was on my third watch shift of the night when the first Mongol stirred. He rose like a ghost from the mist-covered grass, a silent shadow. I pretended to be asleep and lay there watching as he crept with soundless feet to another Mongol and nudged him awake, and then moved on to another.

I knew it! My chain mail and Sam were too much of a temptation.

With shaking hands, I drew my sword, making sure the metal made no noise as it came free of its scabbard. These guys were doing their best to be quiet—they probably figured I'd be an easy target. But Sam and I'd be ready for them.

I turned as if I was stirring in my sleep and put my mouth close to Sam's ear. "Sam!" I hissed. "Wake up. But stay quiet."

Her eyes shot open but she remained still. "What's happening?" she whispered.

"The Mongols are up to something."

"What's our plan?"

"On the count of three, we jump out of this time period."

Sam's fingers inched across to her bow. "What about the time glitch?"

"No time to worry about that!" A figure came creeping toward us. "Go, Sam! Now!" I hissed.

I leaped to my feet and whipped out my sword, intending to protect Sam as she jumped out. In the semi-darkness, I could just make out Temujin's face. His eyes were wide with surprise and he raised his empty hands to shield himself.

"I mean no harm," Temujin said. "I just came to wake you. The sun will soon light our way and we shall ride again."

I peered into the dim gray light and saw shapes saddling horses, eating, relieving themselves. None of them were headed toward us.

I'm an idiot. "Oh . . . um . . . we'll be ready soon," I managed to stammer as I sheathed my sword.

"Good. We have much riding ahead." Temujin began walking toward a group of sleeping Mongols. "You are quick," he called over his shoulder. "I will remember that."

"What the hell?" Sam commented as soon as he was out of earshot.

"I thought he was trying to kill us."

"Why?" she demanded.

"Well . . . uh . . . okay, maybe he didn't actually *do* anything. But look at us, Sam. We're complete strangers here. We don't look like them. We don't know their customs or manners. And we sure as hell don't know if Temujin is actually going to protect us. Sure, he told people to back off, but have you noticed how everybody's been looking at me because of my chain mail? Do you know what that feels like?"

Sam gaped at me. "Awww . . . did poor little Dan get creeped out because a few Mongols looked at him for too long?" She jerked a thumb at her chest. "I'm the only woman in an entire freakin' army! Everyone has been staring at me since we got here. At least you can just take your armor off and—poof—threat's gone. What the hell are my options? But you don't see me flipping out and almost killing the source of the time glitch."

First rule of arguing with Sam: I was never going to win, even if I was right. But this time, I was clearly wrong. "Sorry," I mumbled.

Luckily, Bo'orchu approached, saving me from further stupidity. He had a pair of saddlebags slung over his shoulder and he reached into one to pull out a lump of something wrapped in felt. "The sun begins to rise, so we will be moving soon. Let us share some food before we begin our journey." Unrolling the bundle, he offered Sam and me what looked like half-petrified knots of cheese and hunks of dried meat. "Take some aaruul and sheep meat. It will give you strength."

"Aaruul?" Sam asked, her nose wrinkling as she eyed the food skeptically.

"Dried cheese curd." Bo'orchu motioned for us to take some. "Good for long travels."

It was probably a great honor among Mongols to share food, but I couldn't get over the fact that all the food had felt fuzz stuck to it. To avoid insulting Bo'orchu I selected the smallest piece of dried meat. Mongol cuisine could be described as many things; tasty wasn't one of them. The sheep meat had the texture of day-old chewing gum, and even less flavor.

Sam went for one of the petrified cheese bits. By the way she grimaced as her jaw worked at the hard lump, I figured I'd made the better choice.

"Take more," Bo'orchu urged. "It will give strength for a long ride."

"We're good," Sam and I said in unison.

Bo'orchu shrugged, took a few lumps for himself, and then rewrapped the bundle. "If you need more, just ask." He patted the bulging saddlebag.

Sam waited until Bo'orchu walked away, then she leaned in close. In the weak rays of the rising sun, her usually sparkling eyes were noticeably red-rimmed from lack of sleep. "How much trail mix did you bring? Is your pack full?" she whispered.

"Of course. It will probably last *me* a full week—maybe even two."

"What? You wouldn't share with me, your fake wife?"

"Maybe eating nothing but stale cheese covered in pocket lint will teach you not to give me so much attitude for being paranoid," I teased.

She rested her hand on my arm. "If you want a fake divorce from our fake marriage, I understand," she declared with mock sincerity. "Can we still be friends, though? At least for the sake of the fake kids and . . . the trail mix?"

I laughed and put my arm around her waist, pulling her into me. She wrapped her arms around my shoulders, and for a few seconds nothing else outside of our embrace existed. "No matter what happens, you'll always be my best friend." With my other hand I reached down and picked up my backpack. "And friends don't let friends eat pocket lint."

We shared a quick breakfast, rolled up our coarse wool blankets, then began saddling our horses. The saddles weren't difficult to figure out, but they were still different from what we were used to. Even though we had been among the first people awake, we were nearly the last ones to get mounted. I had just finished tying down my backpack when, from the center of To'oril Khan's tribesmen, a rider raised a felt banner on a pole. The banner depicted a reddish-brown hawk or eagle in flight. On this signal, To'oril Khan began riding along the river's edge, his thousands of Kereyit warriors following him.

From the middle of our grown group, Jelme hoisted a pole with what looked like an upside-down soup bowl on the end of it. From the rim of the bowl hung long strands of black animal hair, making it look like a really ugly lampshade.

"What's that?" I asked him.

Jelme stared at me as if I was a bug that needed to be squished. "Temujin honors you both by naming you Mongols, yet you know nothing of our ways." His voice dripped with disgust. "The banner of nine yak tails is Temujin's standard." He waved the pole so the black strands swung in the air above him. "In times of peace, the tails are white—but now they are black for war." He gave me a disdainful sniff and rode away before I could ask him anything else.

Sam watched his retreating back. "What's his problem?"

"I don't know," I muttered. "Maybe his horse peed on him while he was sleeping." Not that I cared in the slightest about Jelme. I had more important things to worry about, like figuring out how some seventeen-year-old guy on a quest to get his wife back was going to mess up history.

I did a quick scan of the area with the jump device, checking to see if maybe one of Victor's men had shown up and Sam and I could ditch this place, but came up empty.

The last Kereyit had followed after To'oril Khan; now it was our turn. Temujin flicked the reins to start his own horse moving. Jelme fell in directly behind him, and one by one the rest of us followed. Like a long, deadly snake, we began riding hard along the smooth plains that wrapped both banks of the river, winding our way uphill and heading deeper into the mountains.

I'd ridden at stables back home. I'd ridden with the Anglo-Saxon army as it raced across England to confront the invading Normans. I'd led a group of Celtic horsemen against Batavians. I'd thought I was a pretty good rider. But the Mongols shattered that delusion. They were the best I'd ever seen—as if they were born on horseback. They ate and talked and drank while in the saddle, all the while keeping up a spine-pounding pace. After about an hour I was ready for a break, but rest breaks didn't seem to be a thing in the Mongol army. If anyone needed to switch horses or relieve themselves, he did it alone, and then it was his job to catch up again.

Around midafternoon, the river we were following had shrunk to a stream, probably only knee-deep. We were high in the mountains now, above the tree line. The sun shone brightly and a cool breeze whipped past. In the distance a large, dark shape clung like a smudge to the treeless hillside, looking unnatural among the green grass and gray rock of the mountain. "We are almost at the meeting point," Temujin announced, his face lighting up.

Within minutes, the smudge began to take shape: thousands of horses and riders—an army almost as large as Temujin's. Broad grins broke out on men's faces, and they eased their horses to a slow walk as we closed the last of the distance between the two groups.

"More freakin' Mongols?" Sam muttered.

Bo'orchu overheard her and chuckled. "These are the men of Temujin's sworn brother, Jamukha. With them at our side, our army is complete."

As we approached, Jamukha's army formed a line many rows deep, like a dirty, shabbily dressed parade formation. Our own army did the same, with To'oril Khan's larger group taking the center and right, and Temujin's on the left. Bows remained slung over shoulders, and men relaxed in their saddles. At the head of the other army sat a tall man, about the same age as Temujin, with his arms crossed and an annoyed look on his face.

To'oril Khan and Temujin rode toward him. "Jamukha, my sworn brother," Temujin began, his voice loud so it could carry to everyone. "My heart is stronger to see you here."

Jamukha's eyes narrowed and he raised his spear skyward, the sun glinting off its metal tip. "Fair speech from someone who does not keep his oath. As I promised you, I made offerings to the long spear-tipped banner. I have beaten the rumbling drum made from the bull's black hide. I have ridden my swift gray horse and put on my leather-thonged armor." He waved his spear behind him toward his horsemen. "And, as promised, I made ready for war and brought my army to the source of the Onon River." His scowl deepened. "We have been waiting three days! Three days of our horses chewing down the same stalks of grass until they almost eat the dirt beneath. Three days of standing like sheep in a pasture, resting in the sun, when we should have been riding to war." He slammed his spear butt into the ground. "Even if a snowstorm stands in the way of our appointment, even if rain hinders this meeting, we should not be late. Did we not so agree?" He glared at To'oril Khan, but he reserved most of his anger for Temujin. "When we say yes, are we not bound by oath?" He spat on the ground. "Did we not say that we should cast from our ranks those who fall short of the agreement?"

Temujin and To'oril Khan sat mutely on their horses, heads bowed. Finally To'oril Khan nudged his horse forward. "It is as you say. We have arrived three days late at the appointed place. It is for you, younger brother Jamukha, to punish and reprove us."

Jamukha looked past To'oril Khan to Temujin. "And have you no words, my sworn brother?"

Temujin kept his head bowed, offering his submission. "Words will not change what has passed. We were late and I wait upon your punishment. Do as you see fit."

Jamukha nodded and yanked his spear up from the ground, his scowl softening. "Raise your head, brother. I know your thoughts are troubled by fears for Borte. There will be no punishment today."

Temujin rode forward and grasped Jamukha's forearms. "Your mercy is an example to us all."

"My mercy has its bounds. Do not make me wait again." Jamukha looked north. "But I tire of words now. Let us ride. My horses yearn to run, and my men thirst for any sight other than these hills." He kneed his horse and began heading off along the mountain plateau, Temujin and To'oril Khan beside him. As for me and Sam and the rest of Temujin's small army, we had to wait for all the Kereyit warriors to go first, then Jamukha's Mongols, and then finally us—last, so we got to breathe in all the dust thrown up by the horses ahead of us.

I leaned in close to Sam and motioned with my head toward Jamukha, who was riding far ahead of us, tall in the saddle and leading like a triumphant conqueror. "Did you see that guy's spear? It was metal. That's the first one I've seen."

"He has a sword, too, like To'oril," Sam replied, her voice quiet.

I thought back to what little I knew of Mongol history. "Do you think Jamukha could be Genghis Khan?"

"Jamukha?" Sam scoffed. "Why him? If I had to pick anyone to be Genghis Khan, I'd pick To'oril. At least his name ends with 'Khan.'"

"But both To'oril and Temujin were bowing and sucking up to Jamukha. And Jamukha's got a metal spear *and* sword, so he's clearly richer than the others. Even the names are pretty close. Ja-mu-kha. Gengh-is Khan. Maybe his name got twisted over time."

Sam looked at me incredulously. "How do you get Genghis Khan out of Jamukha?"

"There are tons of names that grew apart in time but still mean the same. Elizabeth and Betsy. Robert and Bob. James and Jim. Why not Jamukha and Genghis Khan? It's possible."

"Sure. Hey, maybe I'm Genghis Khan. Sa-man-tha. Gengh-is Khan."

"I'm serious!"

"So am I." Sam had a playful smile on her face. "After your awesome linguistics lesson, I really think I might be Genghis Khan." She sat up straighter in the saddle, raised one arm and waved it about like a queen acknowledging the adoration of the masses. "Maybe that's why we're here, so I can become empress of the Mongols."

I loved that smile, the way it made her eyes light up. Too bad I only ever saw it when she was making fun of me. But at least I got to see it often. "Joke all you want, but the fact is we don't know why we're here. All we know is that Temujin will break history somehow. I'm just trying to figure things out before we end up in a situation we can't handle."

She stopped midwave and raised an eyebrow. "And being surrounded by a Mongol army is something we *can* handle?"

"They're not trying to kill us, at least."

Sam's smile faded. "Give them time."

CHAPTER 10

We finally stopped riding once the sun cast long shadows across the steppe and it became too dark for the horses to travel. I was so sick of riding at the point. My legs were sore, my butt hurt, I was covered in bug bites, and I'd swallowed so much dust that I probably had a flower garden growing in my lungs.

I slid out of the saddle, and my legs buckled under me as soon as they touched the ground. I nearly sprawled in the dirt but managed to catch myself. After a full day of constantly bouncing up and down on horseback, the sudden introduction of flat, unmoving ground under my feet was wreaking havoc on my sense of balance.

Sam climbed down from the saddle and leaned on my shoulder to steady herself. "I need a hamburger and a hot bath," she said.

"Good luck with that." Men were already setting up for the night, removing saddles from their horses and spreading blankets on the grass. Not a single fire burned. "Looks like it's going to be trail mix and cold ground again tonight."

Sam shrugged. "Better than aaruul."

Bo'orchu dropped his saddle on to the ground and sat down next to it. "You do not like aaruul? Perhaps you would like to try the sheep meat instead?" He began reaching into his saddlebag.

"Thanks. But we have food. Do you want some?" I offered him a handful of nuts and seeds from my backpack.

Bo'orchu threw back his head and laughed. "That is food for squirrels, not men."

Belgutei and Khasar came over to see what Bo'orchu found so funny, and they both laughed at my handful of food too.

Khasar nodded to Sam. "If your man is too poor to provide for you, maybe you should think of getting a new husband. I would provide you with only the best if you were mine."

"But she is not yours," Belgutei said, clapping Khasar on the back. "So you can instead offer me your best food. Even I tire of aaruul at times."

Khasar scowled and sat down with Bo'orchu and Belgutei, while Sam and I sat across from them. We ate quietly, no one saying much after a long day of riding. At least Jelme wasn't around to spoil my dinner. He and Temujin were on a nearby hillside, chatting with Jamukha and To'oril Khan. Jamukha's hands jabbed the air as the rest listened quietly from their horses.

I had just finished my meager handful of "squirrel food" when the clop of approaching hooves made me look up. Temujin, with Jelme following closely, came riding toward us. He dismounted in a hurry and limped over to our group.

"I have met with Jamukha and To'oril Khan," he said, "and we have reached a decision of great importance."

My ears perked up. Would Sam and I finally find out why we were here?

Temujin eased himself down next to Khasar. "Soon we will descend from the hills and enter Merkit lands. At all times we have scouts ranging ahead to warn us of the enemy, but the hills are high and the steppes are wide. Our scouts cannot spot every horseman and herder." Temujin tapped his leg nervously. "If just one man should see our army and bring warning, then all will be lost; the Merkits will flee before I can win Borte back. For this many men to enter Merkit lands without being seen, I must divert their eyes elsewhere. The Merkits must be so worried about the one approaching fox that they do not spot the pack of wolves."

Belgutei snorted. "And you want the four of us to do this? Or do you include the fair-skinned ones as well?" He jerked a thumb toward me and Sam. "Either way, the task is impossible. We are too few. The Merkits will not fear us or even notice our approach."

"You are not expected to take this path alone. To'oril Khan and Jamukha are sending their best men too." Temujin pulled an arrow from his quiver and scratched a large V in the dirt. "Three separate groups will precede the army. One ahead of our path, one to the left, and one to the right. Like a spear point they will dig deep into Merkit lands, seeking out the enemy. The rest of us shall follow half a day's ride behind, hiding our true strength. The Merkits are no fools; they know I come to reclaim Borte. But when they see you, they will only be seeing the tip of the spear. They will not see the shaft or the mighty fist that wields it."

Khasar picked at his teeth with the sharp point of an arrow. "Which group shall I lead?"

"None. You have neither the patience nor the discipline to lead." Temujin turned to Belgutei. "You will take two hundred men on the right wing. Jelme will take two hundred men on the left." He rested his hand on Bo'orchu's shoulder. "And you, my friend, shall take fifty men with five horses each—and like an eagle you must fly directly ahead."

"Fifty men?" Bo'orchu's brow furrowed. "Why so small a number when Belgutei and Jelme lead so many? How will we fight?"

Temujin shook his head. "You are not to fight. While Jelme and Belgutei keep their men out of sight in the low valleys, I need you and your men to become the fox. You must ride the high hills, drawing Merkit eyes. And when men see you and rush to tell Borte's captors of your approach, they will report that only fifty men have come."

"Not all men will flee when they see us. What about those who stand and fight?"

"If their numbers are small, kill them. If their numbers are large, let them give chase. Lead them back to the valleys—"

Belgutei clapped his hands together and grinned savagely. "Where Jelme and I will crush them between us!"

Whoa . . . an actual plan. When I fought in England and Wales, the battle plans had been nothing more than *line up in a wall and smash the other guys.* This plan had finesse. It had art.

I thought back to that meeting on the hillside and Jamukha talking with his arms raised while the others listened. This had to be his plan. And more and more it made sense that he was Genghis Khan.

"And what of me?" Khasar demanded. "Am I to stay here with the main army and wander like a sheep through the valleys, while Jelme, Bo'orchu, and Belgutei gain all the glory?"

"Khasar, my eager little brother, I would not dream of keeping you from the chase. You will ride with Bo'orchu and Dan. You will be my arrowhead, driving into the heart of Merkit lands."

A huge grin spread across Khasar's face, while my jaw hung open. *Bo'orchu and Dan?* I was supposed to be bait for a huge Mongolian trap?

"You actually trust him?" Jelme sneered, jerking his thumb toward me. "He is not one of us."

I should have been offended by Jelme's disdain, but right now I was silently cheering him on, hoping he'd win this argument.

Temujin gestured to the thousands of horses grazing in the long grass. "Jelme, look at all these horses around us. Some have spirit and will run long distances. Others are slow yet strong. A wise man will know the difference and will use each horse to its best purpose. Men are the same. Each has strengths and weaknesses a wise leader can use to his advantage." He slapped a hand against his thigh. "And just as I do not care what color horse I ride, I do not care what tribe or clan a man belongs to, or what color his skin is. No, I care about what that man has done for me, and what he can do for me. Dan will go with Bo'orchu and Khasar because I believe that is his purpose." His brown eyes bored into Jelme's. "Do you have further objections?"

"No," Jelme muttered.

"Good." Temujin pulled himself to his feet and began walking away from the group, his sprained left ankle dragging behind him. "Dan, Sam, please walk with me."

Sam raised an eyebrow at me. We didn't have much choice; we had to go with him. But I dreaded the coming conversation. I didn't want to ride with Bo'orchu and Khasar. How could I get myself out of this without sounding like a coward?

Temujin waited until the three of us were out of hearing range of the others before he spoke. "You said you have led men in battle before," he said to me. "Tell me, what is the hardest part of commanding men?"

I thought back to the fighting in Celtic times. The small group I'd led fought well and we did some damage, but we just weren't enough. The Celts had lost the battle—badly. All because they couldn't fight together as one, and the Romans could. "Getting them to stop fighting as individuals and instead fight as a united force."

A smile creased Temujin's lips. "I knew you would understand." He pointed to Khasar and Bo'orchu, barely visible now in the twilight. "These two are my brothers: Khasar by blood and Bo'orchu by deeds. I trust them as I would myself. But I also know their strengths and their weaknesses. Khasar is brave but will not run easily from a losing fight. And Bo'orchu has wisdom but does not know how to lead men. Instead, he is content to be led."

"So why are you even sending them?" Sam asked.

Temujin stroked his jaw, suddenly looking tired, as if the weight of his decision was wearing him down. "Who else could I send? This is the most dangerous task, so I could not leave it to To'oril Khan's or Jamukha's men. And what message would I send to my allies if I do not send my own brothers on a mission of danger?"

"So why do you need *me* to go?" I asked. "You already have Bo'orchu and Khasar."

"Tell me, Dan and Sam, why are you here?"

"Umm . . . to help you," I replied. A weak answer, but the best I could think of.

"Why? For what purpose?"

That was a question I'd already asked myself a few times. In other time jumps there had been a clear goal; Sam and I had figured out exactly what we had to do in order to save history. But here we were still muddling along like rats in a maze, hoping after each turn that we'd finally find the cheese. I looked to Sam to see if she had an answer, but she just stood there with one of her braids gripped in her fingers, twirling it nervously.

"We don't know," I said quietly.

Temujin shook his head in disbelief. "You travel from distant lands, across hostile territory, yet you do not know why you are here! How can that be?" He raised his head skyward and waved his hand toward the few stars shining down on us. "The eternal heaven has a plan for all men and women. For most, it is a simple one: to feed a family and watch them grow. Others are destined for greater deeds: to lead a people or slay a tribe's enemy. But a man must know his purpose; otherwise, his life holds no meaning. He becomes like an arrow launched aimlessly at the sky, drifting in the wind and never finding a target, until he crashes to earth spent. Is that why you are here? Have you launched yourself into the winds?"

I thought back to the past year of my life. Ever since I'd found out I was a time jumper, I'd been running around, trying to figure things out, but never getting anywhere. My dad was dead, murdered by Victor, who seemed more powerful than ever, and I had no definite plan for how to stop him. Even my relationship with Sam was in some awkward state beyond my control. I knew what I wanted but had no clue how to get any of it. "I guess so," I muttered, "but it's not my fault. My last year really sucked."

"Fate throws obstacles in all our paths. We choose how we respond." Temujin clenched his fist. "My father was murdered by the treacherous Tatars when I had seen only nine summers. And my deceitful uncles, instead of taking us in, cast me, my mother, and brothers out onto the cold steppe. For years we survived by eating roots and seeds and whatever meat we could hunt or fish. Men stole our horses. The Tayichi'uts hunted and enslaved me, treated me like a dog. But no matter how much I suffered, every day I woke with a purpose—that I would regain the leadership of the tribe that was rightfully mine." He stood taller at that: a man proud of his accomplishments. "And by force of will, I have claimed my birthright." He tilted his head at me and there was no missing the challenge in his stance. "What tragedy have you suffered that, when compared to my own life, will make me weep with sorrow?"

I bowed my head, avoiding Temujin's gaze. My life sucked, but his was a thousand times worse.

"And what of you, Sam?" Temujin asked. "Do you know your purpose?"

"Vengeance," she replied without hesitation, her usually soft lips curling into a snarl. "I want to kill the bastard who murdered my dad and brother."

Temujin's eyes narrowed. "I understand revenge; I hold it close to my heart as well. The Tatars will one day pay for killing my father and forcing me into a life of exile and suffering." He gestured to the army settling in for the night. "Vengeance must wait, though, for the Tatars are many and my men are few. But one day, when my men have become too numerous to count, and the mountains tremble at their passing, then I will crush the Tatars and make them suffer for the pain they have caused me." He rested a hand on Sam's shoulder. "But vengeance cannot be your only purpose, just as it is not mine. One who lives solely for revenge will find life meaningless once that goal is met. What will you do after you achieve your vengeance? What will be your purpose then?"

"I don't know," Sam shrugged. "I'll figure it out when I get there."

Temujin shook his head. "No wonder the eternal blue sky sent the two of you here to me. You are like flies in a storm, letting the winds scatter you wherever it will, and achieving nothing. That is no way to live."

Was I seriously getting a lecture on responsibility from some uncivilized sheep herder the same age as me? I couldn't figure out what annoyed me more, the way he kept spouting all this mystical garbage as if he was some wise man on a mountain, or that, deep down, no matter how hard I tried to deny it, I knew he was right: I'd lost my direction. "And you think my purpose is to chase after Khasar and Bo'orchu?" I snorted. "What good is that going to do me?"

"I cannot tell you that. Each man must follow his own path in life." Temujin looked to where Khasar and the others were setting up for the night. He leaned closer so his voice wouldn't carry. "But I can tell you that the eternal heaven has set you two in my path for a reason." He turned to Sam. "I still do not understand what role fate has planned for you, since Mongol women are masters of the home and do not venture into war. But for you, Dan, I know." He gripped both my hands. "I saw you in battle against the Merkits. You are brave, but you do not rush headlong into battle. And you have skills in leading men. Your purpose is to ride with Khasar and Bo'orchu so you can provide them with the wisdom and leadership they lack." He looked me in the eyes, his expression pleading for help. "I need you to keep my brothers safe, Dan, and to lure the enemy away from me. The rescue of my wife depends on it."

My shoulders sagged. How could I say no? "All right," I muttered.

Sam sighed. "And what's going to happen to me?"

"You will stay with me. It is not our way to send women into battle." Temujin rested his fist over his heart. "Do not fear; I give you my pledge that no harm shall come to you. I will kill any man who says an unkind word to you or looks upon you as anything other than my sister."

Sam chewed her lip but said nothing.

"All is settled, then," Temujin said. "Rest well, Dan. You leave at dawn." He turned and headed back to the camp, leaving the pair of us standing alone in the near darkness.

"Are you really going to do this?" Sam asked.

"I don't have a choice, do I? You heard him." I pulled Temujin's fur-lined cap off my head and twisted it in my hands. "I don't think these guys accept excuses."

Sam shook her head slowly. "No, I guess not."

"I hate that I'm leaving you here alone." I put my hand on her shoulder. "Are you going to be okay?"

Sam gaped at me. "I'll be surrounded by forty thousand Mongols, and the only thing keeping me safe is the authority of some seventeen-year-old guy we just met." She snorted. "If that's your definition of okay, then yeah, I'll be fine."

"All right, maybe that was a dumb question. But don't forget that we have that new command—you can jump out at any time."

She tilted her head and looked over to where Temujin was getting ready to sleep while Jelme fussed over him. "Actually, I can't. With you gone, I'm stuck watching over Temujin in case the glitch appears."

Damn it . . . For twenty seconds, I'd actually forgotten about the stupid glitch. "At least promise me that if things look really bad, you'll leave, okay? I'll still be in Mongolia. I'll figure out some way to fix the glitch."

"Sure." She put her hand on the side of my face and leaned in close, her green eyes filling with concern. "That goes for you too. If there's anything you can't handle, send yourself straight home."

"You don't have to worry about me. If I see anything more threatening than a chipmunk, I'll be gone faster than my appetite at a Mongol buffet."

She gave me a half smile. "I hope you mean that." Her lips lightly brushed my cheek, sending a charge through my entire body. "I do care about you. I'd hate for anything bad to happen to you." Sam motioned toward the camp. "We should probably head back now. You'll need to get some rest."

"Okay. I'll even take first watch." Between my feelings for Sam and the worries of what tomorrow might bring, I doubted I'd get any sleep at all.

CHAPTER 11

A nudge on my shoulder startled me awake. I opened my eyes to see Sam's two braids dangling just above my face.

"Time to get up," she said, keeping her voice low. "The rest of your group's getting ready."

Lurching to my feet, I glanced at the dim glow on the horizon. "Any idea what time it is?" I asked as I began saddling my horse.

Sam walked around to the other side of the horse to help me tie the two saddle straps. "I'd guess it's around four. Not that time seems to exist here. It's either sleeping time or riding time—and right now it's riding time."

I gave the strap one last tug and stepped back to eye my handiwork. "Toss me your backpack," I said to Sam.

Looking slightly confused, Sam passed me her backpack. I dumped half my supply of trail mix into it. "Can't have you living off Mongol food."

"Thanks." She threw her arms around me. "Be safe."

"I will." I hugged her tightly, wondering when we'd see each other again. "You too," I whispered.

115

"I will."

The thump of hooves rang out in the quiet morning air as Bo'orchu came riding toward us, eight riderless horses trailing behind him. I swung myself into my saddle as he pulled up beside me and passed me the leads to four spare mounts. "Take these," he instructed. "We will need to change horses many times on the long ride ahead." He gestured to where Khasar and the other horsemen waited. "Are you ready to go forth and clear the way?"

I gripped the reins and nodded. *Ready as I'll ever be.*

With a flick of the reins, Bo'orchu guided his horse toward the edge of the camp, the rest of us following. As we passed the sentries, I looked over my shoulder one last time. Sam stood watching us go. I couldn't see her expression, but I knew she was worried. She waved to me and I waved back, then kneed my horse to catch up to Bo'orchu.

We picked our way carefully through the early-morning darkness, keeping the pace slow so the horses would be able to set their feet surely. Once there was enough light to see clearly, we picked up the pace and began riding hard and fast ahead of the main army. Endless distances passed under the hooves of our mounts as we churned our way along the smooth hills, heading toward Merkit lands. In no time, the rest of the army—and Sam—disappeared behind us.

My ears were filled now with the sound of the wind whistling past, the thunder of hooves, and the metallic rustle of my chain mail as it jostled with each step my horse took. I hadn't noticed these noises the day before; with so many riders it had been difficult to hear anything. But now the sound of my chain mail felt like the pealing of a bell.

Bo'orchu and Khasar paid no attention to the noise and continued riding, but some of the others sent curious glances my way.

"What is that sound?" yelled one of the horsemen from Jamukha's group.

Crap. I did not need these guys figuring out that I was wearing a fortune in metal. I scrambled to think up any plausible excuse. "I . . . uh . . ."

"He wears a shirt of iron under his deel." Khasar jerked his thumb in my direction. "He carries a long blade of iron as well."

Damn it! Stupid Khasar!

"A shirt of iron?" the rider asked, his mouth now hanging open. He rode his horse up next to mine and looked me up and down, his eyes wide with curiosity. "Is this true?"

No use lying, since the incriminating rustle of steel links was impossible to muffle while we were riding at such a spine-pounding pace. "Yes." I already knew his next question, so I opened the collar of my deel to show him the dull metal mesh underneath.

His eyes grew even wider. "Menggei! Qada! Janggi! Come look at his shirt!" Hordes of men swirled around me as we rode. Some just took a quick look, while others leaned precariously out of their saddles to run their hands over the links. For a few minutes I became the eye of a hurricane of poking, prodding, and questions. Then, just as quickly as it started, Jamukha's men retreated. They spoke among themselves, every now and then casting glances my way.

I closed my collar and tried to ignore their greedy looks, but all I could feel was their attention fixed on me. *This stupid armor's going to be the death of me.*

I nudged my horse closer to Bo'orchu. Temujin wasn't around to protect me, but hopefully Bo'orchu would back me up if Jamukha's men tried anything. He'd been decent to me so far, at least, unlike Khasar, who wouldn't miss me one bit if I disappeared.

Bo'orchu raised an eyebrow as I neared. "Is something amiss?"

I couldn't admit to him that I was feeling creeped out. Mongols didn't really seem to understand the word *fear.* I just needed to find an excuse to hang around him and pass the time until my racing nerves calmed down.

"Umm . . . How did you end up with Temujin?" I asked. "He clearly trusts you even though you aren't his brother."

Bo'orchu scratched at his jaw and a wistful smile crossed his lips. "I first met Temujin a few years ago, when he was still wandering the steppe as an exile. He had been cast out and was living in the wilds, with no clan to protect him." Bo'orchu looked up at the sky and his eyes softened. "A pack of thieves stole the few horses his family still owned. So he, just a boy of my age, chased after the bandits on the only horse left to him. I felt sorry for him and offered to help. Together we found the thieves and stole back the horses." He chuckled. "That was an adventure: two boys against so many men, but we survived to tell the tale. After that, I decided to stay with him. My father is rich and I am an only son, so I had no shortage of sheep or pasture, but the life my father intended me to live held no interest for me. There will always be more sheep and more pasture to be had. Temujin brings something . . . more. He is like a rock dropping into a still pond: the ripples from his actions spread far and wide and are seen by many. One day I may tire of the adventure, and then I will take over my father's herds. But for now, the wide steppe and the high hills call out to me, telling me to be more than just the owner of many sheep."

"And what about Jelme?"

Bo'orchu's smile faded. "A different path brought them together. Jelme's father presented him to Temujin as a gift on Temujin's birth."

"Gave him? You mean he's a slave?"

"Not a slave. A trusted companion."

"Why would Jelme's father do that? Was he in debt or something?"

"Debt?" Bo'orchu's brow furrowed. "No. Temujin was born noble. It is a great honor to give one's son to a man of noble birth. Just like those who are closest to the fire benefit most from its heat, so those fathers hope their sons will gain in stature by being close to those of high rank."

Made sense, I guess. Kind of like an apprenticeship. "So that's why Jelme's always hanging around Temujin?"

"Yes. Jelme would give up his own life for Temujin." Bo'orchu turned to me. "But what of you, Dan of the iron shirt? What brings you from far-off lands to ride here beside me now?"

"It's complicated."

"Life is simple. Complications exist only in our minds." Bo'orchu tapped the part of his fur hat that covered his temple. "Banish all the thoughts that cloud your head and tell me, what brings you here?"

Good question. I wasn't sure I even knew the answer. True, I hated Victor, and wanted to see all his plans fail miserably, but what did I really hope to achieve by time-jumping? "I guess I came here looking for answers, but I don't know what the question is."

Bo'orchu tilted his head back and laughed. "All men undergo the same quest at least once in their life. And what of your woman—does she share your journey?"

"She does." I thought of Sam among the army of Mongols. "Is she going to be safe?"

Bo'orchu's face turned serious, and his brown eyes held level with my own. "Yes, Temujin will see that no harm comes to her. Men may flit about her like flies around a horse, but none will dare touch her."

Khasar pulled his horse closer to Bo'orchu's. "But *there* is something that might bring harm." He pointed to a trio of horsemen in the distance. They watched us from a hilltop, keeping pace with us but not drawing near.

"Merkits!" Bo'orchu declared. He reined in his horse and looked to me and Khasar. "How shall we proceed?"

"The path is clear," Khasar said. "We are fifty; they are only three. You heard what Temujin said: we must drive them away from here!"

Wrong answer! "No. We need to keep riding," I said. "Let them follow us until we know for sure if there are more of them."

Khasar gave an irritated shake of his head. "I will find out how many there are when I count their bodies." He snapped his reins, and his horse took off like a bolt.

"Wait, Khasar!" Bo'orchu yelled. "The horses are tired. We need to change mounts."

But Khasar didn't listen. He kept riding toward the distant Merkits, his extra mounts trailing after him.

Bo'orchu pounded a fist against his saddle and looked at me and the rest of the riders, struggling to determine the best course of action.

"We need to change horses," I suggested. "That's what Temujin would want us to do."

He glanced again at Khasar. "No. We cannot let Khasar attack alone." Bo'orchu snapped his reins to gallop after him.

I groaned and shook my head. A good leader should never sacrifice the whole group for the sake of one hothead with suicidal tendencies. No wonder Temujin wanted me along. Good leadership was in short supply in this group—and so was common sense. The rest of the horsemen now tore along the grassy field, chasing after the fleeing men.

"Stop!" I yelled. "We need to keep together." But my words were drowned out by the thunder of hooves and the eager shouting of the men as they sensed the thrill of a chase. I sat alone on my horse in a cloud of dust until I nudged my mount in the ribs and began chasing the blood-thirsty idiots, my tired horse barely keeping pace with the slowest of them.

We rode over hills and through valleys, never catching up to the three Merkits ahead of us. And the farther we went, the more spread out our group became as we charged after Khasar. A sense of impending disaster began to weigh in my gut. Everything about this chase was wrong. We should have slowed down, changed horses, and scouted the area carefully. Instead, we all chased after Khasar, who remained far ahead, bow in hand, striving to get close enough to bring down the Merkits by himself.

In the distance, the Merkits ducked over the ridge of a hill and into a valley, disappearing from my sight. Seconds later Khasar chased after them and quickly became hidden by the hillside as well.

As the main body of Mongols approached the ridge, Khasar reappeared, barreling back toward us. He flailed at his horse with his reins, trying to urge more speed out of the exhausted animal. He was yelling something, but I was too far away to hear. But by the look of panic on his face and the way he kept looking over his shoulder, I knew it wasn't good.

What has Khasar gotten us into?

Almost instantly I got my answer. Behind him, galloping hard on his heels, came a swarm of horsemen at least double our number.

"Head for the forest paths!" yelled the rider closest to me, a squat man with a long drooping mustache. He wheeled his horse around and rode madly toward a tree-covered hillside.

I chased after him, desperate to get away from the Merkits. Over my shoulder, I saw Bo'orchu and the other Mongols scattering in different directions. As for Khasar, he kept turning in his saddle and firing arrows as he rode. With deadly accuracy, each one dropped a man out of his saddle. As much as I couldn't stand the guy right now, I still felt a touch of admiration at his incredible skill.

"Faster!" urged the squat rider as he bent low over the neck of his panting horse and galloped toward a small path leading into the forest.

I plunged after him into the gap between the trees. We rode like madmen along the twisting forest trails, some no wider than rabbit runs. The trees were thick around us, and I ducked constantly under branches or pushed them away with a hand. Twigs and leaves lashed at my face, but I pressed forward, straining my ears for the dreaded sound of Merkits gaining on us. I heard nothing except the slapping of leaves, the thumping of hooves, and the snapping of branches.

Finally, the man in front of me guided his horse down yet another narrow path and stopped in a small clearing. "We must switch horses." He leaped from his saddle and began untying its straps.

I dismounted and began doing the same. My poor horse needed the rest. It drew in deep gulps of air, its sides heaving. I patted its nose and rubbed my hand along its flank.

"You must hurry," the Mongol panted, his voice thick with fear.

Untying the saddle was easy. Tying it back up on a fresh horse was near impossible. My hands shook and I kept looking back, expecting to see Merkits. "Almost done," I said as I struggled to knot the first of the two straps.

Without the noise of riding assailing my ears, I could now clearly hear the Merkits in the forest behind us. They called out to each other, searching for our trail.

"We do not have much time left," the Mongol said.

"I know," I snapped. I turned my back to him and began tying the second strap around the body of the horse. My fingers trembled so much that the leather kept falling out of my hands.

Just another minute.

Behind me came the unmistakable creak of a bow. The Mongol sat on his fresh mount. He had an arrow drawn, and his brow was creased with fear. He looked like he was about to abandon me there.

"We'll get out of this," I insisted, trying to calm him down as I returned to tying the straps.

"One of us will," the Mongol replied.

A blinding pain lanced through my upper back, just below my right shoulder. It felt as if I'd been punched and stabbed at the same time. I spun around, looking for the source of the attack, only to find the Mongol reaching over his shoulder for another arrow.

"Stop!"

All in one motion he drew and fired again but his speed threw his aim off. The arrow sailed past my head and clattered among the trees.

I ducked behind one of my horses for cover, then pulled my sword from its sheath. I could barely hold the blade up—every move sent a spasm of pain through my back and shoulder.

I peeked over the back of the horse as the Mongol drew another arrow. "Give me your iron shirt and sword and I will let you go," he declared. "You can hide in the forest while I take the horses and lead the Merkits away."

Fat chance. My sword and chain mail were the only things keeping me alive. As soon as I gave them up, he'd fill me with more arrows and leave me face down in the dirt. "Ride away now, and I won't tell the rest of the Mongols what happened here," I called out.

His eyes flicked toward the trees, as if expecting Bo'orchu, Khasar, and the others to come galloping along the path at any minute. He turned back to me and his face hardened. "The wolf has already stolen the lamb. It is too late to put it back."

"The Merkits are almost here," I bluffed. "You'd better run."

He cocked his head and listened to the forest sounds. In the distance horses neighed and men shouted, but nothing sounded close. A slight smile crept up his face. "We still have some time, I think." He released again. The arrow flew low under the belly of my horse and straight into my right calf, digging so deep that the arrowhead poked out the other side of my leg.

Every inch of me wanted to howl but I bit down on my sleeve to stifle the cry. Merkits were still out there, searching for us; I couldn't scream and lead them here. *Desperate* didn't begin to describe my situation—Merkits in the surrounding forest and a Mongol trying to kill me. He had a bow and I could barely hold my sword. Fighting was out, and with an arrow in my leg, so was running. Only one option left—hide. With my right leg dragging, I limped into the bushes as fast as I could, pushing past tree trunks and thorny bushes and into the deepest part of the forest.

An arrow whizzed past and buried itself in a tree beside me, its feathered end vibrating from the impact. I dropped to the ground and hid behind the largest tree I could find, my wounded leg stretched out in front of me. I lay there with my good shoulder against the rough bark, biting down on my lip to still my ragged breathing.

"Hiding will do no good," declared the Mongol from somewhere behind me. "I will find you and take your weapons of iron. Then I will flee and become a rich man. Do not fear, little lamb. I will tell everyone you died a heroic death at the hands of the Merkits. The men will drink airag in your name and sing songs about your bravery."

I heard the soft pad of his boots as he leaped off his horse and began creeping through the underbrush. My back tingled in anticipation of his next shot. Blood seeped from around the arrow embedded in my leg.

With my left hand, I pulled the jump rod from my waistband. I had only one chance: either the command worked and I got the hell out of this place—or I was dead.

Come on, Dan.

With my hands shaking, I spun the rod sections into position. Sweat dripped into my eyes, blurring my vision, but a swipe of my dirty sleeve wiped it away.

"Come face your death like a man." The Mongol's voice sounded closer.

The last section clicked into place. "*Arbah rastvas orokol biradelem,*" I said softly.

The sighing of the wind through the branches was the only response. My stomach lurched. The jump rod didn't work.

"*Arbah rastvas orokol biradelem,*" I said again, this time louder.

Too loud.

"The wolf hears you, wounded lamb," the Mongol said, crashing through the underbrush.

My heart pounded in my chest. Why wasn't it working? Did I have the combination wrong? Was I saying the words incorrectly?

I thought back to when I had learned this command—right after my Celtic adventure, when Cenacus the druid had pushed a piece of paper toward Sam and me as we sat together in a coffee shop. The symbols on the page had been written clearly, but the words had been a bit messy—especially the second word. I had always assumed that he had scribbled down *a*'s. What if they were *o*'s?

Just a few feet away, a twig snapped. I whipped my eyes to the right and saw the Mongol's fur-covered head moving back and forth as he scanned the forest for me. Our eyes locked and his went wide. He drew his bowstring to his chin.

"*Arbah rostvos orokol biradelem*," I yelled, just as the Mongol released his bowstring and his arrow flew straight toward me.

CHAPTER 12

My body sagged with relief as Mongolia disappeared in a super-nova of light. The brilliance of the time stream enveloped me, carrying me along to the safety of my own time.

So close.

One more second and the bastard would have killed me. Of course, he still might. There was no way of knowing how deep the arrow in my back had embedded itself. It might have nicked a major artery and I could be bleeding internally as I drifted through time and space. What would happen if I died in transit? Would my body show up at home? Or would that strange wind I experienced on my second jump drag me off into the void?

Before I could panic any more, the glare vanished and something solid materialized beneath my feet. For a second I stood there, my ears alert for danger, then the dizziness of time travel hit me and I fell to the ground, jarring the arrow that still pierced my calf. Daggers of pain stabbed through my leg, and I buried my face into the crook of my sweaty, dirty elbow to smother my cries.

Only when the agony subsided did I open my eyes. Purple spots swimming in my vision made it hard to see, but the hazy outline of a familiar sofa, coffee table, and chair appeared, and there was no mistaking the smells of stale pizza and oiled steel that hung in the air.

Home.

I sat on the tiled floor outside my bathroom and exhaled as the last bits of time-travel sickness passed and everything came into focus.

Step one: assess my injuries.

The arrow through my calf looked like something out of a horror movie. In one side, out the other, my pant leg drenched in blood. At least it hadn't hit bone. Some stitches and antibiotics would probably take care of this one. The arrow in my back was the big question mark.

Using the wall for support, I pulled myself up off the floor and then half hopped, half limped into the bathroom, taking care not to jostle either of the arrows.

With the bathroom mirror as my guide, I gritted my teeth and went for the arrow in my back. I reached around with my left hand, my fingers roving over my right shoulder to find the point of entry. But no matter how much I twisted and stretched in every direction, I just couldn't grasp the shaft. If I hadn't been wearing my under-tunic, the chain mail, and my Mongol deel over everything, I probably could have reached it. But with this much bulky clothing on, my arm just couldn't stretch far enough.

I slumped over the bathroom counter. I needed help. But Sam was still in Mongolia . . .

Sam!

Fear snaked down my back. Sam had the wrong words for jumping out. And, because of the weird way time passed in history compared to real time, who knew how long she'd been in Mongolia without me by now. Half a day? A day? She could be stuck there, yelling the wrong words, trying desperately to return home as bloodthirsty Mongols surrounded her. I needed to get back!

Ignoring the pain shooting through my leg, I stumbled into the kitchen and snatched my phone off the table. But who was I going to call?

The hospital was out of the question. If I showed up at the ER looking like a human pincushion, the doctors would call the police for sure. And how could I possibly explain this? I was cleaning my bow and it accidentally went off? *Twice?* Even if by some miracle the police didn't get involved, I still could end up in the hospital for days. Sam didn't have days.

I hit the number for my lawyer and guardian, Mr. Morris. He'd been a good friend of Dad's and helped me through everything after Dad died. He'd told me to call him if I ever needed help. Had he known what he was offering?

"Morris and Rothstein. How can I help you?"

My adrenaline buzz was already beginning to wear off, and the pain in my leg and back was becoming excruciating; it took every bit of my strength not to yell into the phone. "This is Daniel Renfrew. I'd like to talk to Mr. Morris, please. It's urgent."

"I'm sorry, Mr. Renfrew, but Mr. Morris is on vacation until next Monday. Would you perhaps like to talk instead with Mr. Rothstein?"

"No, it's okay." I ended the call and cradled the phone limply in my hands. *Who else?* It takes a certain type of friend to pull arrows out of you without asking questions. Besides Sam, I didn't have any friends I could trust to that level. Hell, who was I kidding? I had only one friend here, and no matter how much I liked her, I barely knew her. I was not about to ruin the one potentially normal thing in my life by roping her into the height of my abnormality.

I thought back to my dad. He'd always seemed to have some part of himself bandaged up. I'd believed all his lame explanations—chopping onions, hedge-trimming accident—because I didn't know any better; I just thought he was the world's clumsiest person. But he must have gotten those injuries while time-jumping. So who had patched him up? Professor Gervers might know, but I already knew how that call would turn out.

Just then, my eye was drawn to the lone white rectangle on the stainless-steel refrigerator door. Victor's card. The one he'd given to me after Dad's funeral. I didn't even know why I'd kept it. But there it was, reminding me that Professor Gervers wasn't the only time jumper I knew. Victor would be able to pull strings and get me stitched up in no time. Unless, of course, he just pushed the arrows in even deeper. Was I desperate enough to go crawling to my worst enemy? For Sam's sake, I just might have to.

The phone vibrated, sparking a flicker of hope. Had Sam somehow made it back on her own?

Nope. Just a message from Jenna. In fact, all the messages I'd missed while I was gone were from her. According to my phone, it had only been about eight hours since I'd jumped out, but she'd texted five times already, the oldest ones saying that she hoped I had fun camping and wishing me a good night, while the newer ones were telling me what she'd been doing with her Saturday morning, and already trying to make plans for next week.

She was clearly into me. But how much? Jenna was the poster child for normal, and my current situation wasn't anywhere close to normal. She might end up so freaked out that she'd never talk to me again—or worse, get the police involved.

My fingers hovered over the keypad.

A vision of Sam, surrounded by Mongols and screaming for help, made up my mind. Good morning. I texted.

Seconds later: RU back?

Yeah

What happened to camping?

I hesitated before sending my reply. What could I say that would convince her to come to my place alone? Accident. I need your help.

The seconds dragged as I waited for her response.

Then my phone rang. "Hey, Jenna." Despite the pain, I tried to keep my tone light so she wouldn't freak out.

"What happened?"

"I can't get into details. I just . . . I'm hurt, and I can't go to the hospital."

"Why not? Hospitals still have to treat you even if you don't have insurance."

"Look, I just can't. Can you please come over?"

"Okay," she said without hesitation. "I'll bring my mom. She knows first aid."

"No!" I shouted. "Can you just . . . come alone?"

"I don't know," Jenna said, her voice wary. "Why don't you want my mom to come with me?"

Sam would have had me cleaned and bandaged by now. "Please, Jenna, I know this sounds messed up, but can you please come alone? It's . . . embarrassing. I swear, you'll be out of here in ten minutes."

An awkward silence followed, and I thought for a moment she'd hung up on me.

"All right," she finally said.

"Thanks! You're awesome! I'll text you the address." I hung up before she could change her mind.

I sent her the details, unlocked the front door, then limped slowly back to the living room. I sat down sideways on an armchair, so my shoulder arrow wouldn't hit the back, then carefully propped my heel on the coffee table, keeping my other leg well clear of the calf arrow.

Heading out now, came Jenna's text.

It would take her about fifteen minutes to get here, meaning I had time to look up Temujin and hopefully find out how some kid with a missing wife could mess up history so badly. I googled *Temujin Mongolia*, and stared in shock as the results filled the screen.

Temujin *was* Genghis freakin' Khan! I scanned the first website and my shock turned to horror. He, Khasar, Jelme, and Bo'orchu weren't simple sheep herders—they were the most ruthless mass murderers in all of history. Millions of people killed. Entire cities destroyed. Countless women and children led into slavery. Rivers of blood followed him wherever he went. And his raid into Merkit lands in 1179 to win back Borte was the start of his rise to power and the ruthless destruction of his enemies.

Sam was in huge danger. I couldn't wait for Jenna; I needed to fix myself up and get back to Mongol times—now!

I fumbled behind my back again, determined to yank that arrow out. My arm felt close to dislocation, but I still couldn't reach the arrow's shaft.

I slumped back into the chair, defeated, and panting heavily from my exertion.

The knock on the door startled me. "Come in," I called.

The door inched open, and Jenna stepped hesitantly into my apartment. In her bright yellow coat, with her raven hair pulled back in a ponytail, she looked so fresh and colorful—the complete opposite of me in the disgusting Mongol deel that clung to my sweaty skin. Her eyes went wide when she caught sight of me slumped awkwardly in my chair. "What the hell?"

No use sugar-coating it. "There's an arrow in my leg and one in my back. I need you to pull them out."

She glanced down at my leg and her face paled as if she was going to throw up right there in the doorway. She clamped her hand over her mouth and turned her head away. "I'm calling an ambulance," she said, the words barely intelligible through her fingers.

"No, Jenna, please! The police will get involved, and I don't have time for that. I need *you* to do this for me."

She lowered her hand from her mouth and peeked my way. Her eyes didn't drop from my face. "Why don't you want the police involved?" she asked, her voice quaking. "Who did this to you?"

Great. More questions. Too bad I couldn't answer them.

"Jenna. Please listen," I began, trying to keep my voice calm enough to cut through her panic. "I'll explain everything to you, but I'm in a huge amount of pain, and I need you to pull these arrows out of me."

She hovered at the doorway with both hands clenched in front of her. She glanced at my injured leg and then turned to the hallway behind her.

I'd made a mistake asking her for help. Scared and clearly grossed out, she looked like she was about to cry, run away—or both.

"Forget it," I said. "Just go home."

Jenna unclenched her fists and smiled in relief. "So you'll go to the hospital?"

"No, I really can't. But I don't have time to answer your questions or wait for you to get over your fear of blood. Don't worry, I'll figure something out."

"Wait!" She bowed her head and blinked a few times, as if psyching herself up to do something awful. "I'll do it."

"Are you sure?"

Jenna took one last look back into the hallway, then nudged the door shut behind her. "Yeah, I am. You look awful. I can't let you do this yourself. You could end up making things worse." She took off her shoes, arranged them neatly by the door, then came over to kneel on the carpet beside my chair.

She reached for the arrow in my calf.

"Stop!" I yelled, as I moved to block her hand.

Jenna jumped back, jerking her hands away. "W-w-what? Tell me what to do."

"You can't just pull it out." I tried to sound calm. "The arrowhead will rip muscle on its way back out." I pointed over to the kitchen. "You need to get a sharp knife and use it to trim the feathers off the shaft of the arrow. Then you can pull the arrow out by the tip. Okay?"

She bit her lip and nodded, then disappeared into the kitchen.

Drawers slammed. Cutlery rustled. Then she returned with a small paring knife and a dish towel in her hands. "You ready?" she asked.

"Pass me a magazine first."

She gave me a curious look. "You're going to read?"

"No. Just . . ." I held out my hand.

She picked up *Military History* and passed it to me. I rolled it into a tight tube and bit down on it. "Ready," I mumbled through gritted teeth.

Jenna knelt beside the chair, wrapped the towel carefully around my leg, and then began sawing at the strings that held the arrow fletches in place. Every knife stroke became its own separate agony as the arrow shaft was pushed back and forth in my leg. I clenched my fists until my knuckles cracked, and ground down on the magazine until my mouth was a soggy mess of chewed paper. I didn't scream, though, and that's all that mattered. The last feather fell to the floor and Jenna rested her hand on the arrow's horn tip. "This is probably going to hurt," she said. "You going to be okay?"

I took a few quick breaths to prepare myself then nodded.

With one hard yank, Jenna pulled the arrow shaft out of my leg. It felt as if my entire calf was being ripped off and I pounded the chair back with my fist, trying not to scream. Jenna wrapped the towel tight around the wounds, and as quickly as the pain had started, it faded away.

One down. I spat the soggy magazine out and panted heavily. Sweat dripped off the tip of my nose. "The one in my back didn't go all the way through," I gasped. "So don't worry about the feathers. Try to pull it out as straight as you can, so the tip doesn't cut me any more than it already has."

Jenna nodded and walked around behind my chair. "Ready?" she asked.

"Sure. Just give me a—Aaaaah! Craaaaaap!" She had yanked the arrow out without waiting for my response.

Jenna sat down on the edge of the coffee table in front of me, the blood-tipped arrow still in her hand. She didn't look nearly as timid as before. Her eyes had narrowed, and her jaw had an angry set to it. "Okay. Now are you going to tell me what the hell happened to you?"

"Can you go get the first-aid kit from under the bathroom sink, please?"

She glanced toward the door but didn't move. For a second I thought she'd say no, but then she padded over to the bathroom and came back with the kit. "Do you really think a Band-Aid is going to stop that bleeding? You need stitches."

"I don't have time for stitches." I pulled off the towel and rolled up my pant leg, revealing pencil-sized puncture wounds on both sides of my calf. Dried blood clung to my leg all the way down to the ankle. From the first-aid kit, I opened the bottle of ibuprofen and swallowed four tablets. Then I found antiseptic wipes, gauze, and crazy glue. I reached down to swab my leg and grunted as the wound in my back shifted.

"Here, give me that." Jenna snatched the first-aid supplies from my hands. A few quick swipes with the antiseptic set my teeth clenching again from the sting, but she deftly cleaned the wound, hopefully enough to prevent infection. She patted the twin holes dry with the towel and glued them shut, squeezing each repair for a count of thirty to make sure they'd hold. She wound a few layers of gauze around my calf to keep things in place, then put the first-aid kit back on the table.

"Wow!" I said, admiring her handiwork. "Can you do my back?"

Her dark eyes bored into mine. "First, tell me the truth. Is this about gangs or drugs? I can't go out with you anymore if you're into either."

Despite the pain, a smile crossed my lips. How many gangs ran around dressed up like Mongols and shooting each other with arrows?

I grabbed Jenna's hand and gave it a reassuring squeeze. "I promise you, this isn't about gangs or drugs. Now can you please hurry?"

She licked her lips and nodded. "Fine. But you need to take that coat off."

With my left arm I untied my deel and pulled it over my head, revealing the chain mail underneath.

Jenna raised an eyebrow, but to her credit, she didn't ask for an explanation, just unbuckled the leather straps that held the chain mail in place. I raised my arms above my head and she pulled both my armor and tunic off me, leaving me naked from the waist up. As the chain mail dropped to the floor in a jangle of metal, Jenna took a step back. Her gaze ranged over my body. "You work out, huh?"

"Every day." I turned around so she could see my back. "How bad is it? Still bleeding?"

"Your armor must have helped. The arrow didn't go too deep." A second later came the unmistakeable sting of the antiseptic wipe hitting my back. I clenched my teeth until my jaw ached, and then the pain passed. A few wipes with the towel followed, then a long pinch as Jenna glued the wound before squeezing it shut. "All done," she said, as she patted my undamaged shoulder.

"Thanks, Jenna. I really appreciate it." I began pulling my tunic back over my head.

"What are you doing?" Jenna put her hands on her hips. "That's filthy. Your wound is going to get infected."

I pulled the heavy chain mail over my tunic and began tightening its straps. My right arm had recovered some movement now, but not much, so the straps would take forever.

Jenna didn't make any moves to help me. "Dan. Tell me what's going on."

I needed to keep my excuse short and simple so I could get her out the door quickly. "Umm . . . Sam and I got carried away," I began. "We were dressed up like Mongol warriors, play fighting. There was an accident." *Sounds plausible?*

She tilted her head and gave me a side-eyed glance. "You mean *two* accidents? And in one of them you got shot in the back? I don't believe you. And where is Sam, anyway?"

I knew Jenna was smart. But why'd she have to make a thing of it now?

I shrugged my one working shoulder. "It was just one of those crazy things. But I'm good now, thanks to you. You're truly a lifesaver." I squeezed her arm, then went into my bedroom and began rummaging through my drawers, tossing shirts, shorts, and pants everywhere.

"What are you looking for?" Jenna stood in the doorway, watching me.

"Something made out of natural fiber that I can turn into a bag."

"Pillowcase?"

Of course! Just like Halloween. I dumped my pillow on the floor and flipped over the label of the pillowcase to inspect it. Cotton. "Thanks!" Just what I needed: something that would biodegrade if I lost it in history.

I squeezed past Jenna on my way to the kitchen. The pain in my leg had scaled down a notch, most likely because of the ibuprofen. I began rummaging through the cupboards: crackers, potato chips, cookies . . . anything dry that would travel well was emptied from its packaging and tossed into the pillowcase.

Jenna had followed me into the kitchen and stood watching, bewildered. "What are you doing now?"

"Provisions." I poured a full box of cereal into the mix.

Jenna rested a hand on my arm. "I really think you should go to the hospital, Dan. Did you get hit on the head?"

"I'm fine." I retrieved a spare water skin from the cupboard and filled it up from the tap. "In fact, I'm better than fine. You did an awesome job. So great, in fact, that I'm ready to head back out already. You should probably go home."

She crossed her arms and tapped a foot on the tiled floor. "I'm not leaving until you tell me what's going on."

With my full pillowcase in hand, I slid past her into the living room, where I picked my deel up off the floor and slipped it on over my armor. "I'm sorry, Jenna. I do owe you an explanation, but it isn't going to happen now. When I get back, I promise I'll take you out for a nice dinner and tell you the whole story. But right now, Sam is in huge danger and needs my help. So I need you to go."

Jenna stomped to the door, but instead of leaving, she locked it and slid the security chain in place. "I'm not letting you go until I get an explanation, Dan. If Sam needs help, call the police."

Who knew that cute, bubbly Jenna had this much fight in her? I was kind of impressed, but she was also in the way. "Please, Jenna. Go home." I picked my sword off the floor and sheathed it, then began spinning the sections of the still-cold jump rod into the combination for jumping back to the past.

Her focus narrowed on to the jump rod. "What's that?"

"Just *go*. Please."

"No!"

I had enough practice fighting with a determined woman to know I wasn't going to win this argument.

"I really do like you, Jenna," I said. "But I'll understand if you never want to see me again after this." I motioned to a row of hooks hanging by the door. "The last key is for the door. Please lock up when you go. I don't know when I'll be back."

The last rod section clicked into place. "And don't bother telling anyone about this, because no one will believe you."

She opened her mouth to reply just as I shouted, *"Azkabaleth virros ku, Haztri valent bhidri du!"*

The last thing I saw before the blinding light hit me was Jenna's face, her mouth gaping and her eyes wide as I disappeared.

CHAPTER 13

The bright glow of the time stream surrounded me once again as I drifted through time and space. In roughly thirty seconds, I'd be back in Mongolia.

But where would I land?

Would the jump rod dump me right back in the forest with the Mongol still trying to kill me? Or would I land a few minutes later, with the place swarming with Merkits? Or would I end up back where Sam and I first met Temujin, except now Sam would be days of travel away from me? My back stiffened as all the horrible possibilities piled up. So much potential danger, and I'd be confused and disoriented for a few seconds when I touched down.

I drew my sword and held it ready in my left hand. A few wild slashes as soon as I landed might be enough to hold off any attacker long enough for the dizziness and blindness of time travel to pass. Like most of my plans, it was sketchy and relied heavily on luck, but it was the best I had.

My feet hit the earth and I cast out my senses, searching for any sign of attack. The scent of greenery filled the air, the wind blew, insects buzzed, and a distant bird was calling, but there were no sounds of Merkits. Wherever I had landed, it wasn't in the middle of a battle. Dizziness pushed me to the ground, and I felt knee-high grass under my hands.

Slowly I opened my eyes and let the purple spots clear. A wide, grassy plain stretched around me on all sides. In the distance, a few gentle hills interrupted the flatness, while small white clouds dotted the sky. Staying low, I shielded my eyes from the sun and scanned the entire horizon, checking for horsemen.

Nothing. Just grass and sky.

I exhaled slowly. *So far, so good.* Not that I believed I was safe. Trouble would find me soon enough. But hopefully not before I found Sam.

I spun the sections of the jump rod to search for other rods. Like a magnet, it pulled weakly toward the horizon. Somewhere across the endless hills and fields, I'd find Sam's jump rod. The big question was: did she still have it? After everything I'd read about Temujin and his gang of killers, I severely doubted it. As soon as I left the army she'd probably been married off to some smelly Mongol, her jump device taken as a shiny metal status symbol that was now hanging around his neck.

A lump formed in my throat as I thought of Sam being held captive—trapped in this time period. I could almost see the horror on her face. I had to find her.

But what would I even do? She'd be surrounded by forty thousand of the most feared horsemen in history. Getting her out of their clutches would take cunning and good planning—too bad I was short on both.

An even bigger gap in any rescue plans was my lack of a horse. How could one guy with a bum leg catch up to an army moving on horseback? I scanned the grassland again, hoping that somehow a herd of horses was just magically standing around.

Yup. Optimism was for suckers. No horses anywhere.

I put one foot in front of the other and began limping in the direction the jump rod pointed. Each step hurt like a fresh stab wound, but Sam was in danger, so I sucked back the pain and pushed my feet forward.

After about an hour of stumbling across the endless plains, I still hadn't thought of any genius plan to rescue Sam. And soon a more pressing issue arose—my own survival. The sun beat down relentlessly, making the steppe a thousand times hotter than the hills. My armor felt like it was made of lead, and my two layers of clothing only helped increase the sweat factor.

To top it all off, the pain in my calf had spread as the rest of my muscles were forced to compensate for my limp. I wasn't really walking now; my body kind of lurched forward, like a zombie in a horror movie. I'd have to start ditching gear soon if I wanted to keep moving; my strength was fading fast. I needed a horse badly—it was the only way to gain any ground on this endless steppe.

I stopped to wipe the sweat from my brow and take another drink. Flies buzzed around my face as I squeezed a few precious drops of water into my mouth. Already half my water was gone. Swatting away the flies, I peered into the distance, searching for a creek or maybe a pond.

Huh?

Ahead of me, just before the horizon, stood a white dome-like shape. With one hand shielding my eyes, I squinted, trying to make out further details. Smoke curled up from the top of the dome, suggesting that it was some sort of dwelling. But it was the few large brown shapes standing next to it that had my heart pounding.

Horses!

But just as quickly my excitement faded. Whoever lived there was obviously not going to just hand over a perfectly good horse to me. And even if the Mongols used some sort of currency, I didn't have any. Only one option left—I had to steal one.

Gritting my teeth, I limped forward. The little hut was probably a good twenty minutes away, but with luck I'd be able to sneak over, steal a horse, and ride away without anyone noticing.

I froze in my tracks as a man emerged from the building. I suddenly became aware of how visible I was out here, just a lone dark speck on an empty steppe—anyone who even glanced my way would be able to see me.

Don't look this—damn it!

The distant figure had turned in my direction. He didn't move, just stood and stared. He'd clearly seen me; what happened next was up to him.

He went back inside and reappeared a few seconds later with a saddle. He glanced again in my direction, as if making sure I was still there, then quickly began saddling one of the horses.

Soon he was riding toward me, the clomp of his lone horse's hooves sounding strange to me after the rumble of thousands of horses galloping together.

I pulled my cap lower on my head to hide my clearly non-Mongolian features. Temujin might have been tolerant of foreigners, but who knew how this guy would react? As he approached, I twisted the jump rod sections to the jump-out setting, and then tucked it into my sleeve. The last thing I wanted was to leave Mongolia and Sam, but I had to be ready for all possibilities.

He reined in his horse about twenty paces away. He was probably about thirty years old, with ruddy cheeks, tanned skin, and an outfit matching all the others I'd seen here. He had a bow slung over his shoulder but made no motion to draw it. Instead his brown eyes peeked out at me from under his cap. "A man without a horse on the steppe is as good as dead," he declared. "How do you come to be here?"

"My horse was taken from me and I'm lost." No use trying to make up complicated excuses.

He nodded. "And where are you heading?"

I pointed in the direction the jump rod had pulled me.

The man ran a thumb along his chin. "What tribe do you come from? I have not seen people with your features before."

"I belong to a tribe far to the west."

"And yet you head east?"

"Yes."

"How are you called?"

"Dan."

He said nothing, merely staring for a few seconds as if deciding what to do with me. The tension hung in the air, like the flies and the heat, and my hand slid into my sleeve to clutch the jump rod.

Finally, he shrugged and moved his horse up next to me. "I am called Senggum." He reached down and offered his hand. "Come to my ger. There you will find food and shelter. No man should be left alone on the steppe."

"Thank you." I reached up, grasped his hand, and then managed to awkwardly drag myself up into the saddle in front of him.

With a click of his tongue and a tug on the reins, Senggum turned his horse and began heading back to the white dome he'd called a ger. The horse proceeded at a gentle pace, but still faster than I could have achieved on foot. With my good hand I held on to the saddle, while I rested the other arm close to my body, to keep my chain mail from rustling. It still rattled a bit, but not enough to cause Senggum to comment.

"I see that you have a few horses," I said. "Is there any way I could um . . . borrow one?"

"We will talk about such matters once we reach my ger."

"But I really need a horse. It's an emergency."

Senggum slowly waved his hand in a broad arc in front of us. "The days are long on the steppe and the distances are great. I am sure that whatever draws you away can wait for you to have some tea."

Sam didn't have time for me to sit around taking leisurely horseback rides followed by tea and crumpets. "Can't we at least—"

"Patience," Senggum interrupted.

Every second I wasted here was another second Sam could be in danger. If only Senggum wasn't sitting right behind me, I could have pushed him off the horse and just ridden away with it. But he'd been smart—he put me in front of him. So I was stuck doing things at Senggum's glacially slow pace. And he seemed blissfully unaware of my agitation. He just kind of sang under his breath but so low I couldn't make out the words.

As we neared his ger, its shape became more defined. It wasn't actually a dome, but rather a circular tent of white felt with a sloping roof—almost like a small circus tent. Except where circus tents had a peaked roof, the center of this one had a smoke hole. A small herd of sheep grazed nearby, and two boys, their faces and hands covered in dirt, watched us from the middle of the herd, their eyes wide with wonder.

Senggum reined in his horse next to the ger and we both dismounted. "Khorchi, come take my horse," Senggum said to the boys. The older of two, who looked about ten years old, rushed forward and took the animal by its bridle. As Khorchi led the horse away, Senggum went over to a thin post hammered into the ground beside the tent. A leather bag hung from the post, with a heavy stick attached to a leather strap hanging next to it. Senggum grasped the stick and hit the bag hard, twice, and it jostled as if full of liquid. He pressed the stick into my hand and looked expectantly at the bag. I took two quick whacks at it, which seemed to please him.

"Airag?" I asked.

He smiled and nodded, then flicked back the embroidered flap of the ger, motioning for me to go inside.

I hesitated before stepping into the tent. Even though Senggum and his sons looked like a simple family, I couldn't let my guard down. The last time I did that I'd ended up with two arrows in me. With one hand on my sword hilt, I stepped through the opening, Senggum behind me.

In the center of the tent, between the two posts holding up the ceiling's central ring, lay a circle of round stones and a pile of dried dung. A small fire burned within the circle, and above it roasted something that looked like a half-deflated leather ball. I wasn't sure what they were cooking here, but it smelled good, especially since I'd been surviving on trail mix for the past few days. Smoke from the fire drifted up through the smoke hole, which provided the only source of light in the ger.

As my eyes grew used to the dim interior, I noticed a woman standing among shelves covered with wooden bowls, buckets, and wicker baskets of different sizes. She was roughly the same age as Senggum and wore a long deel richly embroidered with scenes of birds. She welcomed me, and then poured some steaming liquid out of a copper kettle into a small bowl. She added some milk to it, then handed the bowl with both hands to Senggum.

He held the bowl out to me. "Drink and be welcome." The aroma of tea wafted up.

I took the bowl in both hands and drank a few sips. The tea spread a warmth and comfort through me that plain water just couldn't match. The thought that it might be poisoned crossed my mind for a second, but rapidly vanished. Senggum could have easily killed me by just leaving me out on the steppe. His friendliness seemed legit.

Both Senggum and the woman were watching me. Clearly I was supposed to do something with the tea. There was too much to just chug, so was I supposed to hand it back?

I offered the bowl to Senggum and he grasped it with both hands and took a sip as well. As he gave the tea back to the woman, the tent flap flew aside, pulled by the two boys. Their eyes flicked with uncertainty from me, to Senggum, and back to me. Then the boys rushed past me and ran clockwise around the ger until they were standing next to their mom on the right side of the tent. The three of them sat down cross-legged next to the fire and eyed me with curiosity.

Senggum smiled a toothy grin. "Khorchi. Ogele. This is Dan. He is a traveler from the west." Senggum turned to the woman. "And, Dan, this is the fire of my heart, Toregene."

"It's a pleasure to meet all of you." I bowed my head to them, then turned back to Senggum. "Now, can we talk about the horse?"

"Patience," Senggum repeated. He sat down cross-legged next to the fire on the left side of the tent, underneath two shelves that held bows, extra arrows, leather bridles and straps, a few leather sacks of what was probably airag, and a short knife. "Come, sit with us. Tell us a tale of your land. It is not often that we have visitors."

My entire body was practically trembling. Sam didn't have time for all this. But unfortunately, this was Senggum's house, so I had to live with his rules. No matter how much I wanted one of his horses, I clearly wasn't going to get one until I at least provided them with some entertainment. I took a seat next to the fire and stretched out my aching leg so the sole of my boot rested next to the fire pit. A bit of heat might do my sore calf some good.

A sharp intake of breath from Senggum and Toregene filled the air.

"The man puts his feet toward the fire," the younger boy, Ogele, observed, the tone of his voice hinting that I'd just committed some huge cultural crime.

I pulled the leg back instantly, grimacing from the pain. Only now did I notice that everyone else was sitting cross-legged. "Sorry! Sorry!" I blurted. "I didn't mean to offend anyone."

Senggum's brow creased. I couldn't tell whether he was angry, scared, or confused. He pointed to the flames. "Fire is the source of life. You must never dishonor it by showing your feet to it. But you come to us from distant lands, so your actions are forgiven."

"Thank you. Thank you." I bowed my head repeatedly, greatly relieved that I hadn't messed up my chance of getting a horse. I resolved to sit still, smile, nod, and not do a single thing unless I was either told it was okay or I'd seen Senggum doing it first.

Senggum smiled and passed me the bowl of tea again. "So, tell us about life in your land."

I raced through the briefest of overviews of life in Celtic Britain, which had the closest lifestyle to something he'd understand. While I spoke, Senggum and his family sat next to the fire paying rapt attention.

The boys asked me lots of questions, and I gave them the shortest answers possible without being rude. "So, that's what life is like where I came from," I said, once I'd finished. "Now . . . uh . . . about that horse?"

"Food first," Senggum said.

I forced a smile to hide my irritation. Every second I spent here was another second Sam was in danger. But I had to do things at Senggum's pace, which seemed to be somewhere between that of a glacier and a snail.

He took the weird leather bag off the fire and split it open with his horn knife, the aroma of meat wafting out. He reached in to pull out a morsel of meat with his fingers, then motioned for me to do the same.

I took a small piece. It was greasy but tasted pretty good. I thought with all the sheep roaming around we'd be eating mutton. But this was definitely not mutton. "What are we eating?" I asked casually.

"Marmot," Senggum replied.

"What's that?" I asked, even though I had a feeling I wouldn't like the answer.

"They live in the grass and dig holes in the ground. Any man who rides the steppe will have seen them."

Oh, yeah . . . I knew what I was eating now: Mongolian groundhog.

I shrugged and took another piece. It was better than the stuff Bo'orchu had given me.

To accompany the marmot, Senggum's wife passed around yogurt and some cheese. Normally I would have been a good guest and offered them some of my own food but, with the way my luck was running, I couldn't risk giving any of it away.

After lunch, Senggum licked his fingers clean and then wiped them across the front of his deel. He rested a hand on his belly, smiling happily at his wife and kids.

"Can we talk about horses now?" I asked, half expecting him to find some other excuse to delay things.

"Yes, but you cannot have one of mine. I have only enough for my sons and myself to look after our sheep. I do not have any to spare." He pointed toward the doorway. "Two days' ride to the north, there is a man who has plenty of horses. Perhaps he can help you."

Un-freakin'-believable! Senggum had been stringing me along all this time? "Please. I don't have much time. My horse wasn't the only thing stolen from me. My wife was stolen as well. I have to rescue her."

Senggum glanced at Toregene and his eyes softened. "I feel your loss, but I still cannot give you a horse."

With a slow hiss, I drew my sword from its scabbard and laid it across my lap. The long steel blade glowed orange as it reflected the firelight.

Toregene clutched Khorchi and Ogele to her chest, while Senggum visibly paled. "I am a peaceful man," he said. "I brought you to my ger and offered you tea and food. Why do you bring violence to me?"

"No, no . . . You don't understand." I held the sword by its blade and offered it to him hilt first. "I want to offer you a *trade*. My sword for a horse."

Senggum's mouth dropped open as he gazed at the weapon, his eyes ranging over its more than two feet of polished steel. "You are sure of this?" he asked, his voice cracking.

"I am." I passed him the sword. "You can sell it to whoever you want. I'm sure it's worth more than one horse."

Senggum bowed his head, and I could swear there was a tear in his eye. "I accept your generous offer. I will give you a horse and saddle." He reached up the wall and pulled down a bow and a quiver. "I also give you this so that you may replace your weapon. A man cannot ride the steppe unarmed. There are wolves out there—both real and in human form."

I wrapped my fingers around the string and gave the bow a test pull. The string didn't budge. I tugged harder but my injured shoulder couldn't take the strain, so I gave up.

"You cannot pull the bow?" Senggum asked.

"My shoulder is wounded."

He nodded and clapped his hands. "Khorchi! Give him your bow."

"I don't need a bow," I said. "I just need the horse. Can I get it now?"

"Are you sure?" Senggum looked down at my bloodstained pant leg. "A wounded man can fall prey to many troubles on his path. You should stay here with my family for some days and rest."

He was right. In an ideal world I'd stay here with him and his family, rest up, heal, and be able to use a kid's bow without wincing. But I didn't have that luxury. "Thank you, but I can't. I need to go."

Senggum bowed his head again. "Come with me, then, and I will give you your horse. It is not for me to delay a traveler from his path." He grabbed a saddle and bridle off the wall and led me out of the ger. A few minutes later, one of his horses was ready for travel. He passed me the reins of the animal and pointed toward a distant hill. "You will find a stream half a day's ride that way. Follow that stream to the north and you will find a cluster of gers. They will take you in when you grow tired."

I bowed deeply to Senggum. He had literally saved my life, and I owed him so much. "Thank you for all your help."

He bowed back to me. "Be well, Dan of the western lands."

I carefully pulled myself up into the saddle and then nudged my horse in the direction the jump device had last pointed.

I'm coming, Sam.

CHAPTER 14

Senggum's white ger grew smaller and smaller as my horse clipped along. I wished I could be galloping across the steppe, with the wind in my hair and the distance separating me from Sam vanishing beneath my horse's hooves. But if there was one thing I'd learned from the Mongols, it was how to pace a horse so it didn't burn out, so I held him to a steady gait. Flies buzzed around my ears and eyes, and the heat was just as oppressive as before, but on horseback everything seemed better. I wasn't alone; I had a companion. And catching up to Sam didn't feel like an impossibility now.

Around me stretched endless grasslands and hills, with the occasional smattering of trees or a small forest to break the monotony. Time seemed meaningless in this land, as did distance. It was a strange place for someone who had grown up in a city where every block presented something different. I often glimpsed other white gers dotting the steppe, but I steered clear of them. I didn't know whether Senggum's hospitality was the norm here or a fluke.

After about an hour, I reached a little trickle of a stream and stopped for a rest. While my horse drank, I pulled the jump rod out, switched it to the search setting, and scanned for Sam. The pull was uncomfortably faint, meaning that that she was still far away.

Damn it . . . Come on, Sam. Be safe.

I was about to jam the jump device back into my sleeve, where I'd been carrying it ever since I met Senggum, when I paused. The stupid thing had been constantly sliding loose, and twice I barely caught it before it fell out completely. What I really needed was an archery bracer like Sam's.

I tore some strips off one end of my pillowcase and twisted them into a makeshift rope, and used it to strap the jump rod tightly against my left forearm. Then I raised my arm and swung it around in a slow circle. It again pulled in the same direction as before.

Much better.

When my horse finished drinking, I hopped back into the saddle and began riding again. As the sun inched across the sky, I slowly pieced together some ideas for getting Sam back. The first part of the plan was to follow Temujin's army from a distance and locate her—which was going to be a humongous task considering that she would be obscured by forty thousand riders dressed exactly like her. Hopefully, whoever took her jump device was traveling close to her so I could at least narrow down my search area.

The even harder part would come after I found her. I'd have to sneak into camp at night while most of the Mongols were sleeping, avoid the sentries, find her, and jump out before anyone noticed. Sure, we'd end up leaving her own jump rod stuck in history, but at least she'd be alive.

The rapid beating of hooves carried over the breeze, interrupting my train of thought. I whipped my head around and felt the blood drain from my face. Six horsemen armed with lances and bows were bearing straight at me, weapons at the ready.

Crap! Crap! Crap!

I'd been so focused on what was in front of me that I hadn't paid any attention to what was behind—now these guys were almost on me! Even if I had my sword, there was no way I could take on six guys at once. There was only one option—I'd have to jump out again.

I snapped the reins of my horse. "Come on! Move!" I screamed. The little horse flew forward at my command, clods of dirt flying from its hooves. With my left hand on the reins, I reached my right hand inside my sleeve to untie the cloth straps that held the jump rod in place. My fingers bounced all around the knots as my horse continued galloping across the steppe, but I came nowhere close to untying them.

Desperately, I tore at the cords, trying to snap them apart, but the damn things wouldn't budge. I yanked up my sleeve and began gnawing at the twisted strips of cloth that held the rod in place.

Behind me, the hoofbeats were getting louder—the horsemen were almost on me. I leaned forward in my saddle and tried to urge more speed out of my little horse.

Come on . . . I just need to get this damn jump rod out.

Suddenly, a rope looped around my neck, jerking my head back. I groped at it, trying to free myself, but the noose tightened around me even more. A sharp yank sent me flying off my horse. My body thudded into the ground, knocking the wind out of me.

I gasped for breath and dragged myself to my feet, my long, loose sleeve falling back into place over the jump rod. In front of me, a horseman held a long pole attached to the lasso tight around my neck. The other riders had turned their horses to form a circle around me, penning me in like a runaway sheep. Each had a bow drawn with an arrow pointed at me.

Escape wasn't going to happen.

The man with the lasso looked me up and down. He had cold, angry eyes and a thin mustache that drooped around his mouth. "You do not look like a man of these lands. What tribe do you come from?"

"Who cares?" shouted another man. "We have his horse. Let us take anything else he has and leave him to the steppe."

The guy holding my leash motioned to another rider. "Muqali. Search him."

Muqali dismounted and swaggered toward me, gripping a knife.

My entire body quivered with fear, rooting me to the spot. I couldn't fight these guys and I couldn't outrun them. If I didn't think of something quickly, they'd steal my armor and jump rod and leave me to die alone on the steppe.

Then it hit me. I had one other thing of value that they'd want.

Please let these be Merkits.

"Wait!" I yelled. "I need to talk to the Merkit chief! His people are in terrible danger."

That stopped him. He glanced over his shoulder toward the man with the lasso. "Should I believe his words, Chiledu?"

Chiledu leaned low in the saddle and nudged his horse closer to me. With a cruel sneer twisting his lips, he rubbed a hand along his jawline and stared hard into my eyes. I met his harsh expression, trying not to show my fear.

He yanked on the rope around my neck, sending me flying face-first into the grass. "You will tell us what you know, and *we* will decide if our khan needs to hear it."

Our khan. I'd guessed right: these guys *were* Merkits. I had to walk a fine line here. Tell them too much, and I'd mess up history. Tell them too little, they'd kill me. "Temujin of the Mongols has gathered an army and is coming this way."

The noose tightened around my neck. "Tell me. Where is this army?"

"No." I pulled myself to my knees, my lungs gasping for air. "You'll kill me as soon as I tell you. I'll tell only your khan."

Muqali placed the blade of his knife against my throat. "Speak now, or your corpse will feed the vultures."

Sweat dripped down my back in rivers and I was two seconds away from pissing my pants, but I held myself up defiantly. "N-n-no," I stammered, "I won't tell anyone but your leader."

Muqali's knife hovered next to my throat, the sharpened blade digging into my skin. He turned to Chiledu, waiting for instruction.

Chiledu tilted his head to the side and tapped his lips with a finger, clearly unsure what to do with me. "Tie his wrists," he finally said, then he motioned to a tall, lanky rider. "And Guchu, fetch his horse."

"What are we going to do with him?" Muqali asked, his knife still pressed against my skin.

"We will take him to our main camp. If what he says is true, we will be heroes, and he might live to see a reward for his information. And if he lies . . ."

His look of sadistic glee sent a shudder through me. No delusions here—once we reached the main camp, I either told them everything I knew or I was dead. I couldn't let them take me to their chief—I needed to escape.

As Guchu went to fetch my horse, Muqali pulled a long strip of leather from his saddlebag. When he returned, I obediently put my forearms together to make my wrists easier to bind. Hopefully he'd think I was sucking up, but all I really cared about was keeping the jump rod in my sleeve hidden.

Muqali wound the long strip of leather tightly around my wrists. The leather pressed into my skin, barely allowing blood to circulate. When he was done, Muqali tugged once on my leather shackles and nodded in satisfaction.

As Guchu returned with my horse, the rest of the Merkits began to rifle through my gear. One took a sip from my water skin and spat it out immediately. "Water?" His lips curled in disgust. "What type of man drinks water?"

Another opened my pillowcase, grasped a handful of the kitchen-cupboard surprise it contained, and sniffed at it, his nose wrinkling at the smell. "What is this?" he asked me, his eyes narrowing in suspicion.

"Food." Should have told him poison.

The man selected a potato chip and tentatively bit into it. His mouth worked slowly, crunching with each bite. He swallowed the whole chip and began searching for more in my pillowcase. The other Merkits joined in, wolfing down handfuls of my food and comparing the different bits as they ate. The potato chips and cookies were big hits, the cereal and crackers not so much. My stomach growled as I watched them eat. My last decent meal had been hours before, and that was only if I counted a few morsels of roasted marmot as decent. That pillowcase was supposed to last me days, and it was now emptying in seconds. As a final insult, when the food was gone, one of them even took the pillowcase.

Chiledu wiped his fingers clean across the front of his deel, adding to the stains already there. He motioned to my horse. "How fares his animal?"

"It is tired." Guchu patted my horse on the neck. "If we want to travel with speed, we will need to give the prisoner one of our own."

Chiledu removed an airag skin from his saddle and swallowed a few mouthfuls while scanning the horizon. "Let him ride his own horse for now. It looks strong enough to get him to the river. We will keep our mounts fresh and rested in case he tells the truth and this army nears our lands." He hoisted a foot into a stirrup and mounted his horse. "We should have little to fear. None of our scouting parties have spotted an army."

"Not all have returned," one rider protested.

Chiledu scowled and wheeled his horse around. "Get into the saddle," he barked at me. "We leave now!"

Slowly, making sure my chain mail made no noise, I pulled myself up, wincing at the strain on my wounded shoulder. Despite being tied up and a prisoner, I felt a flutter of hope pass through me. They had searched only my horse; the jump rod remained snugly tied inside my sleeve. If I ever managed to get my hands untied, I could send myself back home.

We began heading north with the six Merkits in a protective circle around me. While a torrent of sweat ran down my back, they laughed and joked with each other, and guessed at all the different tortures I'd have to endure if I was lying. I could only ride along, hunched over with my arms pressed tightly against my ribs to prevent my chain mail from making noise, while I listened to each gruesome detail and silently plotted my escape.

As the sun began to set over the distant horizon, we arrived at a wide river that cut the steppe in half. Chiledu pulled up his horse close to the south bank and dismounted. "We camp here."

The rest of the men dismounted and unsaddled their horses. Then a group of them headed to the river and began searching the shoreline for frogs. Another Merkit started a fire with reeds and sticks he gathered from along the riverbank. Before long, the aroma of roasting frogs began to waft over the camp.

I sat down next to the fire and performed a slow sweep with my arms, making it look casual as if I was just stretching out the kinks after a long ride. The jump rod tugged directly away from the river. The force of the pull was stronger now, which meant Sam's jump rod was closer. And that meant that Temujin and his army were closer too. But by how much? Two days? Four?

Chiledu sat across the fire from me. He took one of the frogs from its spit, tore off a leg, and popped the meat into his mouth. He jerked his thumb toward the river. "We cross the Kilqo tomorrow. We are now only a day's ride from the main camp. There you will be able to tell your story to Toqtoa Beki. Let him decide the truth in your words. Just know this: you will not live long if these words are false."

"I'm telling the truth," I protested. I tried to sound confident, even though my insides were quaking.

One day?

I sure as hell couldn't tell the Merkit leader about Temujin's army—that would mess up time royally. And stalling was definitely out of the question. If I so much as stuttered or paused to catch a breath, these guys would torture me. I wiped the sleeve of my deel across my brow. No matter how I looked at it, tomorrow was judgment day. I had to escape tonight.

His eyes never leaving me, Chiledu wolfed down the rest of his frog. I was so hungry that my mouth watered at the thought of a small piece of frog meat, but he didn't offer me any.

As for the rest of the Merkits, they ignored me as long as I sat next to the fire and did nothing but sip from my water skin. They joked, laughed, boasted, and were generally loud. But any time I shuffled to stretch my sore leg, all heads turned toward me and conversation stopped. Escape was going to be tougher than I thought.

One thing in my favor was the amount of airag that passed their lips. Each man drank at least a full skin of the alcoholic milk. As the fire died down, and the moon rose to light the steppe, their laughs and boasting grew louder. Even Chiledu looked drunk. His eyes, normally filled with suspicion, now drooped half shut.

He stretched out next to the fire and nudged one of the other Merkits with his foot. "Cha'adai, you take first watch," he said groggily. "Make sure our prisoner does not escape."

Cha'adai looked at Chiledu with bleary eyes. "We all grow tired. Why must we watch him? We should just tie his feet together so he cannot run."

Chiledu pinched the bridge of his nose and shook his head to clear his thoughts. "Fine, but lash them tightly. And tie his hands behind his back."

Cha'adai pulled some leather strips from his saddlebag, then knelt beside me. "Give me your hands."

I again played the part of the obedient prisoner, holding my hands out so they were right in front of him. The less he had to touch me, the less chance he'd find the jump rod.

He sliced through my existing bonds with his knife, then with sadistic efficiency retied my hands behind my back. Using another leather strap, he tied my feet together. I ended up facedown with all my limbs bound even tighter than before.

"There . . . he will not run away." Cha'adai nudged me in the ribs with his foot. "Try not to piss yourself while you sleep."

My cheeks burned as the rest of the Merkits laughed at my humiliation. But I just gritted my teeth and let their laughter wash over me.

Just fall asleep, you bastards, and stay sleeping.

Two of the Merkits were already snoring loudly, and the other four had lain down. Only a matter of time now. As I lay there, waiting for all of them to fall asleep, my thoughts drifted to Sam. Wherever she was, I hoped she was in better shape than I was. I couldn't believe how lousy my "rescue" was going.

I snorted quietly and shook my head. Time-jumping seemed to be just one near-death experience after the other for me. There had to be more to it than this. After all, Dad had been a jumper for decades, and I couldn't imagine him continuing with it if he'd nearly died every time. And I sure as hell couldn't imagine him in my current situation, tied up like a calf at the rodeo. As for Sam, she definitely wouldn't be stuck like this—she was way better at time-jumping than I was. Victor? Professor Gervers? The time jumpers who had kidnapped me? None of them would be stuck like this either.

The conclusion was obvious—the problem was me.

I craned my neck and looked up at the stars blanketing the sky. *If I survive this, I promise to do better. To think first before acting. Just please, give me another chance.*

I don't know who I was praying to; I just hoped that someone or something out there was listening and had my back one more time.

CHAPTER 15

Not surprisingly, the universe didn't bother responding to my plea. I shut my eyes and buried my face in the grass. Around me, the drunken snores of all six Merkits wafted through the night.

I took a deep breath and exhaled slowly. *You can do this.*

Slowly I curled my legs in until the heels of my boots were touching my butt. While my ears strained to catch any changes in snoring, I reached for the knotted leather around my ankles. In the dim glow of the dying embers, my fingernails dug into the shapeless knots, trying to loosen them. I scrabbled at them for probably ten minutes, then gave up in frustration.

Clearly I wasn't getting out of here without cutting the straps. I needed something sharp.

I lay flat on my stomach, hoping to feel a nice jagged rock sticking into me like I did on most camping trips. Nothing. The ground around me was completely smooth.

The obvious solution was the Merkits—each man carried a blade tucked into his belt. But realistically, what were my chances of stealing one without being noticed? In the dark, with my hands tied behind my back?

My eyes darted over to the fire, where a few half-burned sticks still glowed red at their ends. *That might do it.*

I slithered on my belly to the fire and grasped one of the sticks by its unburnt end, pulling it out of the fire. By lying on my side, I managed to curl my legs around until the stick's glowing tip touched the leather strap binding my feet. No sizzle. No pop as the leather snapped. Just a feeling of warmth near my ankle that I could soon feel through my boot.

Five sticks later, the leather strap around my ankles had a definite indentation from the repeated singeing. If I kept up the routine, the thin strip of hide was bound to snap. Unfortunately, the fire had died down to the point where only a few small embers remained. My supply of smouldering sticks had run out.

I tugged at the straps binding my ankles but, no matter how I pulled, the leather would not break. How could I break these stupid straps? *Come on, Dan. Think!*

My eyes fell again on the pile of sticks, and an idea hit me. I selected the thickest one and slid it under the strap until a roughly equal length stuck out on both sides. Slowly I began to rotate the stick in a circle, twisting the leather strap tighter and tighter. My ankles jammed together, bone pushing against bone, even through my boots. I gritted my teeth from the pain and twisted again. The stick became harder to turn as the leather grew even tighter. Something had to give soon: stick, strap, or ankle.

I threw my head back and twisted one last time. With a quiet pop, the weakened leather strap snapped apart. I froze in place, straining to hear whether any Merkits had woken up at the sound. Their loud snores assured me they all still slept. I allowed myself a small grin as I removed the leather straps and wiggled my feet to get some circulation going. My legs were free—time to get away from here as fast as possible.

I began heading toward the horses but stopped. How the hell was I going to ride a horse with my hands tied behind my back? Plus, the Merkits were using all the saddles as pillows.

Damn . . .

Running was my only option. I'd be getting a few hours head start, so I hoped I could at least cover enough distance to find a new hiding spot before the Merkits woke up and started searching for me.

I rose to a crouch and tiptoed away from the camp, making sure not to step on any discarded sticks.

Wait . . .

These sticks had been gathered from the river, but there were no trees on this section, so they must have floated down from somewhere else. Forget running. I could use the river.

I changed direction and headed for the water. With achingly slow steps and with every nerve on edge, I crept past the sleeping Merkits. At the riverbank, the croak of frogs and the buzz of insects drowned out the noise of snoring. Tall reeds lined the banks, and I pushed them aside to step into the water. An icy chill bit into my legs, but I plunged forward until the water was chest height.

A shiver arced through me, and not just from the cold; the dark water and tall reeds could be hiding anything. Mongolia was probably too cold for alligators and crocodiles, but poisonous snakes or deadly fish could have been swimming right next to me and I wouldn't have known it. In the darkness, everything looked menacing.

Come on, Dan, suck it up. It's either this or the Merkits.

I took one more step so that the water reached my neck. The current swirled around me, trying to draw me downstream. With my hands tied and twenty pounds of chain mail covering my torso, I had the swimming capability of a large rock. But luckily I didn't need to swim to move.

I pushed off with my uninjured leg and let the current carry me. I traveled a few feet downstream before my boots touched bottom again.

Like an astronaut on the moon, I made huge leaps from the river bottom, each one moving me farther and farther downstream, much faster than I could have run. As a bonus, the chill water numbed the pain in my leg.

For the first time in hours, I didn't feel paralyzed with fear.

Woo-hoo! Suck it, Merkits!

It was impossible to know how long I bobbed along in the dark, pushed by the current. But as the moon traveled across the sky, it became harder to fight the current pulling me toward deeper water. If I didn't get out soon, I'd drown. With my last bit of strength, I flopped onto the bank and dragged myself into the middle of a thick clump of reeds. I was cold, wet, and alone, but I was free. With that thought in my mind, I curled myself into a tight ball and closed my eyes.

A harsh croaking close to my ear jarred me out of my sleep. I jerked upright, expecting to see the cruel, mocking face of Chiledu. Instead, a large green frog, its morning disturbed by my sudden movements, hopped quickly toward the river. Insects hummed all along the bank, and birds chirped. The sun hovered just above the horizon, giving the sky a red and orange glow.

Crap . . . I'd slept too long. Chiledu and his band of thugs would be on the move soon—I needed to get going before they found me. I tugged again at the cords binding my hands behind my back but, to no surprise, they didn't budge.

Okay. Where the hell am I going?

I poked my head over the top of the reeds. Except for the river, there was nothing but grass and gently rolling hills in all directions—no Merkits in sight. I turned in a slow circle until I felt the familiar tug of the rod pointing away from the river, toward a group of low hills in the distance.

With a few shaky steps I emerged from the reeds and began stumbling in the direction the rod had pointed. My clothes were still damp and muddy, while my stomach was practically caving in from hunger—I hadn't eaten since I'd left Senggum's the day before. But I had to get away from the river before the Merkits came searching for me.

I began half jogging, half limping in the direction the jump rod had indicated, trying to use the gentle rolling contours of the ground to keep me hidden. My soggy clothes chafed, and a stab of pain ran up my leg with each step, but anything I suffered now would be nothing compared to what I'd endure if the Merkits found me.

When the sun was directly above me, I decided to see how far I'd gone. Keeping my body crouched low, I climbed a small hill and then lay flat on my stomach to survey the area. To the south stretched yet more hills and wide valleys, and the distinctive green of a forest about a twenty-minute walk away. To the north, the river had become a distant ribbon, glittering like a jeweled snake in the sunlight. As I gazed along its bank, my heartbeat quickened. A horseman was riding down the river's edge, leaning low from his saddle to search the ground. He couldn't see me way over here, but he didn't have to. A steady trail of flattened grass led from my hiding spot all the way back to the river. Any second now he'd notice it. I had to make it to the forest!

I leaped to my feet and began racing for the trees as fast as my injured leg could carry me. I'd covered only a few steps before a loud horn rang out. Seconds later, answering calls came from farther upstream.

Fear gripped me. I had to make it to the forest or I died, plain and simple. Drawing on my last reserves, I forced myself to run even faster, struggling to keep my balance without the use of my arms.

You can do it, Dan!

I'd covered about three quarters of the distance when a shout echoed behind me. A quick glance over my shoulder showed a Merkit cresting the hill. He pointed in my direction as he looked back and shouted something over his shoulder to those behind.

Faster!

The safety of the forest was about two hundred paces away. My lungs heaved for air and my right leg ached with every step, but there was no stopping; I had to reach the trees.

The ground shook behind me as the beating of hooves grew louder and louder.

I didn't look. The forest was so close. I had to make it.

At the edge of my peripheral vision, a horse's head came into view. I twisted my head sideways and saw Chiledu leaning low in his saddle, an amused smile on his lips. "You run well, and you gave us good sport." His eyes narrowed. "But now that sport is at an end."

He veered his horse into me, sending me sprawling into the grass. I rolled a few times and came to halt with my back on the ground.

I lay there gasping, too tired to move. This was it. Game over.

Chiledu and the others formed a circle around me with their horses.

"What shall we do with him?" Muqali asked.

Chiledu spat on the ground beside my head. "We take him to the khan, for his words may still have some truth in them." He took out a knife from his belt and tested the edge with his thumb. "But this time we make sure he will never run again." He slid down from his saddle and swaggered toward me, his lips curved in a cruel smile.

I could only lie there and cower in fear as he loomed over me, a menacing figure surrounded by a halo of sunlight.

"You don't have to do this," I pleaded. "I won't run again. I promise."

Chiledu threw back his head and laughed. "Your words are like the bleating of a lamb, quickly forgotten. But a severed heel tendon is something you will always remember." He pointed with his knife first at my right foot and then at my left. "But I am a fair man. You may choose which foot will forever be crippled."

My stomach lurched and bile filled my mouth. "Please . . . I'll tell you what you want to know."

"I gave you that chance before, and you refused. Now give me one of your feet, or I will cut both."

A whimper escaped my lips, and I slowly raised my injured right leg off the ground.

Chiledu grabbed my foot and wrenched my boot off.

"I bet you a skin of airag he pisses himself," one Merkit said.

"I bet you two that he cries like a newborn babe," added another.

More bets and counter bets followed, filling the air with shouts and laughter.

I shut my eyes and turned my head away. My teeth ground together and every muscle in me tensed as I waited for the knife to slice into the back of my ankle.

Over the constant shouts and cheering of the Merkits, I heard Chiledu grunt, and his grip on my foot loosened.

"Come on, don't play with him," Muqali laughed. "I want to hear his screams."

Chiledu grunted again and let go of my foot. I opened my eyes to see him standing open-mouthed, tottering slightly as if in the breeze, his eyes vacant. Then, like a tall tree in the forest, he slowly fell forward and crashed to the ground beside me. Two arrows with bright red fletching jutted from his back.

In the sudden silence that followed, the steady beat of a lone horse's hooves rang out.

"There!" Cha'adai yelled, pointing to a single rider galloping toward us down a distant hill. The figure stood up in the stirrups and fired again, waiting for the exact moment when all four of his horse's hooves were off the ground.

Khasar?

It had to be him. I knew only one person who used red-fletched arrows and could shoot with such accuracy. Not to mention that the rider had the same small build, cocky way of riding, and complete lack of concern for personal safety. But what was he doing here? And where was Bo'orchu and the rest of the group?

Khasar's intended target ducked just in time and the streaking arrow sailed over his head.

"Get him!" Muqali yelled.

The remaining five Merkits galloped toward Khasar, hugging the necks of their horses to offer him less of a target. Despite the odds, Khasar kept coming at them, firing a steady stream of arrows.

The Merkits lowered their horn-tipped spears as they closed the distance on him. Even if Khasar dropped one or two more Merkits, he'd never be able to fight all of them. But he kept charging, a solitary madman against a much stronger foe.

What is he doing?

The ground began to tremble with a dull vibration that sent shivers through me. I recognized that feeling; I'd woken up in a sweat so many nights, imagining it in my dreams. Horsemen were coming. Lots of them.

Behind Khasar, a wave of Mongols surged over the crest of the hill, and I let out a sob of relief.

The Merkits wheeled their horses around and began to race away, lashing their mounts for speed. Their flight only spurred Khasar on. He howled a bloodthirsty cry and raced after them, with the rest of the Mongols chasing behind, tumbling down the hillside like a tsunami— straight toward me.

The blood drained from my face and my sobs of joy changed to cries of panic. I scrambled to my feet and began hobbling toward the forest. My legs felt like jelly, but if I didn't get out of the way, I'd be trampled.

I made it only a few steps and then stumbled face-first into the grass. The swarm of hooves and horse legs was almost on me; I needed another plan quick.

My eyes fell on Chiledu's body, the two arrows still sticking out of his back. In life he'd been a complete asshat, but maybe in death he could actually be of some use. With my feet I pushed him over onto his side so his back faced the onrushing stampede. Then I curled myself back-first into his corpse, trying to make myself as small as possible. One wrong step and I'd be crushed or killed. *Come on, Chiledu, you useless lump, protect me.*

Three Merkits shot past my location, one barely clinging to his saddle because of the arrow in his back. Seconds later, Khasar roared past, his bow thrumming as he fired again. The ground quaked as the main body of Mongols began thundering past. Clods of dirt flew into the air, spattering me with mud. An endless flow of hooves and legs flashed in front of my eyes as horses swept around my human shield.

CHAPTER 16

I pressed myself into the ground, wincing as each horse and rider raced by, hooves flashing dangerously close to my head. I lay there for what felt like an eternity before the stampede ended and the last horseman rode past. I let out a huge breath and pushed Chiledu's corpse aside. Somehow I'd survived without a scratch. Chiledu had been good for something after all.

A few paces away a lone rider watched me. A familiar face peeked out from under a fur-lined cap. "Dan?" Bo'orchu asked in disbelief.

I dragged myself to my feet and eyed him warily. After all I'd read on the internet about Temujin, Bo'orchu, and the others, I'd be a fool to trust any Mongol. "Yeah, it's me, Bo'orchu."

"You look well for someone who is dead," he said with a smirk.

What did he mean by that? Was that a threat?

He slid off his horse and came toward me, a knife in hand.

"Y-y-you don't have to do this, Bo'orchu," I stammered as I stumbled back a few steps. "You can have my armor. You can have whatever you want. Just please, don't kill me."

"Kill you?" He stopped and blinked in confusion. "I shared my food and airag with you. I gave you my only spare deel. We rode together into battle. I call you friend, Dan of the western lands. And I am not one to throw aside bonds of friendship for a mere shirt of iron." He pointed his knife at me. "Now turn around so I can free you."

I tried to shut my mind to all the horrible things I'd read about the Mongols and just focus on the facts. Bo'orchu had been decent to me and Sam—there was no reason for him to stop being decent now. I turned my back toward him, and with one quick slice, he severed the cords that bound my wrists.

After a full day of having my arms pinned behind my back, there was no better feeling than being able to move them again. I massaged my chafed wrists and tried to work the kinks from my shoulders. "Thanks, Bo'orchu. Sorry for doubting you. I've . . . been through a lot the past few days."

"No need to apologize. I am glad that you have returned to us from the ranks of the fallen."

"Why do you keep saying I died?"

"One of Jamukha's men said a Merkit spear had pierced your back and he had seen you fall." Bo'orchu shrugged. "When you did not return, why would anyone doubt his words?"

"The guy who told you this, was he short, kind of fat, with a long mustache?"

Bo'orchu nodded.

"Is he still alive?"

"Yes." Bo'orchu motioned in the direction that the Mongols had come from. "He was wounded in the arm, but he will live to fight again. I sent him back to ride with the main group. Why do you concern yourself so much about this man?"

"He's the one who attacked me!"

Bo'orchu's eyes narrowed. "That treacherous dog told us a different tale."

I pointed to my pant leg, where the faint outlines of a bloodstain were still visible despite the amount of time I'd spent in the water.

"Whatever he said, he lied. He shot me in the leg and again in the back. He was about to kill me so I . . . um . . . left."

Bo'orchu's brow furrowed. "How do you leave a battle? And how do you reappear days later, so far ahead of us?"

"I don't think you'd believe me if I told you."

Bo'orchu chuckled and clapped me on my good shoulder. "You are probably right. But no matter, it is good to see you again."

"What about Sam? Do you know if she's all right?"

Bo'orchu shook his head. "We have been separated from Temujin and we have not heard anything." He looked over to the river in the distance. "But now that we have reached the Kilqo, our journey ends. We will wait here for the rest to join us. Do not fear for her; you will see her soon."

I sat down on the ground and pulled my knees to my chest. Bo'orchu's news had hit me like a one-two punch to the gut. The guy who'd betrayed me was still alive, and Bo'orchu didn't know a thing about what had happened to Sam.

He sat down next to me and unrolled a wad of felt. "Here, take some food. You look like you have not eaten in days."

"I'm not hungry," I muttered.

"Starving yourself will not bring her here quicker." Bo'orchu pushed the felt toward me. "Now eat, so when she does come, you will at least have the strength to stand."

"Fine." I popped a piece of leathery dried sheep meat into my mouth and began chewing. It's amazing what a day of starvation did to my appreciation of Mongol cuisine. The petrified chunk tasted delicious— and I didn't even care about the lint.

By now the Mongols had finished chasing after the fleeing Merkits and were returning to where Bo'orchu and I sat. In one fluid movement, Khasar brought his horse to a halt next to us and slid out of the saddle. "Bah! I only got five of them. One of Belgutei's men struck the last one." He flopped to the ground right beside Bo'orchu, a skin of airag in hand.

"Thanks for saving me, Khasar," I said.

"I did not save you." He brushed aside my thanks without even looking at me. "I killed some Merkits. Who are you, anyway? Kereyit? Tayichi'ut?"

"It's Dan. Remember me?"

"No . . ." Khasar jerked back as if he had seen a ghost. "The great blue heaven cannot hate me this much." He leaned across and stared at my face in disbelief. "It *is* you underneath all that mud." Scowling, he got up and stomped off in the direction of his spare horses and began separating the small herd into two groups.

"What did I do to him?" I asked Bo'orchu.

Bo'orchu chuckled. "Just wait." He cupped his hands around his mouth and shouted toward a cluster of riders. "Belgutei! Come here! It is important!" Bo'orchu nudged me in the arm. "Stand up and take your hat off so that Belgutei can see your hair better."

I struggled back to my feet and yanked off my hat as Belgutei rode closer, with Jelme following.

Belgutei grinned and his eyes lit up with amusement. "Dan!" He halted his horse next to me. "It is so good to see you *alive!*" He turned to Khasar. "Little brother! Did you hear that? Dan is *alive!*"

"The whole valley can hear your bellowing, you great ox."

"Our bet was so long ago," Belgutei said. "Please refresh my memory. Was it for two horses? Three horses?"

Khasar scowled. "You know it was five." He pointed to the small group of horses he had just separated from his own herd. "There are your horses. May they all run slowly and throw you at every chance."

Belgutei laughed. "Just remember, little brother"—he patted his chest smugly—"I always win."

Khasar scowled once more and stalked off.

"You bet on whether I died?" I asked incredulously.

"Of course," Belgutei said. "You ride with fear on your face. A man cannot live long if he is always afraid." He shrugged. "But I bet that you would die *after* the Kilqo. Khasar was the one who said you would die *before* we reached it."

Jelme had dismounted and now directed a sneer in my direction. "So you live," he said with his usual disdain. "At least Temujin will be pleased."

Good old Jelme, the one rock of consistency among the Mongols.

All around the valley, men sat on the grass while letting their horses rest after their long ride. They passed around skins of airag and food.

"So what do we do now?" I asked.

Bo'orchu lay back on the grass with his hands behind his head and looked up at the sky. "We wait. The river blocks our path forward, so we will rest here, hidden in the shadow of the hills, until Temujin arrives."

Rest? Impossible. How could I rest now? I still hadn't seen Sam, and the guy who'd tried to kill me was on his way to meet up with us.

"Can I borrow your knife, Bo'orchu?"

He nodded and passed me his blade. I stuck it up my sleeve and slit the straps tying down the jump rod, leaving it loose inside my sleeve. Now I was ready. As soon as Sam appeared, I was going to grab her and jump out of here.

I returned the knife to Bo'orchu and then lay down on the grass, determined to conserve my energy as I waited for her. Every part of me felt tired and sore. I fought to keep my drooping eyelids open. But the sunlight beating down was almost blinding, and I closed my eyes for a moment just to give them a rest . . .

Something hard jabbed me in the ribs. "Wake up."

Huh? I opened my eyes to see Khasar leaning out of his saddle with a spear in one hand, the butt of it hovering just above me. "Temujin is coming," he said. "His scouts have already reached us."

I bolted upright and wiped the sleep from my eyes with the heel of my palm. Everyone else had resaddled their horses and now milled

about the valley, waiting. The sun had nearly traveled across half the
sky while I slept.

"How long . . . ?" I began but stopped. The ground vibrated, and a
dull rumble emanated from the south. Temujin's army would be here
any minute.

"Where are your horses?" Belgutei asked me.

"I don't have any."

He pointed to the small group of five that he had won from Khasar.
"Take those as a gift," he said.

"Really? Are you sure?"

He waved a hand dismissively. "Horses come and go. Knowing that
I beat Khasar is a much greater prize to me."

I mounted the only horse with a saddle. I still didn't have a weapon,
but it felt great to be on horseback again. Now I just had to find Sam.
The rod tugged fiercely in the direction of the approaching rumble.

Nervously I tapped a fist against my thigh as the first wave of horsemen crested the hill and came into view. To'oril's men charged down
the slope, thousands of dust-covered riders streaming ahead of their
khan's banner. After them came Jamukha's men, turning the hillside
into a wildly careening jumble of horses and men. Shouts filled the air,
and the grass was trampled into mud.

Finally Temujin rode into view at the head of his troops. My eyes
skirted past him and flew over the swarm of sweaty, grimy men that
followed him.

Where's Sam?

The jump rod pointed toward the center, where Temujin's standard of nine black yak tails hung over the army. I shielded my eyes
with a hand and searched for her, but it was so hard to see anything
through the dust in the air and the mass of wild riders, each leading
multiple horses. The rod pointed consistently toward the center of
that swirling horde, to where the standard bearer rode, with a wide
space around him.

Had he claimed her for himself and taken her jump rod?

Hold it . . .

My stomach fluttered as I peered closer at the standard bearer. He wore a Mongol hat and deel and had a bow slung over his shoulder like everyone else, but his dirt-covered face looked slightly paler. And his hair?

I could feel my lips curling into a big, goofy smile, but I didn't care. I'd recognize that flaming red hair anywhere, even tied in ponytails, darkened by dust, and smashed under a furry hat.

Judging by the bow slung over her shoulder, she had managed to avoid becoming the wife of some smelly Mongol. After all my fears and my struggle to find her, I wanted to rush over and sweep her up in my arms, but I held myself in check. Belgutei and Khasar already thought I was a cowardly little nothing—rushing off to Sam would probably sink me even lower in their opinions. Besides, Temujin and his troops were heading our way. Just a few more minutes and we'd finally be together again.

Bo'orchu pulled his horse up next to mine. "See! Your woman holds our war banner. I told you no harm would come to her."

"Yes," Khasar added from the other side of Bo'orchu, his tone heavy with longing. "She still looks as beautiful as when I left her." He sighed wistfully and shook his head. "I was ready to claim her when we met again. I had a string of Merkit horses to offer her, and tales of bravery in battle that would have melted the ice around any woman's heart. But then her man showed up alive."

"Hey! I'm right here," I protested.

"I know. I have not gone blind," Khasar said to me, his eyes not leaving Sam. "Your wife is a fine woman, with a fair face and fiery hair. You should be glad that I find her worthy of my attention. It is a sad man who has a wife no one else longs for."

"Are you set on giving him all your wisdom, Khasar?" Belgutei asked. "Just do not give him too much or you will have none left."

"And what do you know about women, you sheep head?"

"More than you," Belgutei said. "Look at her ride. She has a proud back and a warrior's eye. She is not interested in some boy who simply brings her horses and tells stories. She is like a great hunting eagle. She can only be tamed by the greatest of men."

Jelme snorted and jerked his thumb in my direction. "Then why is she with this heap of dung?"

From Khasar, Belgutei, or Bo'orchu, I would have taken the comment as good-natured. Not from Jelme. "What's your problem?" I snapped. "You've been on my case ever since I got here."

Jelme guided his horse so that it was right beside mine and our knees almost touched. He looked me up and down, not bothering to hide his disdain. "If not for Temujin, I would have killed you long ago. He thinks you are sent by the spirits to guide him, but I know better. You are just a scared boy who will piss himself at the first sign—"

The edge of my hand chopped across Jelme's Adam's apple. Instantly he began coughing and his face turned red as his throat constricted. Summoning all the strength in my wounded body, I launched myself at him and knocked him out of the saddle. We crashed to the ground, with Jelme landing back-first and taking the brunt of the impact. All my pain, fear, and anger channeled itself into one target—Jelme's ugly face—and I began raining punches down.

Jelme swatted at my fists with his left hand, trying to block the blows. With his right hand he pulled a sharpened antler from his belt and slashed at my face. I jerked back so its sharp prongs passed right in front of my eyes.

The bastard almost blinded me!

I put his arm in a wristlock and twisted. His features contorted with pain and the weapon fell from his hand. A new look appeared on Jelme's face—fear. One more twist and I'd snap his wrist.

"Enough!" boomed a powerful voice.

Rough hands grasped my shoulders and wrenched me off Jelme. I turned around to punch whoever had restrained me and found Bo'orchu. My fist stopped mere inches from his face.

My rage fizzled away, and I dropped my hand to my side. Only then did I become aware of Temujin sitting on his horse, watching us. And, judging by the scowl on his face, he wasn't happy.

"You are my most trusted brothers," Temujin began, his chastising glare alternating between Jelme and Bo'orchu. "The ones I relied on to stand by my side to help me win Borte back. My heart soared on eagle's wings to hear of my brothers' return. But now I find you fighting like dogs over scraps of meat." He nudged his horse closer and stared down at me. "And who are you to quarrel with Jelme? When you quarrel with Jelme, you . . ." Temujin stopped himself and he peered closer at me. "Dan?" The harsh lines of his eyes softened, and the light of recognition shone in his eyes. "You are alive? I was told of your death."

It felt weird seeing Temujin again. Before I'd left Mongolia, he'd been some ignorant seventeen-year-old sheep herder on a quest to get his wife back. But now he was Genghis Khan, the most bloodthirsty conqueror in history. "Yeah, I'm alive," I said, trying my hardest to push away thoughts of all the death and misery he would cause and instead focus on the man I knew. "The guy who told you I died was the one who tried to kill me."

Temujin's eyes widened as if he'd been slapped, and his nostrils flared. "All of you," he barked, "come with me." He snapped his reins and began heading toward Jamukha's group, which was currently setting up camp next to the river.

Jelme pulled himself to his feet and wiped the blood away from his lip with a sleeve. He fixed me with a baleful glare. "One day, foreigner, Temujin will see you for what you truly are. When he does, I will kill you."

I tried to return his stare and seem confident, but inside I was shaking. Sam and I were way out of our depth here. The jump device never should have dumped us in this strange place. "Whatever." And with that brilliant rebuttal, I got back on my horse.

Then I chased after Temujin, catching up to him as he reined in his horse in front of a large group of riders led by Jamukha.

"I must speak with you," Temujin said to Jamukha.

Jamukha looked past him to the rest of us. "When does my sworn brother need guards to speak to me?"

"They are not guards. They are here to make sure that justice is done."

"Who has wronged you, my brother?" Jamukha's back stiffened. "I will make sure he suffers."

Khasar pushed himself forward. "You sent a man with Bo'orchu and me to scout ahead. He was wounded in a fight with the Merkits and was sent back to recover. Where is he?"

"Bayan?" Jamukha frowned. "I have known him since we were boys. He is not a man to betray my trust. What do you accuse him of?"

"He tried to kill one of my men," Temujin said. "And he then lied to all of us about the deed."

An angry mutter rippled through Jamukha's men.

"Find me Bayan," Jamukha snapped to one of his followers. "But tell him nothing of what you have just heard."

The man nodded and rode off into the mass of Jamukha's army, disappearing quickly from our sight.

Wait . . . We're doing this now?

No. We couldn't. I wasn't prepared. I knew nothing about Mongol law. How did they even figure out who was guilty? Did Bayan and I just fight it out? Or did it go to a vote, and the guy with the most friends supporting him won? Either way, I was screwed.

From the corner of my eye, I could see Jelme watching me, eagerly anticipating my execution.

CHAPTER 17

Jamukha's messenger returned, and behind him rode the greedy little backstabbing bastard who had attacked me. He rode straight toward Jamukha, not looking in my direction.

"My lord," Bayan asked him. "What do you wish of me?"

Jamukha motioned to Temujin. "Speak, my brother. What claim do you have against him?"

Temujin rode forward a few paces so that he blocked Bayan's view of me. "When the Merkits attacked you," Temujin began, "you claimed that the man with the white skin and golden hair was killed."

"Yes," Bayan said. "I saw him fall with my own eyes. A Merkit spear took him in the chest. He fought bravely before he died."

Temujin nudged his horse to the side so that I was now in clear view. "Dan. Tell us what really happened."

Bayan went pale and his eyes cast about desperately. "I—I—I must have made a mistake," he coughed.

"You shot me!" I yelled. "Twice! With the same white-fletched arrows you now carry on your back." I leaned down and rolled up my pant leg to reveal the bandage around my calf.

"I never struck you, outlander," Bayan replied. He had recovered quickly from his initial shock and his face was now a calm mask. "You confuse me with one of the Merkits."

"I saw *you* shoot me! Not a Merkit."

Jamukha turned to me, his expression unreadable. "And why would he attack you, outlander?"

"Because he wanted this." I pulled up one corner of my muddy deel to show the chain mail underneath.

A gasp went up from the group surrounding us. Jamukha's eyes went wide for a second, but he recovered. "Can anyone support your words? Khasar? Bo'orchu?"

"Your man *did* know of the iron shirt," Khasar said. "It makes a great noise when riding."

"Did you see Bayan fire the arrow?" Jamukha asked.

"No," Khasar said. "I was too far in front."

"And I fled along a different path," Bo'orchu said.

Jamukha rubbed his jaw. "Bayan. Do you swear by the great blue heaven that what you say is true?"

Bayan nervously licked his lips and nodded. "I do, Jamukha. I would never lie to you."

"And you, outlander. Do you swear by the great blue heaven?"

"I do. It was him who attacked me—not a Merkit."

"One of you lies," Jamukha declared.

"Jamukha! You know me," Bayan began. "I would never—"

"Silence! I must think." Jamukha lowered his head and began idly tapping his fingers on his saddle.

What? That's it? Trial over already? No, there had to be more. I'd barely said anything. I opened my mouth to speak but Jamukha shot me a warning glare.

Crap . . . I already knew who Jamukha was going to trust. There was me, the complete stranger, versus the friend he'd known for ages.

I reached into my sleeve for the jump rod.

Jelme nudged his horse closer. "What are you hiding in your sleeve?" he asked, his eyes narrowing.

"N-n-nothing. Just scratching an itch." I pulled my hand out.

Sweat dripped down the side of my face. I needed about five seconds to set the jump rod to the *get the hell outta here* position and recite the words to send me home. With Jelme nearly salivating at the thought of stabbing me, I clearly didn't have that much time. I inched closer to Temujin. As soon as Jamukha's verdict was delivered, I'd throw myself on Temujin's mercy and hope he'd spare me.

"I have decided." Jamukha pointed toward me with his spear. "You, outlander. You do not look like us. You do not ride like us. And you do not know our ways. I do not know you, yet you bring me words of treachery." Jamukha's spear shifted to Bayan. "You I have known many years. We hunted side by side as boys and have grown into men together. I have learned to trust you like a brother."

Jamukha's eyes narrowed in on me and then shot back to Bayan. In a blur of motion Jamukha buried his spear into Bayan's chest. Bayan's mouth parted in shock as blood gushed from the wound. "And that is why your betrayal strikes deep." With a sickening crunch of bone and flesh, Jamukha wrenched the spear out, and Bayan dropped out of his saddle.

"Take his body far from camp and leave it for the wolves," Jamukha ordered; then he locked eyes with me. "Your coat of iron has cost me a trusted friend. Be wary of what other treachery it will bring."

"I . . . I will," I stammered, unable to take my eyes off the bloody hole in Bayan's chest.

Temujin grasped Jamukha by the arm. "Thank you, my brother." With that, he released Jamukha, turned his horse around, and began riding back to the main Mongol camp. Jelme followed, not bothering to say a word to any of us.

"I think Temujin is right," Bo'orchu said to me. "The great blue heaven does smile on you. I have never seen a man avoid the wolves as well as you."

Khasar shook his head at me and scowled. "Because of you, I just lost *another* five horses to my sheep-head of a brother. Why do you not die?"

Belgutei chuckled and clapped him on the back. "You are lucky I did not bet you ten."

Khasar's face twisted as if he was sucking on a lemon. He paused as if to say something, but instead he changed his mind and rode off after Temujin. The rest of us followed at a slower pace.

We headed downstream toward the camp along the riverbank. I veered away from the others and homed in on the Mongol standard. It hung lower than before, as if it had been stuck into the ground.

Where's Sam?

Men and horses milled about, blocking my view. I pushed past them and finally spotted her, seated by herself, a wide ring of empty grass between her and the men. She looked so lonely, quietly chewing on a handful of trail mix, her eyes cast to the ground. I'd never seen her so sad. What unspeakable hell had she suffered while I was gone?

I slowed my horse to a walk and stepped it into the empty circle of grass surrounding her. Suddenly, every Mongol within twenty paces of her jumped to his feet, and the creak of countless bows being drawn to full extension filled the air, all of them aimed at me. I jerked my horse to a halt and froze in place. All conversation had stopped. In the eerie silence, the men kept their bows trained on me. Watching. Waiting.

"Just go away," Sam said in Mongolian without looking up. "I don't want any horses or sheep, and I'm sure you're brave and would make a great husband, but I'm not interested."

Huh?

"Sam!" I hissed. "It's me."

Her head snapped up and she stared at me incredulously for a few seconds, as if doubting her own eyes. "You're alive?" Blinking back her shock, she stood and began walking, almost as if in a daze, toward me. "It's okay. He's with me," she called out to the men in a distracted tone.

Not quite the hero's welcome I expected. As the men dropped their arrows back into quivers and returned to their drinking and eating, I slid off my horse, but my injured leg buckled under me.

Sam's eyes dropped to my bloodstained pant leg and her lips drew thin.

"Don't worry," I reassured her. "It's just a scratch." I raised my arms to hug her, but she held out a hand to stop me.

"Please . . . don't." She seemed almost afraid to touch me.

Something was up. This was not the Sam I'd left here. There was no light in her eyes, no joy in her dust-covered face. And she didn't seem excited at all that I had returned. "What's wrong?"

She bit her lip and hesitated before giving me her response. "I'm fine," she finally said.

"Don't lie to me, Sam. I know you. What did they do to you?" After everything I had read about the Mongols, I couldn't believe that they had just left her alone.

"Nothing," she replied.

"Then what's wrong?"

"Nothing's wrong. I'm *fine*," she said with a finality that I knew meant she *wasn't* fine, and also that I wasn't going to get anything more out of her. She motioned to me with her chin. "How are you even alive?"

"Just a misunderstanding. I was attacked and had to jump out. But I came back to rescue you."

"You came to rescue *me*? Seriously?" She shook her head incredulously. "You're the one who looks like you need rescuing. What's with all the mud?"

"Well . . . I kind of got captured by a band of Merkits. I managed to escape them, but I slept on the riverbank last night."

"Always the same old Dan," she sighed.

I wasn't quite sure what she meant by that, but the disappointment was clear in her tone. This conversation was going downhill faster than a yeti on skis—time to change the subject. "Why are you in charge of the standard?"

"That was Temujin's idea. He knew I might have some issues being the only girl around, so he figured the best way to keep me safe was to make me the most visible person in his army. But just to be on the safe side, he also made a rule that if any man comes within ten steps of me without my approval, he's to be killed on the spot. And if any Mongol allows another man to come close to me without my consent, then both of them will be killed."

"Oh . . . I guess that explains the warm welcome I got back there. But it worked, right? You've been safe?"

"Couldn't have been safer." She motioned without enthusiasm to the circle of men surrounding her. "Except it also means that I can't go to the bathroom without a thousand men watching, and that every idiot who feels like offering himself as my husband knows just where to find me."

"Sorry . . . Sounds terrible."

"I've managed." She pointed at the bloodstain outlined on my pant leg. "Clearly you can't say the same. That looks like more than a misunderstanding. What *really* happened to you while you were gone? Don't skip anything."

Oh boy. I sat down and patted the grass beside me. "It's going to be a long story."

She sat down, but much farther away from me than usual. Something had changed, but I knew she wasn't going to tell me anything until she was ready. So I launched into the entire story of how Khasar had galloped ahead, and we were attacked by Merkits, and how Bayan shot me in the forest. I told her about my jumping back home, having Jenna patch me up, getting captured by Merkits, my escape, and my rescue, then the fight with Jelme, and Bayan's execution. "And that's it," I said. "That's where I've been the past few days."

Sam stared at a piece of grass in her hands from which she was slowly ripping shreds. "That's a lot of near-death experiences, even for you," she finally said.

"I know. Trust me, I didn't go looking for them."

"At least your little girlfriend came to save you." Sam stood up and walked around behind me as I sat. "Let me make sure she did a decent job. It would kind of suck if you managed to survive everything else only to end up dying because of an infection."

I pulled off my deel, chain mail, and tunic, leaving myself naked from the waist up. Sam's fingers skimmed my back, prodding gently at the wound. This was the Sam I needed, the one who cared about me. I didn't know what had happened to her while I was gone, but clearly something was different between us. I just hoped we could get back to the way we used to be.

"It looks good enough." Sam patted me once on the shoulder. "But if you had a bandage on it, it's gone."

"It probably fell off when I was in the river."

She sat down again, this time facing me. "So how did you explain your porcupine impression to her?"

"I didn't. I just made up some garbage about a camping accident, then jumped out before she could ask any more questions."

"Wait . . ." Sam leaned forward, hands on her knees. "She saw you jump out?"

"Yeah." The look on Jenna's face crept into my mind—complete shock mixed with disbelief. "I don't know how I'm going to explain it to her."

Sam threw her hands in the air. "What were you thinking? Why would you do that?"

"She refused to leave, and you were stuck here alone with the wrong words for the jump device. And there was so much horrible stuff about the Mongols on the internet—cities being wiped out, entire peoples being killed or enslaved. I was worried about you."

"Damn it, Dan!" Sam's cheeks turned red and her eyes flashed with anger. "I don't need you to save me! I survived plenty of time jumps without you, and I've managed to do it without being shot, stabbed, enslaved, or whatever mess you always seem to find yourself in."

I'd never seen Sam this angry before. But I didn't think me jumping out in front of Jenna was the issue. Something else was bothering her. She'd been distant ever since I got back. "Sorry," I said quietly. "So what do we do now?"

"The exact same thing we were doing before you left. We stick to Temujin like glue, fix the time glitch, and then get the hell out as soon as we can." She fixed me with a glare from red-rimmed eyes. "Do you think you can manage that?"

"Yeah," I muttered glumly. There was nothing else to say.

"Good." She wiped her eyes with her sleeve, leaving a streak of moist dirt across her face. "So did you learn anything while you were a prisoner of the Merkits?"

"No," I sighed. "But while I was home I did some quick research. And I was right, this time jump is all about one of these guys becoming Genghis Khan. And you'll never guess which one."

"Temujin," she declared matter-of-factly.

"Okay . . . maybe you could guess. How'd you know?"

"I've spent the last few days with him. He has more focus than anyone I've ever met. He knows what he wants and exactly how to get it." She pointed at the valley swarming with Mongols and Kereyits. "Just look what he's doing to get his wife back. Do you think this massive army is here because they care about Borte? Nope. These men, they can feel his strength, and they know he'll lead them to greatness. So they listen to him and obey without question. How else do you think I could have lasted as the only female in this army? Imagine what happens when he starts telling them about his plans to form an empire."

"I don't need to imagine—I read about it. This attack into Merkit territory is the beginning of his rise to power. It shows to the other tribes he's a leader who can get things done. But if he fails here, there'll be no Genghis Khan—and without Genghis Khan, the history of the entire world gets completely rewritten."

"So if everything's going according to the history books so far, what's the glitch?"

"I don't know. The website I looked at covered this raid in just a few sentences." I took the thick cap from my head and ran a hand through my sweaty hair. "All we know for sure is that the glitch involves Temujin. The jump rods have pointed to him ever since we got here."

"But why?" Sam asked.

"No clue." I shrugged. "We'll just have to wing it."

Sam let out a long loud sigh, full of disappointment. "We always do."

"Come on, Sam, I'm really trying here. I know you think I'm some idiot who runs into danger at any chance I get, but I can't see a plan—"

"Lady Sam," someone called. "May we approach?"

Sam and I turned to see Temujin on horseback at the edge of the ring of men surrounding her. Alongside him were Jelme, Belgutei, Khasar, and Bo'orchu, none of them daring to venture into the cleared space around Sam.

Sam's right; he is a good leader. His rule was that no one could enter the circle without Sam's permission, and he followed it just the same way he expected his men to.

Sam waved them on. "Sure, come on in."

Temujin rode forward, with the others following. Jelme passed me slowly, his eyes never leaving mine. I'd never felt a glare so full of hostility and contempt. I tried to match it.

"Jelme! Call the men!" Temujin said.

Jelme lifted the banner and began waving it in tight circles, high above his head. On this signal, a sudden hush spread across the Mongol camp and all heads turned toward Temujin.

He stood up in his stirrups and looked out over the assembled warriors. The only sound was the wind blowing through the grass and the impatient stamping of horses. An air of anticipation seemed to hum throughout the valley. The Mongols and their Kereyit allies were like a bowstring pulled back to the chin, just waiting to be released.

"We have ridden for many long days and finally reached the Kilqo River," Temujin called out, his voice strong and loud enough to carry across the river valley. "Beyond its deep waters lie the Merkit summer pastures. But now is not the time to rest. Now is the time for us to cross the Kilqo while the Merkits are not here to oppose us." He raised his fist high for everyone to see. "Then the Merkits will know our fury. And I will reclaim my wife!"

CHAPTER 18

The roar of the assembled Mongols and Kereyits echoed through the valley. Temujin lowered his fist and then began guiding his horse toward the riverbank, with Jelme following, standard in hand. Bo'orchu, Khasar, and Belgutei rode right behind them, while Sam and I grabbed our horses and raced to catch up. With a low rumble of hooves, the rest of the army began surging forward like a huge wave, ready to destroy anything in its path.

At the river's edge, Temujin reined in his horse and then leaped out of the saddle. His weak ankle buckled under him, and he stumbled to one knee. Instantly, Jelme was at his side, helping him up.

"Leave me!" Temujin snapped, pushing Jelme away. "Organize the men to cut down reeds and make rafts. We must ferry our bows and arrows across without getting them wet." He glanced at the far shoreline. "And we must hurry! We cannot be caught while we are crossing."

Bo'orchu leaped off his horse and pushed into the reeds, slashing his knife at the base of a clump of them. "Sam. Dan. Come with me," he called.

As I dismounted, he tossed me a long strip of leather without looking up. "I will cut. You will tie."

As I began lashing the reeds together, I glanced over at Temujin. He and Jelme were still onshore, busy tying together a bunch of reeds large enough to carry both their bows and quivers, as well as the Mongol standard.

What are you going to do wrong?

It was totally eating me up that Sam and I still hadn't figured out the time glitch. On my first jump, things had been easy, I knew enough about Anglo-Saxon history that I'd easily figured out the glitch. And on my second jump, Cenacus flat out told me what it was. But here? Temujin was a mystery. I'd barely spent any time with him, and most of it had been riding. And the few things I learned about him from the internet weren't enough to tell me what the glitch could be. There was obviously going to be one—Sam and I wouldn't be here otherwise. But what?

Think, Dan. What are you missing?

"Hey," I called to Sam, who was busy tying the other end of the reeds. "Do you think Temujin can swim?"

"How should I know?" she muttered.

"Come on, Sam!" I snapped. "I don't know what the hell's going on with you right now, but I need you to start acting like my partner so we can fix this damn glitch! You've spent more time with Temujin than I have—did he ever mention anything about swimming?"

"Sorry, you're right," she said quietly. "And no, I don't know if he can swim. Why?"

"What if that's the glitch? What if he drowns?"

Her brow furrowed as she looked over at Temujin. "Anything's possible, I guess. And he does have that bad ankle. Do you want to go with him?"

I raised my hands defensively. "Hell no! Jelme will probably try to drown me if I get too close."

"Of course he would," Sam grumbled as she shook her head. "Fine. I'll help Temujin." She laid her bow and quiver in the reeds next to me. "Can you keep my stuff dry?" Without waiting for my response, she ran out into the river until the water reached her waist. With one hand holding her hat in place, she plunged under the surface. For a few seconds she remained hidden, and then her head emerged from the water at a point close to where Temujin and Jelme were about to enter it.

"She swims through the water like an eagle glides through the air," Bo'orchu observed. He hefted a bundle of reeds in front of himself. "Me, I swim like a sheep. Are you ready to cross?"

I grabbed Sam's bow and quiver, and then my own bundle of reeds. "Ready."

We led our horses into the river and then tossed each of our reed bundles into the water. Around us, the other Mongols and Kereyits were busy turning the riverbank into a wasteland of churned-up mud and jagged reed stumps.

A few of them were already in the water, clinging to their rafts for dear life and propelling themselves forward with splashy kicks. I chuckled to myself. These guys were the most feared horsemen in history, but none of them looked even the slightest bit confident in the water.

I made sure Sam's bow and quiver were resting perfectly in the center of my mini raft to keep them dry, then Bo'orchu and I pushed our reed rafts toward the deepest part of the river, where the current swirled around us, pulling at our legs. Bo'orchu took small, tentative steps, as if afraid of the water. But the Kilqo and I were good friends. It had saved my life once already and now it would rinse me clean of all the mud and dirt I'd been dragging around.

"Just relax, and do what I do," I called out to Bo'orchu. I held on to my raft and kicked. With my feet off the bottom, my armor was like an anchor trying to drag me under, but fortunately the raft kept me afloat.

Bo'orchu gripped his own raft and took a few hesitant kicks. He hugged the clump of reeds to his chest, while his anxious eyes kept darting back to the receding shore. But as he entered the deeper water, his kicks got stronger and he stopped looking back. He wasn't going to win the Olympics or anything, but the guy would make it across.

Around us the river erupted into an explosion of sound and bodies. Men flailed at the river, splashing everywhere, while riderless horses surged ahead and swam across. My eyes kept drifting to the horizon, where at any moment I expected to see a huge horde of Merkits appear, ready to shoot us full of arrows as we emerged from the water.

"Faster!" Bo'orchu yelled.

"Why?"

He pointed far downstream where the river was narrower and the current ran faster. On the far bank, wrapped in the shadows of early evening, two men were dashing through the tall reeds toward waiting horses. Each held a net in one hand. The lead man stumbled as his net became tangled in the plants. He wrenched at it twice before giving up and leaving the net behind. The fishermen then sprang onto their horses and began galloping away from shore.

Oh . . . crap . . .

Were *they* the time glitch? Was Temujin's grand plan to get Borte back now going to get messed up because these two guys end up warning the Merkits about the Mongol approach? I kicked as hard as my sore leg could handle, trying to get myself across. I had to stop the fishermen from escaping.

Despite my efforts, Khasar was the first to reach the far shore. He clambered onto one of his horses while it was still belly-deep in the river. With water pouring in torrents from his clothing, Khasar snapped the reins, and his horse ran out of the water, galloping in the same direction the fishermen had run.

Go, Khasar!

He made it only about a hundred paces from the shore before a strange, high-pitched whistling sound emanated from above. An arrow arced through the air, flying directly over Khasar's head and landing in the grass in front of him.

He jerked his horse to a halt and wheeled it around, a foul expression on his face. Wordlessly, he locked eyes with Temujin, who had reached shallower water and stood with his bow out.

"What's going on?" I asked Bo'orchu.

"Temujin summoned Khasar back," he explained, his breath coming in gasps as he continued kicking.

"With an arrow?"

"Yes." Bo'orchu didn't explain further but, considering how much he was panting, I was lucky I'd gotten any explanation at all.

A few more kicks and the water was finally shallow enough for me to touch the bottom. I splashed ashore, only too aware of the fact that I had no weapon. If the Merkits appeared now, I'd be useless in a fight. Silently I willed the rest of the Mongol army to hurry up. We couldn't be caught crossing the river. We were too exposed. Too weak.

Bo'orchu staggered ashore and collapsed on his back, his chest heaving. His horses milled around him, and one even prodded Bo'orchu with its nose. "I will ride to the end of the Kilqo River itself before I ever try to cross it again," he panted.

With water still dripping from her long braids and the hem of her deel, Sam splashed through the shallows toward us and picked up her bow and quiver from our raft. She did her best to avoid eye contact with me, but she chuckled at Bo'orchu as she slung her quiver over her shoulder.

"Did Temujin handle the swim okay?" I asked, desperately trying to get things normal again between me and Sam.

"Yeah. He's fine."

"Do you think those fishermen are the glitch? Did Temujin screw up by calling Khasar back?"

She raised her left arm and passed it through a slow arc in front of her. She stopped with it pointing a short way downstream at Temujin and Jelme, who were wading the last few steps to shore. "No. Still pointing at Temujin."

Khasar rode his horse back and forth directly in front of Temujin and Jelme. "Why did you call me back?" he demanded, not hiding his frustration. "We must go after the fishermen!"

"No," Temujin said firmly. "They have strong horses and a long lead on us. We will not catch them."

Khasar tossed his hands in the air. "Of course we will not catch them . . . we do not chase them! Why do you let them flee and warn our enemies?"

"Have you lost your senses, brother? Did you think that we would appear in the middle of the Merkit summer grounds and just take Borte back? An army of this size could never hope for stealth. At some point the Merkits were bound to hear of our coming. We have done well in hiding our approach until now."

Khasar hammered a fist into his other palm. "So let me go after the fishermen. I will catch them and the Merkits will receive even less warning."

"We are in Merkit lands now," Temujin said, "where every man we meet is an enemy, and I do not know where the Merkit armies hide. I will not let my brother ride alone into danger."

"Fine! Send someone else."

"Enough!" Temujin roared. "These men chose to follow me, so they are *all* my brothers. I am responsible for their safety, and I will not throw their lives away. Will you be the one who tells their wives they are not coming back? Will you tell their sons that their fathers are dead?"

Khasar looked away and didn't say anything else.

It took about an hour to get all the men across. Only about a third of them had crossed in the first wave; there hadn't been enough reeds along the shore to provide rafts for everyone. So men who could handle swimming better than Bo'orchu collected all the rafts and swam them back to the opposite shore for others to use, twice.

During this time Sam and I stood on the shore, both of us swatting at flies and constantly scanning the horizon for any sign of approaching Merkits. I had tried to start a few conversations with Sam, but after her third single-syllable answer delivered in the same detached monotone, I gave up. Idle chatter about the weather and Mongol swimming ability wasn't going to fix whatever had happened to her while I was gone.

Around us, the Mongols and their Kereyit allies began setting up for the night. Now that we'd been discovered, they didn't bother with stealth, but instead lit thousands of fires, almost like a warning to the Merkits that an immense army was coming their way.

"Do you want me to take first watch?" I asked Sam as I spread my blanket on the ground.

"Sure." She spread her own blanket far away from mine, then lay down, her back to me.

I felt my chest tighten. Sam and I had started out this time jump as something more than friends, and now it felt like we were complete strangers.

To solve the time glitch, we would both need to be at our best.

I'd be ready. The big question was: would Sam?

CHAPTER 19

At dawn we began our spine-rattling ride into Merkit lands. No more hiding. No more stealth. Just forty thousand warriors thundering across the open steppe—an open challenge to the Merkit army.

No matter how hard I tried to fight it, a part of me was excited. The steady rumble of thousands of hooves hammering the earth was like a war drum that sent a rush of adrenaline through my veins. But the saner part of me was terrified. There was no way the Merkits would let an army just storm across their lands. And when the fighting did start, I'd be completely useless. Arrows would be flying through the air like rain and I didn't have a single weapon—not even a rock to throw. I desperately hoped Sam and I could figure out what the time glitch was before battle began, but she was still barely talking to me.

I did everything I could to break the wall of silence around her. Jokes. Comments about the weather, or the dust, or the crappy food, or saddle sores, or whatever. But unless I was talking about the glitch, I got only the bare minimum in response. And the more I tried to make things better between us, the more she retreated into herself. She avoided looking at me. She created a larger gap between our horses.

Slowly it dawned on me that it wasn't the Mongols who had upset her—it was me. I couldn't for the life of me figure out what I'd done, and she definitely wasn't volunteering any information. In the end, I gave up trying to return things to how they'd once been between us. Sam would tell me what was wrong on her own time—and that time clearly was not now.

By late afternoon Temujin's army had thrust deep into Merkit territory and still hadn't encountered the Merkit army. Unfortunately, we had found many other Merkits. Herders. Hunters. Families fleeing in wagons. Small groups living in clusters of gers. Any adult male died in a hail of arrows, while every female around Borte's age was brought before Temujin. But none of them were her.

The farther we traveled, the more I felt something was wrong. Where was the army that should be guarding the Merkit summer pastures? Why weren't they challenging us? Was that the glitch? Had Temujin, despite all of his planning, messed up somehow and was now leading us into one huge trap?

And I wasn't the only one feeling on edge about our progress; a current of unease seemed to ripple through Temujin's army. Almost everyone rode with their bows in hand, and some even had arrows nocked. Eyes scanned the hills, searching for danger while the scouts ranged in all directions but could not find the Merkit army.

As the sun hovered just above the hilltops, casting long shadows, we entered a broad river valley. The air stank of manure and the grass had been chewed short, as if thousands of sheep had been grazing there. A few gers still remained, but hundreds of circles of yellow grass showed where an entire city of tents had once stood, and the ground was gouged by the long lines of cart tracks leading away from the area. In the distance, the dust raised by the passage of countless people and horses left a dirty haze in the sky. A huge tribe of Merkits was in full flight.

Temujin rode among the few surviving gers. "Borte!" he called out. "Borte!"

No one answered.

Using his spear, Belgutei nudged aside the felt door of one of the gers. An old woman cowered inside, clutching three small children. All looked up fearfully at Belgutei.

"Where is Borte?" Temujin demanded.

The old woman bowed her head and pointed through the doorway to the distant cloud of dust.

Temujin glanced from the cloud to the setting sun, and his brow furrowed. "A reward of twenty horses to the man who finds her!" he yelled as he yanked hard on his horse's reins.

His cry was echoed by hundreds of voices and the army sped after the fleeing wagons, the evening shadows growing longer by the minute. I stared hard into the distance as my horse surged along with the others, its hooves rumbling across the churned-up steppe. If the old woman could be trusted, then Borte was near.

I nudged my horse closer to Sam's. "My gut tells me this glitch is going to happen soon."

"Yeah, I have the same feeling." She chewed her lower lip. "Any idea what it is yet?"

"No freakin' clue," I muttered. I'd never been on a time jump like this, where I could practically feel the glitch nearing, but still had not even an inkling of what it was. For the hundredth time, I glanced at Temujin, who was riding just ahead of us. He leaned over his horse's neck, as if trying to encourage every last bit of speed from the animal. *Come on, Temujin. How are you going to mess things up?*

Soon, beyond the endless drumming of hoofbeats came the unmistakable creak of wagons and the bleating of thousands of sheep. Ahead of us a cart became visible in the gray of twilight, its frantic owner slapping the reins in an attempt to get his horses to move faster. The cart bounced over the uneven ground, its cargo of ger poles, felt, and clay pots jostling violently.

A pair of arrows sprouted from the driver's back, and he slumped lifeless in his seat. While the rest of the army rumbled past the cart and raced onward, Temujin reined in his horse next to the wagon. "Borte!" he called as he leaned from his saddle and lifted a large piece of felt covering the goods stacked in the front of the wagon.

No answer.

We galloped on, more carts appearing as the leading group of Mongols descended upon them. Arrows whistled through the night, seeking out targets. Men howled, women screamed, and children wailed. And over it all chimed the constant, frightened bleating of sheep.

Sam and I stuck with Temujin as he rode from cart to cart, his horse barely moving as it struggled against the press of sheep. "Borte!" he called out again and again.

Sam, her bowstring drawn to her chin, swung her bow over a wide arc, searching for targets. She raised an eyebrow toward me. "Anything?" she shouted over the din.

"Nothing," I shouted back.

The press of sheep and horses and people slowly drove me away from Temujin. I tried to guide my horse closer to him, but I wasn't a Mongol—born to ride—and the distance between us only increased. I slid off my horse and began following Temujin on foot, squeezing through the flock. Desperately I searched for any little thing that seemed wrong, but it was so damn hard to see anything in the near darkness, and it was even harder to hear anything over the cacophony of bleating sheep, stomping horses, and shouting men.

"Borte!" Temujin called again as he looked into another wagon.

A faint female voice floated back from one of the carts ahead. "Temujin!"

Temujin struggled to edge his horse through the press of sheep. "Borte!"

Two women came running out of the darkness and grabbed the bridle of Temujin's horse. "I am here, my love!" the younger one cried.

"Borte!" Temujin shouted. "I have found you!" He leaped out of the saddle and landed heavily on the ground. His injured ankle twisted and he lurched sideways. He only managed to catch himself from falling by grabbing the wagon frame and holding himself upright.

Okay, he's got the girl, so why isn't the jump rod saying "go home"?

As if in answer, an arrow whistled through the air and stuck itself into the frame of the wagon, vibrating just inches from Temujin's head.

Borte screamed—a high-pitched shriek right in the ear of Temujin's horse. The animal reared in panic, its hooves flailing dangerously close to Temujin's head.

"Run!" Temujin yelled as he gripped her hand and began to limp away. He managed only a few steps before stumbling again, his ankle not able to support him. He grabbed the rear deck of the wagon for support and stood there, grimacing in pain.

With sudden clarity, I knew what the time glitch was. In the real history, Temujin had never injured his ankle. He probably ran off into the night with Borte, and the archer never got another shot at him. But there he was, a sitting duck for the hidden archer. And if I didn't do something quickly, the world's greatest conqueror would be dead.

I raced toward Temujin, with only seconds to save history. I was steps away from him when I threw myself into the air like I'd seen in way too many action movies. My body seemed to hang in midair as an arrow hissed toward me through the darkness.

Please don't hit me in the face.

Something drilled into my ribs and then, with a jangle of metal, I crashed to the ground in front of Temujin. My adrenaline was buzzing way too high for me to determine how badly I'd been hit. And right now I didn't have time to worry. I had to make sure Temujin was safe. I shot my head up to search for the archer.

Come on . . . where are you?

About fifty paces away, hidden among the folds of felt covering a wagon, I saw him. He already had another arrow nocked and had drawn the bowstring to his cheek. His eyes locked with mine.

Suddenly, a gray-feathered shaft sprang out of his chest, and his bow fell from his hands. He slumped forward as blood started oozing out over his deel.

Against my forearm, a slow warmth radiated from the jump rod. I collapsed onto my back and stared up at the night sky. *We did it! We saved history.*

Sam appeared beside me with another gray-feathered arrow drawn back to her chin. "How bad are you hit?"

I frowned. I couldn't feel the arrow at all. Pulling myself into a sitting position, I patted my body. Nothing. Then I spotted the arrow lying on the ground next to me, its tip shattered. "My chain mail actually worked!"

"Looks like you dodged another one," she said in the same distant monotone.

"I didn't plan on throwing myself in front of an arrow," I explained. "It was the only thing I could think of."

"I guess it worked." She shrugged. "Ready to go home?"

I dragged myself to my feet and looked around. Temujin and Borte were locked in an embrace. Jelme was eyeing me from horseback and, for once, wasn't looking at me like I should be killed on sight. Around us, the hiss of arrows and the screams of dying men had stopped, replaced with the pitiful cries of women and children as they mourned their dead or watched their property being plundered by Temujin's army.

"No," I said. "I don't think I'm ready."

"Of course, you aren't," Sam muttered. "Why not?"

I stared down at my empty hands. "The last two time jumps taught us so much about Victor's plans. But this one has been pretty much useless. We haven't interrogated any of Victor's men. We have no new information or jump devices. All I have are more scars to add to my collection. It feels wrong to go home with nothing."

"But that's what time-jumping's all about. You don't get a participation trophy for every little jump. Most of the time, you go in, do the job, and go home. So just be happy there weren't any major battles to fight, and then accept the fact we're not getting anything this time and move on."

"Move on? Did Temujin just move on when life flushed him down the toilet? No. He crawled out of the muck and took whatever he wanted." An idea began to form in my head. "Hey . . . what if he has some ideas for how to defeat Victor?"

Sam snorted. "You're kidding, right? He doesn't understand our world. He'll just tell you to raise an army and kill your enemy."

"Exactly!" I waved my hand toward the darkness, where his army still roamed. "I want to know how Temujin did all this. How does one guy manage to go from less than nothing to ruling an empire? We're getting nowhere against Victor, and maybe Temujin has an idea we'll be able to use. This is our last chance to ask him."

"Last night you couldn't stop telling me about all the horrible things he and the Mongols did, and now you want to ask him for advice?"

"Who else can I turn to? My list of mentors is down to zero. Yeah, maybe Temujin does some terrible things when he's older, but right now he's just a kid like me, trying to get his life together."

Sam gave a sad shake of her head. "You're grasping, Dan. There's no way I'm sticking around for this." She walked into the shadow of a wagon, pulled out her jump rod, and began twisting the sections into place. "If you're smart, you'll leave too."

"You don't understand. I need to get *something* out of this jump. Give me ten minutes."

For a second, she just looked at me, and I could have sworn a tear was running down her cheek. Then she shut her eyes and turned her head away. "Bye, Dan," she whispered. *"Azkabaleth virros ku, Haztri valent bhidri du!"*

In a flash of light, she blinked out of Mongolia.

I stood there, open mouthed, staring at the place where she'd just been standing.

She's really gone . . .

Sam, my best friend, my partner, the one person who I trusted to always have my back, had actually abandoned me on a time jump. What the hell had happened to her while I was gone? As soon as I got back, I'd find out. But for now, I had to find Temujin.

CHAPTER 20

Temujin and Borte still clung to each other, excited words flying back and forth between them, while Jelme, Khasar, Bo'orchu, and Belgutei stood guard.

No better time than the present.

I dusted off my deel and adjusted my furry hat, then walked toward the group.

"Dan!" Temujin exclaimed. "This is Borte, the sun in my sky!" His eyes shone even in the darkness, and he wore a huge grin.

Borte was shorter than Temujin, with a round face and almond-shaped eyes. She bowed her head toward me. "My husband has told me how you saved his life," she began, her voice almost musical compared to Temujin's forceful tones. "I thank you for bringing him safely to me."

Temujin placed a hand on my shoulder and held me with his fierce gaze. "I knew when you saved me from the Merkits that you were sent by the great blue heaven itself to help me. Stay by my side, Dan of the western lands, and we will achieve great things."

Wow.

Genghis Khan, the world's greatest conqueror, wanted me to join him? For a second I couldn't speak. "I—I can't," I finally stammered. "I have to go home."

Temujin shook his head. "I had feared as much. But we can still have many nights of feasting and song while we celebrate the return of Borte."

"I'm really sorry. But I need to leave tonight."

"It is late," Temujin said, brushing aside my concerns. "We shall make camp for now, and then tomorrow I will reward you for all you have done for me. Name anything, and I will give it to you: the finest horses, herds of sheep, Merkit women to serve you and Merkit children to tend your herds. Then you can decide properly whether you wish to leave us."

"I can't. I really must go."

"As you wish." Temujin clapped me on the shoulder. "You are not an ox to be yoked to my cart—you are a free man who can come and go as he pleases. But before you go, tell me, what would you ask of me?"

"All I really want is to know how you did it. How did you pull yourself up from nothing to become leader of the Mongols?"

Khasar snorted. "That is what you want, words? You should ask for horses or slaves."

Temujin bowed his head to me. "Wisdom is the richest gift of all. I will give you what I can." He stared up thoughtfully at the first few stars of the night, as if he was reading the secrets of the universe. "To succeed at anything, you must wake each day and greet the sun with a purpose ready in your mind and an iron will in your heart. You must possess both to succeed. Purpose without will leads to failed ambitions. And will without purpose is simply wasted energy."

He pointed to Bo'orchu, Jelme, Khasar, and Belgutei. "No man can succeed in great tasks without help. The great blue heaven blessed me with worthy brothers and great friends who have traveled with me on my path. Always be generous to those who help you, as generosity breeds loyalty and friendship. But be ruthless and crush those who oppose you, so they never dare to challenge you again."

He tapped his temple. "Lastly, you must always know your enemy as well as you know yourself. For you cannot defeat what you do not understand." He looked at me. "Does that give you the answers you need?"

I flipped through his list to success. *Purpose?* Nope. I had no clue how to stop Victor, only a general idea that I wanted to stop him. *Will?* I guess I had that. *Friends?* Other than Sam and maybe Jenna, no. *Knowledge of my enemy?* A big fat hell no. On the great Temujin path-to-victory test, I scored a measly twenty-five percent. No wonder I was getting nowhere.

"I think so," I said finally.

"Can I give you anything else?"

"No, I'm good," I mumbled.

"You ask for nothing, but I cannot let you go without at least one gift." He undid the ties of his deel and gingerly passed it to me with two hands. "For all you have done for me, I give you this."

Around him men sucked in their breath as if Temujin had just handed over his life savings.

I held the dirty, smelly, sweaty, piece of cloth loosely in both hands. *Ewwwww.*

As a gift it ranked right up there with the Latin grammar book Dad had given me one Christmas. "Um . . . thanks?"

Temujin smiled. "All my energy, my history, and soul is in that deel. The sweat from my hard work. The dust from my countless rides across the vast steppe. The blood that I shed. When you wear this deel, you will always have my strength and spirit with you."

Ohhhh . . . Somehow that made it a lot less gross.

"Thank you," I said again, and this time I meant it.

I could feel everyone's eyes on me. I guess a simple "thanks" wasn't enough when someone gave you a piece of their soul. I probably should give him something back. And since I just received a deel, giving my own back wouldn't be very original—and it wasn't even mine in the first place.

But I did have one thing that had provided me with nothing but grief since I arrived in Mongolia—well, aside from saving my life a few minutes ago—and I'd be glad to get rid of it now. I pulled off my deel and began unbuckling the straps of my chain mail. "I have something for you too." I pulled the heavy shirt off and handed it to Temujin. "This shirt has saved my life twice, but it is time for me to pass it on."

Temujin's lips trembled and his eyes grew glassy as he grasped the steel links in his hands. "You are my sworn brother, Dan," he said breathlessly. "You will *never* want for anything while you are in my lands."

I patted the jump rod in the sleeve of my tunic, just to make sure it still had its nice comforting warmth. *Check.* History hadn't been screwed up by my action—not that I'd thought it would be. After all, Temujin was already on the road to becoming the overlord of everything. One little chain-mail shirt shouldn't be enough to mess things up.

"You, outlander," Jelme broke in. "You have given Temujin a gift beyond measure. For this, I will not kill you."

"Thanks, Jelme. But I'm leaving anyway, so you'll never have to see me again."

"You really are leaving?" Khasar asked. "What of Sam? Where is she?" He cast his eyes around. "She is not dead, is she?"

He looked so much like a sad puppy dog, I almost laughed. "She's already left."

"Left? How? When?"

I chuckled. "You wouldn't believe me if I told you."

Khasar removed the quiver from his shoulder and passed it to me along with his bow. "Please give these to Sam when you see her next. And tell her that Khasar will always have room for her in his ger."

I hid my smile as I slung Khasar's bow and quiver across my back. The kid had guts.

Bo'orchu clapped me on the shoulder. "When are you going?"

"Now."

"Now?" Bo'orchu looked crestfallen. "If you must leave, then let us drink together one more time." He unslung a skin of airag, drank some, and then passed it to me.

I took a quick swig, hid my grimace, and then passed the skin around. Belgutei, Khasar, Temujin, and even Jelme took a mouthful, emptying the skin.

So this was it, the end of my Mongolian adventure. Nothing left for me to do now but jump back into the time stream and return home empty-handed.

Wait a minute . . .

An inkling of an idea formed. And Sam wasn't around to tell me how crazy it was.

"Could I have that empty airag skin? And could I borrow your knife?"

Bo'orchu shrugged and passed both over to me.

With the rest of Temujin's group watching, I pulled as hard as I could on the skin's strap, which was wide and thick, and sewn tightly to the rest of the leather. The stitching didn't budge one bit.

So far so good.

I then cut off the narrow top of the skin, widening the opening enough to insert my fist through it. I looped the strap across my body and clasped Bo'orchu's shoulder. "You always looked out for me, Bo'orchu. Thanks. You were a good friend." I gave him back his knife. "But now it's time for me to go." I then bowed to each of the Mongols, saving the longest and deepest one for Temujin, who bowed just as deeply back to me.

I walked into the darkness until I had reached a semi-secluded spot behind a wagon. Reaching into my sleeve, I pulled out the jump rod and spun it to the setting to jump out.

"Azkabaleth virros ku, Haztri valent bhidri du!"

Mongolia disappeared in a flash of light, and the time stream surrounded me, its radiance near blinding even with my eyes shut. For a few seconds, I floated along, trying to build up my courage. What I was planning on doing seemed like the stupidest idea I'd ever had. So many things could go wrong. And even if I somehow survived, what was I going to prove?

With a shaking hand, I placed the jump rod inside the airag skin but didn't let go of it. All I had to do was keep hold of the rod and I'd be home in seconds. Why was I even thinking of letting go? I'd already traveled through time once without a jump rod, and it had been one of the most horrific experiences of my life. Only by clinging to Sam with all my strength had I managed to not get cast away into total emptiness.

My breath caught in my throat. I felt like a skydiver poised in the doorway of a plane, trying to give himself a good reason to jump out of a perfectly functional aircraft. Except skydivers put their faith in some kind of parachute. I was putting mine solely into Bo'orchu's drink bag and its thick leather strap.

Do it!

I let go of the jump rod.

Instantly the surrounding brightness turned to black, and a strong wind howled around me, tearing at my clothes and my face. The furry hat flew off my head, and Khasar's arrows tumbled out of his quiver and rocketed off into the darkness. The wind buffeted me from all sides, making my deel flap like a flag in a hurricane and nearly tugging my boots off my feet. With a creak of leather, the strap holding the airag bag strained as the jump rod tried to break free of the skin. To my relief, the strap held.

One test down. Now for part two.

As soon as my skin touched the pitted metal surface of the jump rod, the blinding light returned, and I felt like I was floating.

A smug feeling of satisfaction flooded through me. My theory was right: let go of the jump rod and plummet through darkness; hold it and float home.

Now for the final test.

I released the jump rod again and immersed myself in the turbulent darkness. Would I be able to find the city hidden in the time stream again?

For about five seconds, there was nothing but inky blackness. Then, in the distance, a speck of white appeared, like a star in the night sky. It approached rapidly, growing larger by the second until at last the outline of the city appeared. I plummeted toward it from high above, the howling wind never ceasing to bite at me. The city was perfectly circular, with a tall stone wall forming its perimeter, separating the houses within from the narrow strip of sand that lay just outside before the city ended.

With no sign of slowing down, I hurtled toward the city, details becoming clearer by the second. My eyes darted everywhere, trying to register as much as possible. A large building that looked like a temple. Rows of city streets that held houses. A circular plaza in the city center. Everything came faster and faster toward me.

Too fast.

I touched the jump rod again and the city disappeared, replaced by the glow of the time stream.

I drifted along for a few seconds, thinking about all that I'd seen. On my previous time jump, the place had looked like something out of ancient Greece. But that was when I'd been clinging to Sam, trying not to be plucked off and cast away into the emptiness. On this second pass, I could tell the city wasn't Greek. The buildings had tiled roofs like typical Greek buildings, but that's where the similarity ended. The structures looked older and yet somehow newer at the same time, with weird angles and multicolored stonework instead of the straight lines and whitewashed buildings typical of Greek cities.

Great . . . I'd seen a bunch of buildings.

If this city contained some hidden mystery that would help me stop Victor, the only way I'd find out would be to stop chickening out and get closer.

I took three rapid breaths to psych myself up, then released my grip on the jump rod. Blackness enveloped me again as the howling winds swirled around me. The city appeared closer this time, about beach-ball size but growing by the second until it eventually filled my field of vision. The buffeting wind propelled me straight toward the wide, circular plaza at the center.

As I plummeted toward the ground, a huge dark smudge in the middle of the plaza contrasted with the pale stone. It looked like a massive mound of trash. What was that doing there?

At the rate I was falling, I had maybe six seconds left before I was splattered all over the cobblestones. My hand reached around the jump device but didn't grasp it.

Five . . .

Within the huge mound, individual items began to appear. A shield. A sword embedded blade first. Cloaks. Backpacks. Leather bags. Cloth sacks. Boots. Two wooden chests.

Four . . .

And right on top of the pile, a cluster of red-fletched arrows had buried themselves point first.

Khasar's arrows?

Three . . .

The thrill of discovery coursed through me. I'd found the garbage heap of the time stream! But any further exploration would have to wait. I only had seconds left.

Two . . .

A jumble of clothing caught my eye. Near the middle of the heap lay a pair of pants, a tunic, and a pair of boots, arranged like they had fallen there together.

Then I noticed the bones sticking out of the clothing.

Over to one side lay another skeleton.

Then another one . . . And another.

The hair on the back of my neck stood on end. This wasn't just a garbage heap—it was also a graveyard. All the time jumpers who hadn't survived the trip must have ended up here, lost to history forever.

I gripped the jump rod and instantly returned to the safety of the time stream.

"Damn," I muttered as the familiar gentle current carried me home. I'd seen the city. But what was I going to do with it? I still didn't know how to land there without getting a face full of paving stones. And even if I somehow did survive the fall, there was no telling what I might find in all those buildings or in that garbage heap. In the end, all I managed to do was prove to myself the city wasn't just my imagination. I'd still need to figure out how to unlock its secrets.

After about twenty seconds, the glare disappeared, and a floor solidified beneath my feet. It took a few seconds more for the spots to fade from my vision and the dizziness of time-travel sickness to pass, but slowly my furniture and walls started coming into view. I half expected Jenna to be there waiting for me, but the room was empty.

I flopped onto the couch and lay back with my head on a cushion. I'd survived another time jump, but for what? I hadn't done anything to stop Victor, Jenna was probably never going to talk to me again, and I had no clue what was wrong with Sam or how to patch things up between us.

I looked down at Temujin's bloodstained and grimy deel.

All right, Temujin. If this dirty shirt is channeling your spirit, then tell me: Where do I start?

CHAPTER 21

My breakfast plate sat next to my laptop on the coffee table. I crunched a piece of bacon and checked one last time on the history forum, hoping to find a message. After I'd gotten back last night, taken a long bath, and eaten a whole pizza, I had logged in using my special ID and made a post, just like the time jumpers who kidnapped me had instructed. But twelve hours had gone by with no response.

I had nothing new to trade with them, but I didn't care. Temujin had said, *Always know your enemy as well as you know yourself*, and these guys had reams of information about the entire time-jumping community: pictures, names, allegiances. If I wanted to fight Victor, I'd need all of it, whether they wanted to give it to me or not. Which led me to Temujin's other words of wisdom: *Be ruthless and crush those who oppose you*. I couldn't let these guys and their unreasonable demands get in my way.

My phone buzzed with about the twentieth message from Jenna. I hadn't read any of them. It had only been one day since I had jumped out right in front of her. It would probably be better to avoid her for a

217

few more days and let her memories fade. Maybe then, once she started doubting her own experience, I might be able to think up a reasonable explanation for what she had seen. I realized that this tactic was straight out of *Gaslighting for Dummies*, but I couldn't think of any other way to deal with her.

Did you get back OK? I sent to Sam.

That was probably the fifth message I'd sent her. She hadn't replied yet either.

I took another bite of bacon. The waiting was killing me.

My phone buzzed once more. Jenna again. I flipped through her messages, just in case she'd been in a car accident or something.

RU Back?

We need to talk

Call me!

Just more of the same.

The phone buzzed one more time.

I can see U just read my messages!

Stupid smartphones.

No hiding from her now. I sank into my couch cushions. How could cute, bubbly Jenna scare me so much? The mere thought of talking to her made my throat swell. I couldn't tell her the truth.

I sighed and looked over at Temujin's deel hanging on my wall among all my dad's medieval weapons. Even Temujin's words of wisdom couldn't help me here.

Wanna talk? I finally texted her.

The minutes ticked by. Hopefully she'd be busy for the next week— or maybe even the next month.

Mall food court. Noon.

The mall was too noisy. We needed some place where I wouldn't have to talk over the crowds.

How about my house? I sent back.

MALL

The all caps of her curt, one-word answer didn't escape me. Jenna was angry . . . and she clearly didn't trust me anymore. This was not going to be pretty.

I'll be there.

She didn't respond.

I had two hours to figure out what to say to her that was more believable than *I accidentally got shot*. What sucked was that, even though Jenna and I had only hung out twice, I really liked her. She was cheerful and fun and had shown me what a normal life could be like. But I doubted we'd ever hang out again after today.

I showered and changed into my best jeans and a collared shirt, then checked myself in the mirror. My hair wasn't sticking out too much, and a good sleep had removed most of the dark circles from under my eyes. I shook my head at my reflection: I kinda looked like some doofus getting ready for his yearbook photo. But Jenna always looked good, so she deserved some effort on my part.

With spring break in full swing, the mall was crawling with kids from my school. I limped to the food court, barely noticing everyone else around me. My mind kept spinning through scenarios of what I could tell Jenna, and how she'd respond. All of them ended badly. But I owed her this conversation.

Not surprisingly, the food court was packed, so it took me a few seconds to spot her as I rode the escalator down. She was sitting alone at a table between Tito's Tacos and the Golden Wonton, her seat facing the escalator. Her eyes locked on to mine, but she didn't wave or smile.

I pulled up the seat opposite her and beamed a huge smile, hoping to ease the tension. "Hey, Jenna."

"Hi," she responded, her voice icy.

So much for easing the tension.

I placed my hands flat on the table in front of me. "So . . . umm . . . it's great to see you."

Jenna's eyes darted from me to the security guard patrolling the food court, then back to me.

"Where should I start?" I asked.

"How about the truth?"

The truth? How about my most believable lie?

"Okay . . . I belong to a group of historical reenactors," I said. "We go camping in the woods, dress up in medieval garb, and reenact battles using real medieval weapons. Unfortunately one of the guys got carried away—"

Jenna smacked her hand loudly on the tabletop. "Stop lying to me!"

A hush passed over the food court as everyone stared at us. "Please, can you keep your voice down?" I whispered, slinking down in my seat. "I'm telling you the truth."

"You disappeared! Into thin air!" Jenna hissed, her cheeks flushing. "People don't just disappear like that."

Lie one had failed. On to lie two.

"I think you passed out," I ventured, keeping my expression neutral. "You were looking kind of pale when you pulled those arrows out of me. The blood must have gotten to you. You collapsed right there on the floor. I went to get help, and when I got back you were gone."

Jenna's eyes narrowed like I was some animal that had just walked into her trap. "Do you know what's funny?" she said in a tone that implied she was not remotely amused. "That thought did pass through my mind. But I remember every single thing that happened. The weird outfit you were wearing. The arrows stuck in you. And that metal thing you were holding. There aren't any gaps in my memory. And I checked the time on my texts. There were only twenty minutes between when I got there and when you disappeared. I did not pass out. I even wondered if you might have roofied me, but I didn't drink anything at your house. It wasn't my imagination. You disappeared."

I swallowed hard and took a deep breath, trying to buy a few more seconds to come up with some kind of story she would believe. But she wasn't done.

"Oh, and when I finally did leave, the chain was still across the door. So what did you do, go out the window?"

Damn it. Forgot about the chain.

Jenna leaned in with her clenched fists resting on the shiny tabletop. Her dark eyes sparkled with a feral glint. "Those arrows I pulled out of you were the only thing convincing me I hadn't lost my mind. Do you want to know what I did with them?"

A sinking feeling grew in my stomach.

She smiled at me. Not a happy smile, more a baring of teeth. "I took them to the Museum of Natural History. You told me you were playing Mongol, so I tracked down one of the guys in the Asian wing. The museum was crowded, and he was doing everything he could to get rid of me. But you should have seen his attitude change once I showed him those arrows."

My sinking feeling turned into full-blown nausea. She'd shown the arrows to a professional? I'd clearly underestimated her. "Yeah, we do a lot of research so we can make our weapons as authentic as possible."

Jenna continued as if she hadn't heard me. "He took some scrapings of the glue and looked at them under a microscope. It's from a mixture that hasn't been used in centuries. He told me that they were the most accurate reproductions of Mongol arrows he'd ever seen. He wanted to know where I got them."

"Um . . . I . . . uh . . . bought the glue online."

"What website?"

Damn it! She's part of the debate club. "I . . . don't remember."

She leaned in close, her eyes boring into mine. "Do you want to know what the guy at the museum found even more amazing than the glue? The feathers on the arrows."

I gulped and tried to remember anything odd about the feathers. They had looked like plain old white feathers to me.

Jenna now smiled like a cat playing with a mouse. "He brought in an expert from the ornithology department. They're from a Siberian crane."

"So? I got them online also."

"No you didn't!" Jenna pounded the table again. "That bird is practically extinct! It's impossible to get their feathers. And even if you did manage to get your hands on a few, you wouldn't glue them to arrows that you 'accidentally' shoot into someone else."

Oh geez. I'd run out of lies. I could feel my mouth hanging open. "Can we go somewhere else?" I finally asked. "It's kind of noisy here."

"No! I don't trust you. I don't want to be anywhere near you unless I'm surrounded by witnesses."

That one stung. "Jenna, it's me. We went bowling. I had dinner with your family. I'd never do anything to hurt you."

She crossed her arms over her chest. "I have no idea what you might do. As far as I know, every word out of your mouth is a lie." Her voice cracked with anger, and she stared at me through eyes glazed with tears. "If you ever felt anything at all about me, can you please just stop lying to me?"

I exhaled slowly and tilted my head back. I'd dug a hole so deep I couldn't go any farther down. Jenna didn't deserve all these lies—she'd been there when I needed her the most. If this was going to be the last time we ever spoke, she deserved at least some truth. "All right. You aren't going to believe me, but here goes—the honest truth." I turned my head to make sure no one was listening. "I belong to a long line of people who jump through time and fix problems with history." The words sounded crazy even as they came out of my mouth, but I rolled up my sleeve to show her the tattoo on the inside of my forearm. "This is our mark. My father had it, and I've had it for as long as I can remember. That weird metal rod you saw is our means of transportation to different time periods. You want to know how I got those arrows in me? I was in Mongolia about a thousand years ago, and some idiot who wanted my armor tried to kill me."

I paused to gauge her reaction, but she just sat there, one eyebrow raised, waiting for me to go on.

"Those arrows aren't my only wounds from history." I pointed to the scar on my forehead. "I told you this was from a hammer? Well, it was a Norman war hammer during the Battle of Hastings in 1066." I pulled aside the collar of my shirt to reveal the skin between my left shoulder and collarbone, where a long scar was still visible. "This also came from Anglo-Saxon times, when an assassin tried to kill me."

Jenna said nothing, just blinked her wide eyes.

I rested my hands on the table. "That's the truth. I jump through time, save history, and get my ass kicked in the process. I've been stabbed, beaten, chased, shot at, even enslaved by ancient Romans—all in the interest of saving history so the rest of you can sit back, totally oblivious, and lead normal lives."

Jenna still said nothing.

I expected her to laugh at me, or to yell at me for lying to her yet again, or storm out in anger. Her silence seemed worse. "Well? Aren't you going to say anything?"

"You're . . . you're serious, aren't you?"

"Yes. And I can tell that you don't believe me. Hell, I live my life and barely believe it myself. That's why I didn't tell you the truth. It's impossible to believe."

She nodded several times, then said, "I have to go."

I reached across the table for her hand. "I lied, and I'm sorry. But I really do like you, Jenna, and I was afraid the truth would scare you away."

She stood, scraping her chair across the floor.

"Whatever you do," I cautioned, "please don't tell anyone what you saw. No one will believe you either."

She ran for the escalator and was swallowed up by the mall.

I stood there alone in the food court, only too aware of people watching me. Some were even pointing and laughing. Nothing like witnessing someone else's misery to make a person's day.

I sighed and headed for the escalator. Sam was right; you can't have normal relationships if you're a time jumper. Of course, Sam was the only person I knew who I didn't have to lie to, but I couldn't make that relationship work either.

I drove home, going over everything I'd said to Jenna. So many lies, half-truths, and evasion—no wonder she'd left. But what if I'd been open from the start? Would she have believed me? It didn't matter now. I'd blown it and she was gone.

Back at my condo, I flopped on to the couch, popped open my laptop, and checked the history forum. A new message was waiting in my mailbox.

9PM tonight. Back of the Miller Building on Pilgrim Street. Come alone. Don't be late. Make sure you aren't followed.

The Miller Building was in the industrial part of town, with no houses nearby and very few stores. I zoomed in on a map of the area. Same as last time—a dead-end alley behind a bunch of buildings. A great place for a secret meeting where someone might disappear if they asked the wrong questions.

Here we go again.

If I wanted to get anything out of this meeting, I'd need to make it so I was in control.

What would Temujin do? He wouldn't just walk into this and hope for the best, that's for sure. He'd show up early and set a trap of his own. Maybe archers hidden on the rooftops or ten thousand horsemen waiting in the shadows of the nearby buildings. I was a bit short on archers and horsemen, but there had to be *something* I could do.

My fingers drummed on the mouse pad. *How to turn this into a trap?* They had guns, I had swords. There were three of them last time, and only one of me, and I had a bum leg and an injured shoulder. I wasn't really coming at them from a position of strength.

If only I could somehow take away their guns. If I could bring something that would overwhelm them with numbers or firepower, then I'd control the situation.

I thought of every half-baked, cheesy storyline in every movie I'd ever seen, and my mind kept returning to *Home Alone*. Similar situation. Outnumbered. Outgunned. Limited resources. As I replayed the movie in my mind, an idea started forming . . . just a ghost of a thought. But I latched on to the idea and worked at it, trying to foresee all possible actions and reactions. A few internet searches proved that what I was thinking about wasn't impossible. I'd need to make a few trips first, and time might be tight but, if everything worked well, I'd have my trap set.

I grabbed my wallet and rushed for the elevator, all the while going through a mental shopping list: PVC pipe and glue, lighter fluid or something a bit stronger, brick anchors, speaker wiring, model rocket igniters, halogen work lights, car batteries, ball bearings, remote control, servos for a model plane, and a few potatoes.

Yeah, that would do it.

As the elevator door opened, I could feel myself nodding. Today with Jenna might have sucked, but tonight I'd find my redemption. I had one hell of a trap planned, and when the dust settled, the three guys in the van would be begging to answer my questions.

CHAPTER 22

By eight thirty, darkness had long cloaked the alley behind the Miller Building. The buildings with their boarded-up windows loomed over me, almost blocking out the sky. After the Mongolian steppe, with its fresh summer air and open fields, this cold, cluttered alley was like torture. But at least the discarded pallets, strewn newspapers, clumps of dirty snow, and bags of garbage served a purpose—they hid the details of my trap.

Over the constant hum of traffic from the nearby highway, I heard a car approaching.

They're early.

I ran for my hiding spot but had managed only two steps toward the nearby dumpster when a van turned into the alley. Its headlights swept along the brick walls and then passed directly over me. Hiding was out of the question now. The van stopped in the middle of the alley, its headlights blazing right at me.

The sliding door opened, and a man walked toward me, the heels of his shoes scuffing the asphalt. He stopped and stood silhouetted against the van lights, his features completely hidden. In his right hand was the unmistakeable outline of a handgun. "You're early," he said.

"So are you." I gripped the remote control in my pocket, hoping all my wiring was connected properly. The van had parked right in my kill zone. *This had better work.*

He raised his gun and aimed it at me. "Hands up."

"Can't we do this any other way?" I asked, as I flipped on the remote control. "You know, just a civilized conversation between men?"

"I thought we made it pretty clear last time that we call the shots." He jabbed the air with his gun. "Now put your hands up."

Was I faster than his trigger finger? No, I needed a distraction. "What's wrong with your van's tire?" I asked.

He glanced behind him. "I don't see anything."

Sucker. Oldest trick in the book.

I pressed the first button on the remote as I dove to the ground. The work lights I had anchored high around the perimeter came to life and bathed the alley in a blinding light.

The gunman took a step back and raised an arm in front of his face. "What are you doing? Kill those lights or you're dead." He squinted and waved the gun around in the direction where he thought I stood. Not even close.

I belly-crawled outside the ring of lights and into the safety of the shadows, stopping behind the dumpster. I lay on the cold asphalt and took several deep breaths to calm myself.

The first button had worked; now I needed the rest to go without a hitch. I pushed the second button. With a roar of ignition, four potatoes shot out from both sides of the alley. One smashed into the side of the van, spraying little pieces of potato everywhere, and another one glanced off the windshield.

The driver-side door was flung open and a man wearing a hood rushed out. "What the hell do you think you're doing?" he yelled as he ran his hands over the side panel of the van and peered closely at its surface. "If there's a single scratch, you're paying for it."

What the . . . ?

My fear level ratcheted down a few notches. I had assumed these guys were stone-cold killers. But tough, ruthless time jumpers didn't worry about the paint jobs on their minivans. Maybe I'd overestimated them.

"That was the warning shot," I said from the darkness. "Is there anybody else in the van?"

"I'm the one with the gun," the other man said. "Now shut off those lights or I'll shoot you."

"If any of you bastards move, I'll blow you up."

The driver laughed. "With what? Potato cannons?"

"Yep. I have a bunch more ringing this alley, except they're using a hell of a lot stronger gas than the hairspray I had in the first ones. Oh, and I also loaded up each one with a few hundred ball bearings just for fun. They're all pointed right where you're parked. I press a button, and thousands of tiny pieces of steel are going to go blasting right at you."

"You're bluffing, kid," the driver said. But I could tell by the way he swiveled his head around that he was trying to spot the tubes.

"Bluffing? The last time we met, you guys stuck a gun to my head and threatened to kill me. In case you haven't noticed, we're not friends. I'm not bluffing. You have until the count of three to put down your guns and toss me your wallets—or I'll blow you and your precious little minivan to bits."

"Don't do it, kid," the gunman said.

"You know what I want. One . . ."

Could I really go through with this?

I tried to shut out all other thoughts and just focus on the gun in his hands and the sheer terror I felt when it had been pressed up against my head the last time.

"Please!" the gunman begged.

"Two . . ." My thumb trembled over the button. Only now I realized the flaw in my plan. What happened if they didn't cave in to my demands? I either killed them or let them go. I wouldn't get my answers either way.

"Thr—"

"Wait!" The man with the gun tossed it to the ground.

Relief flooded through me, and I moved my thumb away from the button. "Anybody else in the van?"

The former gunman banged twice on the van's hood, and another hooded man stepped out from the passenger side, his hands raised above his head.

"Any more weapons?"

Two pocketknives dropped to the ground.

"All right." I stepped out from the safety of darkness behind the dumpster and into the circle of light, but still outside my kill zone. I held the remote control in front of me for all of them to see. "Kick your weapons over here. Then stand in front of the van and toss me your wallets."

Three wallets landed with a series of smacks on the asphalt. The gunman kicked both the knives and his gun over. The gun slid with a hollow, plastic sound, not the heavy metallic scrape I'd expected. I picked it up. "Is this a toy?"

"We're not killers," the gunman said, almost apologetically. "We just wanted to scare you off."

I switched off the remote and flipped through their wallets. From each one I removed the driver's license and snapped a picture with my phone. One of the licenses showed a kid just a few years older than me with brown hair, whose face looked familiar.

"Hey! I remember you from Professor Gervers's office—you brought me my backpack."

The passenger took off his hood and rubbed a hand sheepishly through his hair. "Yeah," he said. "I'm Eric. But I guess you know that now."

The man who'd flashed the gun took off his mask. "I'm Dave." He was probably about Dad's age. He wore a black jacket and jeans, and his long hair was mostly gray and pulled back in a ponytail.

"Brian," the third man announced. He was taller and thinner than Dave, but about the same age, with a short graying beard and thin-framed glasses. Brown hair peeked out from under his baseball cap. Eric looked a lot like him.

I glanced at their licenses again. Eric and Brian shared the same last name, and all three shared the same address. A family affair.

I fired the gun once at the dumpster and a tiny metallic ping echoed down the alley. I tossed the toy gun back to Dave. "Okay, this is what's going to happen. I've taken pictures of your van and your IDs, and I've emailed them to a friend of mine. So if anything bad *ever* happens to me, you can expect police knocking at your door. Now, can we agree to stop all the threats?"

"Agreed," the three men replied with little enthusiasm.

"All right, let's get down to business." I clapped my hands. "I want information about Victor and time jumping."

"Are you nuts, kid?" Dave said. "Why would we tell you anything?"

"Fine. You don't have to. Just remember, I know who you are and where you live. So either you tell me what I want to know now, or I start coming around *every* day until I get what I want."

"What happened to no threats?" Brian asked.

"It's not a threat, just a fact. I need information, and I'm not going to stop until I get it."

The three of them exchanged glances, then Brian and Eric both shrugged.

"What do you want to know?" Dave asked.

After almost a year of jumping blindly into history—not knowing what I was doing, or who I was fighting—answers would be finally coming my way. I felt like a kid at Christmas about to open a pile of presents.

I hit record on my phone. "How do we stop Victor?"

"We don't," Dave replied. "He's already won."

"No! I refuse to believe that. He's one guy. Sure, he may have a few time jumpers hanging on for the ride, but what can they do in the grand scheme of things?"

"It's not just a few," Dave said. "Victor is supported by hundreds, maybe even thousands of the most influential people on the planet. Military leaders, presidents and prime ministers, CEOs of massive companies."

"What? That can't be true."

Brian shook his head. "I wish it weren't. But even though we don't have our time-travel devices anymore, we still have friends in the community—friends who decided it was better to join Victor than to stand against him. And they tell us what's going on."

"Which is what?"

"He's been mucking around with the time stream." Dave raised his hand to stop the question forming on my lips. "No, we don't know how he's doing it without creating glitches. There's a limit to what people will tell us."

For a second I couldn't answer. Had Victor really figured out how to alter the past? And if he had, how? But there was a much simpler question. "Couldn't you just, like, assassinate him and put an end to all his plans?"

"We've tried. Lots of times. But now it's too late. He has 24/7 security. We can't get anywhere near him."

"There has to be *something* you can do to stop him. The four of us can't be the only ones who are worried. How many people are on our side?"

Brian stroked his bearded chin. "A few others scattered around the globe, but most of them are like Eric—they've got training but have never actually traveled into the past. I'd say we're about fifty in total."

"Fifty?" My shoulders slumped. No wonder these guys couldn't fight Victor.

"How many did you expect?" Dave asked. "As far as we know, there are only a few hundred time-travel devices in existence. And by the time we started recruiting, almost everyone had already gone over to Victor's side."

"Victor's smart," Brian added. "He operated in secret for the longest time, just bringing in friends and those he could trust. Then, once he'd built his base, he started expanding. One by one, he tracked everyone down and gave them an ultimatum: swear loyalty or surrender their device. Faced with those options, most sided with him."

Dave let out a long breath. He looked tired, like a man who'd been fighting a losing battle for a long time. "I remember the time Victor tried to convert Brian and me. He came to the house, all smiles. But those smiles turned to threats pretty quickly. We couldn't join him." Dave shook his head grimly. "Not when we heard what he planned. We handed over our devices that same night."

The first time I ever saw Victor, he was in my living room, a sword in his hand, demanding that my dad either join him or give up his jump device. Dad instead bravely chose a third option and threw me his device. Dad took a sword to the chest to keep his jump rod out of Victor's hands, and Dave and Brian just handed theirs over? My already low opinion of these two men oozed even lower. "How could you just give up? Why didn't you fight?"

A scowl appeared on Eric's face, but it wasn't directed at me. Clearly I wasn't the only one who thought Dave and Brian could have tried harder.

"We saw others try to fight," Brian said, as he rested a hand on Eric's shoulder. "Their whole families were killed. The end result was always the same: Victor won."

"Which is why we're still wary of you," Dave added. "It seems odd that Victor would let you keep your device when he's taken everyone else's."

"Trust me. Victor and I are *not* working together. I'm willing to do whatever it takes to stop his plan. Which is a hell of a lot more than you guys are doing."

"We do a lot," Dave bristled. "We're the archivists of the time-traveling community. We gather information about every time traveler from all the regions. Where they traveled to in the past. Who they went with. What they fixed and how. And we didn't stop once Victor took our devices. Yeah, maybe the information is harder to get now, but we're still doing what we can. We know who's fiercely loyal to Victor and who could flip. We know when they've met, who their friends are, and what their weakness are."

"And this has helped you how?"

"Well . . . it hasn't yet," Dave grudgingly admitted. "But a lot of people joined Victor out of fear. If we can find the right people, we might be able to stop the plot from the inside."

"So let me see if I have this right. You've built a Facebook for Time Jumpers, and yet you're doing nothing with it to actually stop Victor?"

"Exactly." Eric rolled his eyes. "And while my dads are tiptoeing around, Victor and his gang keep getting stronger."

"Eric!" Brian protested. "We can't go rushing into things."

Eric waved his hand dismissively. "Whatever, Dad."

The big pile of presents under my Christmas tree had turned into nothing but old socks and coal. I squeezed the bridge of my nose and shook my head slowly. "If I want to know what Victor is planning, who can help me?"

"Victor," Dave snorted. "If you're so desperate to know his plans, go ask him."

"Fat chance," I muttered.

"So what now, kid?" Brian asked.

Good question. My trap had worked, but nothing else had gone as planned. "I guess we go home."

Dave opened the driver's door. "Sorry we didn't have what you were looking for. But at least now you know how to reach us. And maybe we can skip the pyrotechnics next time?" He climbed into the van.

"Wait!" I said. "What about jump-device commands? Can you tell me any of those?"

"How many do you know?" Brian asked.

"I know how to jump in and out, jump out midmission, find the time glitch, and find another jump rod."

"We have a few more," Brian said. "Eric can show them to you sometime."

Eric scribbled something on a piece of paper and handed it to me. "I'm here every Monday night at eight. It's my medieval club. We dress up in garb, talk about history, practice fighting . . . and just hang out. Meet me there next Monday. We can talk without attracting attention—plus it's fun. I'll introduce you as my cousin."

I put the slip of paper in my pocket. "Thanks."

Brian opened his door then paused. "Tell me one thing, Dan. Did you really rig those things with ball bearings?"

"Yup."

He swallowed hard. "And would you have actually fired them?"

I remembered the indecision, fear, and anger as I had counted to three. "Honestly? I don't know."

He hopped into the passenger seat, then leaned out the van's window. "Do you need a ride?"

In the darkness, the hazy outlines of my potato cannons were visible where they hung from their perches on the alley walls. It seemed a shame to just leave them sitting there.

I picked up the remote again and switched it back on. "Nah . . . I'm going to blow up an alley."

As Eric began walking back to the van, Temujin's words sprang to mind: *No man can succeed in great tasks without help.* And Temujin had been ready to accept help from anyone, even former enemies, as long as they were capable. Even though Eric and I hadn't gotten off to the best start, I had no doubts about his abilities. He knew about time-jumping, was roughly my age, and seemed to want to do more against Victor than the absolute nothing that his dads were doing. Could he be a friend? Only one way to find out. "Hey, Eric! Feel like sticking around and helping me blow up stuff? I can give you a ride back."

Eric stopped and looked at the individual tubes anchored to the walls, then shrugged. "Why the hell not?"

"Cool," I replied casually, trying not to smile.

CHAPTER 23

I got home after midnight, my ears still ringing from the simultaneous firing of multiple potato cannons. But the partial deafness was totally worth it. The abandoned couch Eric and I had dragged into the center of the alley had been completely shredded. Even better, I got to hang out with someone my age who I could just be normal with. I didn't have to hide the fact I was a time jumper, or make up excuses for any of my scars. It was like hanging out with Sam, except with violent explosions and fist bumps.

I went to the fridge to get myself a drink and stopped. Victor's business card was still there on the door, a stark white reminder of how little I had learned.

I could almost hear his laughter, mocking my failures.

I yanked the card off the fridge, about to rip it into confetti—but then Dave's words came back to me. *"If you want to know his plans, ask him."*

Temujin had said a man had to *know* his enemy in order to defeat him, so he sent out scouts and spies. But outside sources weren't getting me anywhere with Victor. Maybe this card could be the answer.

No matter how much my stomach churned at the thought, I had to give it a try.

I pulled up Victor's contact info on my phone.

What the hell am I doing? Calling Victor was even dumber than letting go of the jump rod in the time stream. He'd killed my dad and threatened me repeatedly, but here I was, seeking him out.

Calm down, Dan. You took an arrow for Temujin. You can make a phone call.

The phone rang.

"Ah, young Daniel," Victor answered, his voice arrogant as ever, with a touch of condescension thrown in. "I see that you have finally availed yourself of my business card. What can I do for you at this late hour?"

It's really him. I had expected voice mail or maybe an assistant. What was he doing up so late? What should I say? "Ummm . . . I . . . I . . . I want . . . to talk."

"If you are having difficulty speaking, I would recommend a good speech pathologist."

Arrogant prick.

At least his flippant answer had provided me with the spark of anger I needed to tame my fears. "You know what I mean. I want to talk with you, face to face, about time-jumping."

"Much better; always say exactly what you want. That wasn't too difficult now, was it, Daniel?" The sound of tapping keys came over the phone. "I have a free hour at my private office in Washington this Saturday at seven a.m. Shall I reserve that slot for you?"

"Yeah, I'll be there."

"Excellent. I look forward to meeting with you and shall send you the details shortly. And Daniel . . ." Victor's voice lowered a notch. "I should warn you. If you are entertaining thoughts of anything other than talking, I suggest you banish them right now. Better men than you have tried and failed." The line went dead.

I exhaled slowly and stared at the phone screen. *What did I just get myself into?*

I'd already had the misfortune of meeting Victor a few times, and none of them had been pleasant. But now I voluntarily arranged a meeting with him? On his terms? In his office? For a few seconds I just stood there, while my mind envisioned all sorts of horrible traps Victor might set, each one worse than the last. Men jumping out of a black limousine to grab me. Victor torturing me in his office. An unseen sniper picking me off as I walked down the street.

Don't be dumb. Victor doesn't need you to visit him in DC to make you disappear.

Somehow, that morbid thought actually made me feel better. I took one last deep breath and glanced again at my phone. Just past midnight: it was now officially Tuesday—four days until the meeting, and only five days left to try to salvage something from the world's worst spring break. So far I'd nearly died in Mongolia, traumatized a girl who was actually interested in me, threatened to kill a bunch of timid ex-time jumpers in their minivan, and topped it off by arranging a meeting with the most evil human I knew.

One thing left on my list, and with any luck, it would be a huge improvement over my previous vacation activities—I had to see Sam. It was a long drive to Virginia; I needed to get some sleep.

CHAPTER 24

The drive to Sam's house was about eight hours—farther than I'd ever driven by myself before—but the miles started whipping by once I cranked up the stereo in the Audi and hit the highway. As I traveled south, the last few signs of winter slowly began to fade, until I finally reached Virginia, where not a single flake of snow remained and the gloomy overcast of winter had been replaced by the bright blue skies of spring.

I parked at the end of Sam's tree-lined street, far enough away from her house so she wouldn't see me if she looked out the window. She still hadn't responded to any of my texts, so it seemed like the only way I was going to get any answers out of her was by surprising her. Carrying my backpack and a bouquet of flowers, I walked down the road to the house.

I hadn't been there since November, when we'd come back from our time jump to Celtic times, but nothing had changed. The roof still looked like it would spring a leak at the next rain, and the concrete slabs forming the front walkway were just as broken and uneven. At least the weather felt a lot warmer since my last visit. The forest behind her house was starting to green up as the first buds of spring unfolded, and a few brave weeds pushed through the cracks between the paving stones. Through the front window, I could see Sam's stepdad lounging in his chair, watching TV, a beer in his hand. I'd never seen him in any other position.

I hopped up the concrete steps to the front porch, my finger just hovering over the doorbell. Everything felt so much like after my first time jump. The nervousness, the flowers, the worrying about what she'd say. Back then I'd brought a horse and worn armor, to really make an impression. Now I just had me. Hopefully it would be enough.

I rang the doorbell and waited. The soft padding of feet came from inside. I held out the flowers as the door swung open. "Hi—"

It wasn't Sam but her mom, her lips pinched in irritation. She had long, thick hair like Sam's, except black, and she wore torn jeans and a pink shirt with the words *Bingo Babe* across the front in gold glitter. "What do you want?"

"Uh, hi. Is Sam home?"

She peered at me closely, then her eyes widened in recognition. "Wait . . . you're that rich kid."

Of course that's the way she'd remember me. "I guess."

The scowl switched to a phony smile as she swung open the screen door. "Well, come on in, darlin'! You're always welcome here."

I stepped into the front hallway, where a pile of shoes spilled over the floor and about ten different coats hung on top of each other on a row of hooks next to the door. I suppressed a cough at the musty smell of cigarettes and stale beer. "Is Sam here?"

"She's at work."

My shoulders slumped. "Any idea when she's getting back?"

"Any minute now. Can I get you something to drink?"

"Sure." I began to kick my shoes off.

"No need for that," Sam's mom said. With a wave of her arm, she led me toward the kitchen and motioned for me to take a seat at the table, then began rustling through the fridge. "We got soda . . . milk . . . or did you want a beer?"

"He's not having one of my beers!" yelled Sam's stepdad from the living room.

Sam's mom flashed me a forced grin. "Excuse me for a minute." She stomped off into the living room. "Billy! This is the rich kid," she hissed. "Last time he was here he sent Sam four grand. So be nice."

"Fine," Billy grunted. "But he better not drink 'em all."

Sam's mom came back, still all false smiles. "So what can I getcha, sugar?"

I put the bundle of flowers on the table and sat down. "Just water, please."

Her smile faded. "We ain't got none of that fancy fizzy stuff. I can send Billy out to get you some if you want."

"No, tap water's good."

Sam's mom filled a glass and put it in front of me. "You wanna watch TV while you wait for her?"

I had already been shot full of arrows and captured by Merkits this week—that was enough torture. "Do you mind if I just hang out in the woods out back?"

"You do whatever you want, hon." She stuck out her hand. "I don't think we ever been properly introduced. I'm Marlene."

"Dan." As I stood up and reached over to shake her hand, my sleeve pulled back, partially exposing the tattoo on my forearm.

Marlene's eyes narrowed and her smile faded. With one hand she clung to our handshake, while with the other she pushed my sleeve back completely, revealing my tattoo. "Damn it, I knew it!" Marlene tossed my hand away as if it was a piece of trash. "Y'all ain't nothing but trouble. If you really like my girl, you should just leave her well enough alone."

"Look, I don't know what you've got against tattoos, but I'm a decent guy. I only want the best for Sam."

Marlene's lips drew thin. "You may think you're a decent guy. Hell, you might even be one. But you'll change. Trust me. My ex-husband wore that mark, and so did my son. It meant the end for them, and lies and heartache for us left behind."

"I'm really sorry for your loss," I replied. "But I've never lied to Sam, and I'd never do anything to hurt her."

"You been good to her so far, I'll give you that." Marlene's tone softened a notch. "But it don't matter if you're poor as dirt or flush with dollar bills—all you time jumpers are bad news."

What?

I could feel my mouth hanging open. Sam had always described her mom as a clueless, bingo-crazed alcoholic. There was no way she could know about time-jumping. "I—I have no idea what you're talking about."

Marlene put both hands on her hips and cocked her head. "Don't play dumb with me, boy. I seen your scars. I seen that tattoo. I seen the way you limped into my kitchen. For ten years, I was married to one of y'all. And they was not good years. Never knowing if my man's coming home. Lie after lie. Meetings with shady folk at all hours. I don't want Sam living like that."

"I'm different," I said defiantly.

She gave me a sympathetic smile. "You think you are, sugar, but you ain't. None of y'all can lead a normal life. And I don't want that for Sam. I don't want her going back into the past no more."

"You . . . How do you know about that?"

Marlene laughed. "I wasn't sure." She gave me a smug smile. "But I am now."

Damn it. Marlene was more cunning than she looked.

"Don't feel bad. I knew something was going on. I ain't gonna claim to be the best mom around. Lord knows I ain't proud of some of the things I done. But I know my daughter, and I was pretty sure she'd followed in her father's footsteps. All the more reason you're bad news. Without you around, maybe she'll quit."

I snorted. "You clearly know nothing about Sam if you think I have any influence over what she does. She was doing this before I even started, and she won't finish until she's done what she needs to do."

Marlene sighed, and the confidence seemed to fizzle out of her. She pulled out a chair and sat down at the kitchen table. "Have a seat."

"I can stand."

She pushed the black hair away from her eyes, the same motion I'd seen Sam do a hundred times. "You like Samantha?"

"I do."

She motioned to the chair again. "Well, you might wanna sit, 'cause I got a story for ya."

Warily I settled into a chair.

"When Robert and me was first going out, he promised me the world," Marlene began. "He was handsome, and I was young, so like a damn fool I believed him. Don't get me wrong, it weren't all bad. He was a decent man: he loved me and he loved his kids, and he tried to do his best for us." With her finger, Marlene traced the pattern on the tablecloth.

"But even early on, things wasn't right. He'd disappear for days at a time, and come back with some story about how he'd found some odd job in another town. I believed him at first, because I didn't want to think he was lying. He kept disappearing, though." She paused and took a deep breath. "I was plum certain he was cheating on me. So one day I cornered him and told him he needed to stop. Robert swore he was faithful and promised he'd be better, but he just kept disappearing, and all he ever brought home was more excuses and empty dreams. If I'd had two nickels to rub together, I woulda left him. But Steven and Samantha was both young things still, and I was terrified of being a broke single mom. So I stayed."

Marlene took a cigarette from a pack lying on the table and lit it. "I wish I was stronger back then, but I weren't. When he kept on leaving, it got to be too much for me. First I hit the booze, then whatever pills I could get. It didn't matter none; I lived my life in a haze, and I weren't really there for my kids." She took a long pull on the cigarette. "Then things went from bad to worse. More late-night meetings, phone calls at odd hours." Her eyes glinted with anger. "I picked up the phone one time, expecting to hear one of his tramps. But it was a man. It all started making sense to me then. The meetings, the calls, the disappearing, the injuries. I reckoned he was dealing." She tapped her cigarette against the ashtray to knock off some ash.

"Cheating I could take, but my kids wasn't living with no drug dealer. That night, after enough drinks to build up my courage, I confronted him. Told him I knew everything, that I was going to leave him and take the kids with me if he didn't stop. That's when he told me what he really did when he was gone. I thought it was more lies, but a few days later, he disappeared from right in front of me." She held the cigarette in front of her face and for a few seconds watched the smoke curling up off the tip. "I believed him then, but it was too late for us—I didn't trust him no more. I asked for a divorce, and he was more than happy to give it to me. He wouldn't let me take the kids, though. Steven already thought the world of Robert, so I knew I had no hope of getting him. Those two did everything together. Hunting. Fishing. Practicing with swords. Whispering in secret." She snorted. "And Robert even took Steven to get that damn tattoo. But I at least tried to take Samantha with me, to save her from that life."

Marlene bowed her head and stared at the tablecloth as if ashamed to meet my eyes. "Robert wouldn't let me, though. And I was a mess, so the courts agreed with him. You have to be a pretty crap mom to lose both your kids to a husband who ain't even in this century half the time."

Marlene got up, went to the sink, and poured herself a glass of water. She took a drink and then leaned back against the counter, facing me. "I know I ain't been the best mom, and I know Sam don't think much of me but . . . I do love her. She just don't see it. All she'll ever see is the mom who ran away."

I didn't know to say. I wasn't used to adults telling me their life story. "Um . . . That sounds really terrible," I finally ventured.

"You understand what I'm telling you, son? I want a better life than this for Samantha. But she won't never have it if she keeps messing around with you time jumpers. Now I know she won't listen to me . . . but maybe you can convince her to be done with all—"

The sound of the front door swinging open interrupted her, and Marlene stood up and whispered, "Now you mind what I said." She poked her head through the kitchen door. "Samantha, honey, can you come here please?"

I slid out of my chair and grabbed the flowers. Heart racing, I tried to remember everything I wanted to say to her.

Sam stepped into the kitchen. She was dressed in black track pants and a loose shirt, with her hair tied back in a ponytail. She drew a sharp breath when she saw me.

"Hey, Sam!" I blurted before she could say anything. "I don't know what I did to upset you, but I'm really sorry."

"What are you doing here?" she asked in the same monotone she'd been using in Mongolia.

Not the reaction I had hoped for but kind of expected. "I just wanted to see you again." I held out the flowers.

Sam took the bouquet and tossed it on the table without even glancing at it. "Thanks," she mumbled. She looked from me to her mom, and back to me. "You two having a nice chat?"

"Just passing the time while I waited for you."

Sam stepped past me and opened the back door. "Come on. We need to talk."

We need to talk. The four words of doom in any relationship. Clearly I should have stayed home and given Sam more time to get over whatever was bothering her.

I followed Sam out the door and into her backyard. The wind blew gently through the trees, bringing with it the scents of earth and leaves. Sam headed for the worn path that led into the woods.

"Khasar sent you a gift," I said, trying to lead the conversation toward a relatively safe subject. "I have his bow and quiver for you. I had some arrows too, but I kind of lost them."

"Lost them? How?"

"On the jump back home. I went to see the city in the time stream—I found it again! The key is letting go of your jump device."

Sam stopped and raised her eyebrow at me. "You let go of your jump rod in the time stream? Are you out of your mind?"

"No, well . . . I . . . took safety precautions." Now I just had to hope she didn't ask me what they were.

She walked in silence.

"Where are we going?" I asked, again trying to encourage some sort of conversation from her.

"My usual jump-out spot."

She didn't say anything else, and we continued through the forest until we reached a small stream deep in the woods, where a large tree had fallen long ago next to the water. Its bark had rotted away over time, leaving just a thick, smooth trunk. She stopped next to the tree and crossed her arms over her chest. "Whatever grand gesture you had planned is *not* going to work."

"*Grand* . . . huh?"

"Don't play dumb, Dan. You didn't come all the way to Virginia just to bring me flowers. You're here to whisk me away to some other amazing place, like you did after our last two jumps."

I inwardly cringed at her entirely accurate accusation. "Am I that predictable?"

"Yes."

I sighed. Partly because nothing was going the way I expected, and partly because even my "surprises" were becoming predictable. "All right, you got me. I was hoping we could get out of here for a couple days. Go bowling, maybe? I haven't done a single fun thing this spring break—and I doubt you have either. I just thought we could have some fun before the break ends."

A slight smile creased Sam's lips, but just as quickly it faded and her green eyes returned to the same blank look. "No."

"Why not? When we first got to Mongolia you said there might be the chance of us being together—that you had to think things through. Then, we got separated, and when I came back, you were giving off more frost than a glacier. What happened?"

"Ignore everything I told you in Mongolia," she said, her voice hard. "You and I *don't* have a future. So whatever was going on between us has to end. No more trips. No more gifts. No more talks or texts or video calls about relationships or family or anything else."

Every word was a spear point piercing my chest. "Why are you doing this, Sam?"

She turned her head away from me. "It doesn't matter."

"It does matter!" I snapped. "You're my time-jumping partner and my best friend. You can't just end everything without at least telling me why. Please, Sam." I held my hands out to her, begging. "Tell me what happened."

"You really want to know?" she cried, her eyes rimmed with tears. "You died!"

"But I didn't! That was a lie."

"But it was true to me!" She pounded her chest with a fist. "Do you know how much it hurt when they told me you'd been killed?" Her entire body trembled. "I watched my dad bleed to death in front of me! And I'll never forget that horrible day when the police knocked on my door to tell me about my brother! Then I lost you, too?" Her voice trailed off. "I spent days on horseback, my heart broken. Every heartache I felt before came rushing back again."

She shook her head sadly. "I was so stupid to let myself care about you. I told you from day one that I didn't want a relationship—I didn't want my heart broken again. But you just kept pushing your way into my life, no matter how many times I said no. Homecoming. Wales. The constant texts and calls. And the worst thing is that I let you do it. I could have told you to back off, but I liked being with you. I got sucked into your fantasy. I actually started believing we might be able to have a normal relationship. But we can't, Dan. You're going to die just like my dad, just like Steven. Everyone I care about always leaves me."

"No . . . That's not true. I won't leave you. Look, I'm still here." I reached for her shoulder but she pushed my hand away.

"Don't," she pleaded. "I can't let myself feel anything for you again. I need to end whatever we had."

I could almost see my heart being crushed in her fist. *What would I do without Sam?* She was . . . everything to me. "Sam. Don't do this. Please . . . I love you." The words slipped out before I could stop them. I never meant to say them, but I knew as soon as I had that they were true. I loved everything about her, and I was a fool for not admitting it sooner.

Her bottom lip quivered as tears streaked down her cheeks. "That's . . . not . . . fair!" she cried, punctuating each word with a beat of her fist against my chest.

I caught her hand and pressed it over my heart. "It's true, though. You know it is."

She squeezed her eyes shut and shook her head. "That only gives me more reason to end things."

We were alone in a forest and I'd just admitted my love to Sam. We should be making out, not breaking up. "Damn it, Sam! I'm sorry that your dad and brother died, but I'm not them! Don't push me away because you're scared."

Her head snapped up and her eyes flashed with anger. "I'm not scared. It's the truth. You're going to die."

I opened my mouth to speak, but she cut me off. "You're a damage magnet, Dan. Every time jump, you just rush in, not thinking anything through, and hope that somehow you'll magically survive. Getting shot? Stabbed? That's just a normal day for you." She yanked her hand from my grasp and her back stiffened. "Dumb luck has kept you alive so far, but you're going to get yourself killed one day. So I can't let myself care about you anymore." She gave her head a sad shake. "I can't be hurt again."

I wanted to tell Sam she was wrong, that I'd always be with her, that she shouldn't throw our relationship away. But I knew that hard look in her eyes, that set to her jaw. She'd made up her mind, and there was no changing it. This was it. Game over. Somehow I'd managed to get dumped by someone I'd never even dated. I stared glumly at the tops of my running shoes, too embarrassed and hurt to meet Sam's eyes. "Does this mean you're quitting time-jumping also?"

"No," she scoffed. "There's still an evil madman out there who needs to be stopped . . . and some dead relatives of mine who need avenging." She placed a hand on my cheek, and her stance softened. "I can do it alone, but I really do hope you'll jump with me. I need all the help I can get."

My head snapped up. "Really? Are you sure?"

"I'm sure. You're still my time-jumping partner. And we do make an awesome team."

"We weren't an awesome team in Mongolia. You barely talked to me."

"Yeah . . . Maybe I could have handled things better there. But if we just keep things professional and focus on the end goal, then maybe we can get back to how things were on the first jumps."

"And you don't think things are going to be weird?"

She gave a small shrug. "At first. But hopefully over time I'll forget that I actually thought you and I had a future. And you can forget what you feel about me."

I snorted. "I seriously doubt that's ever going to happen."

"You can do it. You have Jenna. Take her bowling. I'm sure she'll love it."

"I guess," I said without conviction.

"You'll be fine." She gave me an expectant look. "So? Will I see you on the next time jump?"

Did I really have a choice? "Sure," I muttered. "Just give me a call whenever you're ready to go."

"Thanks, Dan." She began leaning forward as if to kiss me on the cheek, but changed her mind midway. Instead, she turned and began walking quickly back to her house. I stood in the forest, watching her, with my heart lying trampled and bloody on the ground.

Once she disappeared from view, I sat on the tree trunk and stared at the water trickling in the stream. I'd now officially hit the lowest point in my life. Sam had dumped me. Jenna wasn't talking to me. My dad was dead, and I still wasn't any closer to stopping Victor.

I tossed a pebble into the stream. It plopped into the water and spread out a few ripples that quickly faded away. I grabbed a much larger rock and heaved it at the water. It splashed noisily and threw waves up against the banks. All my life I'd been a pebble, too scared to achieve anything of value. Because of it, everything had been taken from me.

I stood up and dusted the muck off my hands. My pebble days were over. It was time to make some waves.

CHAPTER 25

The streets of DC were nearly empty so early on a Saturday morning. The crowds of tourists were still in their hotels, and I doubted if any politicians bothered working on weekends. Dad had brought me to the capital once when I was younger, and we'd seen some pretty cool things, like the Air and Space Museum and the Washington Monument. It was supposed to be a vacation, but Dad still tried to sneak in history lessons for me every second he could. Even with the subliminal lectures, though, the trip had been fun. Who could have imagined that my next trip to Washington would be to meet with Dad's murderer?

The address Victor had given me didn't lead to one of the regular congressional office buildings. Instead, I ended up at a squat old stone structure just a few streets away from the Capitol. That kind of figured. Victor didn't seem like the type of guy who would be happy with some junior office in a huge public building where every other politician could easily see who he met with. But this place, with its tinted windows, security cameras, steel doors, and concrete barriers, looked great for meetings he wanted to keep private.

I stood on the sidewalk outside the front entrance, snapped a selfie, and posted it, just like I'd done a dozen times already today. If anything bad happened to me here, there'd be a long photographic trail leading right to Victor's doorstep.

6:55 a.m. *Last chance to chicken out.*

But I couldn't run away. Temujin had said that to beat your enemy you had to truly know him, both his weaknesses and his strengths. And when I got down to it, I didn't know much about Victor at all. This was my one chance to learn something I might be able to use.

I walked through the front door to be instantly confronted by a pair of security guards seated behind a desk. "Do you have an appointment?"

"Yes. I'm here to see Victor Stahl."

He gave me a disinterested grunt. "And you are . . . ?"

"Daniel Renfrew."

The other guard scanned his screen. "Third floor. Remove all keys and other metal items from your pockets and proceed through the metal detector. Leave your backpack behind."

I got into the elevator and hit the button for the third floor. Other than the security camera in the corner—watching my every move—the elevator was empty. I half expected it to plummet downward into some underground lair, but it climbed to the third floor and opened on to a hallway straight out of a museum. Paintings of battles covered the walls, and suits of armor stood at intervals, like sentinels. At the far end of the polished marble hall, a massive pair of double doors beckoned. The corridor was eerily quiet, the only sound the squeak of my running shoes as I headed toward the imposing doors.

On reaching them, I pressed the buzzer on the intercom. Instantly my face and the hallway behind me appeared on the display.

"Welcome to Congressman Stahl's office," came a female voice. "Do you have an appointment?"

"I'm Daniel Renfrew."

As the door buzzed, I pushed it open and stepped into a richly carpeted waiting room furnished with four leather chairs and a coffee

table. An older woman in a navy-blue suit peered at me from behind a
desk. "Good morning, Mr. Renfrew. Please have a seat. Mr. Stahl will
be with you in a few minutes. Can I get you anything to drink? Coffee?
Tea? Water?"

"No thank you."

I sat down in one of the chairs and tapped my foot on the floor as I
flipped through several of the world's most boring magazines. Of course
Victor kept me waiting. At seven fifteen, the woman finally rose from
her desk. "Mr. Stahl will see you now."

She pushed open a door, revealing a large room with a monstrous
desk directly in the center. Bookshelves lined the side walls and a large
floor-to-ceiling window gave a panoramic view of the street below.
Victor sat in a leather chair behind the desk, intent on the sheet of
paper in his hands. In the corner, still as a statue, stood Drake, Victor's
bodyguard and constant shadow. The room smelled like a library, with
the distinctive odor of paper, old wood, and leather.

Victor studied the paper a bit longer, then lifted his gaze and gestured to one of the two chairs in front of his desk. "Master Renfrew.
How good of you to come. Please, sit."

Even at too damn early on a Saturday morning, he was dressed
like he was going to the opera: gold cufflinks, little handkerchief in his
suit pocket that matched his tie, graying black hair perfectly styled. I
wanted to hit him. I sat down, though, and kept my hands firmly on
the armrests. Victor didn't bother offering his hand for me to shake,
which was good, because I wouldn't have taken it.

He leaned back in the chair and steepled his fingers. "So, what
brings you to my office?"

"At my father's funeral you said to call you if I ever came to my
senses. Well, I haven't come to my senses, but I'm getting tired of fighting you and not knowing *why* I'm fighting. So I'm looking for information." No use in pretending—with Victor, the direct approach seemed
to work best.

He raised an eyebrow. "I suppose I *could* help you. However, information does not come for free. What are you willing to offer me in return?"

Dealing with Victor was like bargaining with the devil. "What do you want?"

"Like you, what I truly need is information." He leaned forward and raised an eyebrow. "Why don't you and I play a game?"

A game? With Victor? Whatever he had planned, I already knew it wouldn't be fun. "What kind of game?" I asked warily.

"A simple one. For every question I ask, you are allowed one question in return. If I feel you are lying to me, I will stop the game immediately, and that will be the end of your visit. Do you agree?"

"Do I have a choice?"

"Of course. The world is full of choices. Some are just less palatable than others. Your current choice is to either accept my terms or leave."

Bastard. "Fine. I go first."

Victor wagged a finger at me. "My game, my rules. I go first." He brushed at the sleeves of his suit jacket. "Last June, two of my associates ventured into history and failed to return. Their disappearance coincided with your own first foray into the past. What happened to them?"

I swallowed hard and tried to mask my discomfort by pretending to clear my throat. About half a year ago, he'd asked me this same question, and I had told him I knew nothing about their disappearance. Clearly he hadn't believed me. I gripped the chair's armrests as I tried to figure out an answer truthful enough to satisfy his curiosity. "They died," I finally said.

"Really, Daniel? A two-word answer?" He gave me an amused smile. "Just remember that I will answer your questions in kind. Unless you will be satisfied with a similar answer, I suggest you elaborate."

As shown by the Jenna fiasco, I wasn't a good enough liar to wing it. "Fine. The short guy with dark hair died when he barged into my tent one night. He threatened to kill me if I didn't convert to your cause. An Anglo-Saxon friend of mine sank an ax into his back."

I expected Victor to display some sort of anger at this admission, but he merely nodded. "Typical. He always thought himself a larger piece of the puzzle than he really was. His death is no loss." Victor tapped his lips with his fingers. "But what of the larger man—you surely encountered him as well?"

"When is it my turn to ask a question? You've already asked three."

"Patience, Daniel. I assume that whatever questions you put forward will require considerable detail. Allow me my details, so I can wrap up all loose ends. And then I shall answer yours. So tell me, what happened to the other man?"

If it was possible to sink deeper into my chair, I would have. But I couldn't hide from the truth: the face of the man Victor was asking about would always haunt my memory. "I killed him," I said quietly. "I knew the two of them were working together—they had tried to kill me a few days earlier. I set a trap for him, and we fought. I stabbed an arrow into his throat."

Victor stroked his chin. "I am surprised that you managed to ambush him like that. Unlike his colleague, he was quite capable, and not so likely to fall for a trap. Who helped you?"

"No one," I blurted. "I did it alone."

Victor's icy-blue eyes bored into me. "I warned you about lying." The menace in his voice was unmistakable. "You possess neither the skill nor the strength to have defeated a man of his experience and size. If you are trying to hide the culpability of Ms. Cahill in this endeavor, please do not. Rest assured, she will never come to any harm from me."

I sat there, too stunned to answer. Not only had he caught me out in my lie, but he knew Sam was involved and didn't care. First, he let me keep my jump device because of Sam, and now this? What was Sam to him?

Victor chuckled. "I can tell by your stupefied expression that my assumption has hit the mark. I will forgive your transgression because I know you are trying to protect Ms. Cahill, and I admire the nobility of your gesture. However, I need the truth—or you will not get your answers."

"Yeah, all right," I muttered. "She was there, too. She shot him in the leg. That just kind of made him mad, though. I was the one who killed him, because it was either him or me."

"There. Was that so difficult? Now, what would you like to know?"

I had passed his little honesty test, but would he be honest with me? How would I even know if he was lying? "My dad died when his breathing tube was dislodged. Did you murder him?"

"No, I did not."

"Bull!" I jumped up from my seat and slammed my fist on the desktop. "He was in a coma! How else would his breathing tube come out? It had to be you!"

Drake lurched forward but Victor waved him away. "If you are asking me whether I arranged to have his breathing tube removed, thereby causing his death, then the answer is yes," he said calmly. "But 'murder' implies malice—and my actions had a much nobler intent."

"It doesn't matter how you justify it to yourself—you still murdered him!"

Victor ignored my response as he reached into a desk drawer and placed a picture in front of me. It showed about twenty smiling men at what appeared to be a picnic. They were dressed in shorts and T-shirts and all had the time-jumper tattoo on their forearms. Victor was off to one side, and my dad and Sam's dad were standing near him. Dad looked like he might have been in his late twenties. "Like you, your father belonged to an elite brotherhood of warriors—and we take care of our own. None of us should suffer the fate of lying helpless in a hospital bed, breathing only with the aid of machines. Like a Roman gladiator after a valiant battle, he deserved a heroic end to his glorious career." Victor tapped my dad's face in the photo. "I know you will find this hard to believe, but he was a good friend of mine. It pained me to see him a shell of his former self."

I sniffed back the tears welling in the corners of my eyes. I couldn't let the bastard see me cry. "Maybe you shouldn't have stabbed him, then!"

"I regret that day." Victor's tone was heavy with remorse. "It should not have ended the way it did, but he forced my hand. And I must admit that the surprise of seeing you affected my aim. I had hoped to merely wound your father, but my blade landed too low." Victor glanced at the photo and then back at me. "I know you are full of anger toward me—I would not expect otherwise—but understand that when I had your father's life support removed, it was in honor of the warrior he had been. He would never have wanted to survive in that state—a financial and emotional drain on you. I did what was necessary to fulfill the unspoken wishes of my friend."

"But he *could* have survived!"

Victor shook his head gently. "In the unlikely event that he had woken up from his coma, he would not have been in any way the same man. His life would have been a constant struggle, and shame would have overwhelmed his heart at becoming such a burden to you. I did not want that for you or for him, so I gave him a merciful death. I would have expected the same from him had our roles been reversed."

I wiped the tears from my eyes and sat there without saying a word. Victor slid a box of tissues across his desk to me. "Does that answer your question?"

Of all the possible answers I had expected, that wasn't one. "Yeah," I muttered, ignoring the tissues.

"Then, if you feel fit to continue, I would like to ask my next question."

I sniffed back the remaining tears and focused all my hatred across his desk. "Go ahead."

"I know you met with Professor Gervers. What did he tell you?"

"Nothing. He was terrified of you. My entire visit lasted maybe five seconds."

"And did you have contact with any other people in the chrononaut community?"

Chrononaut? Leave it to Victor to find the lamest possible term for something incredibly cool. "I arranged two meetings with these guys named Dave and Brian. They were completely useless. The first time, they kidnapped me and threatened to kill me. The second time, I caught them in a trap, but they still didn't tell me anything useful. That's why I'm here now."

Victor chuckled softly. "Ah yes. Dave and Brian." He pointed to the far side of the picture, where the two of them stood, arms over each other's shoulders. "They were quite the fighters at one point. They cost me several dear friends before I finally convinced them of the wisdom of stepping aside." He nodded to me. "Your next question please, Daniel."

Now was the big one: the point of this entire meeting. "I want to know what you're planning."

"Come, come, Daniel, that isn't a question. It would be truly sad if you did not get the answers you seek solely because you lack the simple ability to formulate a question properly."

Was he seriously giving me a grammar lesson? "Sorry. Can you please go into full detail about your plans to rule the world? There, is that better?"

"Much better." Victor nodded. "And very wise of you to ask." To my surprise, he got up and walked over to the window. "Could you come here, please?" He stood admiring the view of the city with his back to me.

I stepped toward the window. How strong was that glass? Could I kick Victor through it? It was probably bulletproof, meaning the worst he'd get would be a broken nose. Not worth the pain Drake would inflict on me.

I stopped beside Victor, making sure to keep a large space between the two of us, and Drake on the far side of him. Victor pointed toward the street outside. "Tell me, what do you see out there?"

"Buildings."

"Look closer."

A normal city street. A few people walking. Some cars. "Whatever you expect me to notice, I don't see it."

"No. Very few people do. It lurks beneath the surface, eating away at society like a cancer. What you cannot see is the corruption, the fear, and the pettiness of humanity." He turned to face me. "Here, on this serene-looking stretch, there were two shootings, a stabbing, and a woman assaulted, all within the last week, and all within a few blocks of the Capitol." He gestured to the wide expanse of the city visible outside his window. "And this is just one street. Our entire nation suffers from the same fate. We give the illusion of good health, while beneath that facade lies foul corruption. Tell me, Daniel, do you think it right that we are one of the richest countries in the world but so many of our people live below the poverty level? Or that we can afford the most advanced military force in the world but not free health care for everyone?"

"No. But you can save your campaign speeches. There's no chance in hell I'm voting for you."

"We are a nation of rich and poor," he continued, "and the gap between these two is ever widening. But we are not alone when it comes to this imbalance. You would be hard-pressed to find any place in the world where greed and self-interest have not taken hold. The root of our world's problems lies in the self-centered and narrow-minded attitudes that have led us down this path." He turned to me. "Do you disagree with anything I have said so far, Daniel?"

"Are you ever going to answer my question? You just keep yammering on about stuff I can't change."

Victor clenched his fist triumphantly. "But you *can* change the world, Daniel! We are at a turning point in history. The world is in desperate need of a body of people who will unselfishly work together to impose universal changes for the betterment of society."

"Um . . . hello? Ever heard of the United Nations?"

Victor laughed. "The UN is an organization of fools. They are so bogged down by petty self-interests that they have done nothing beneficial for the world in the last sixty years. Nations still wage war on each other, millions of people each year die of disease and starvation, and pollution and climate change threaten our very existence. To save this world, drastic measures must be implemented. Leaders need to come forth—visionaries who can see the greater picture and save the world's people from themselves."

He was slicker than a salesman on a late-night infomercial. He just kept stringing me along with problem after problem to make me desperate to buy his product. "Great speech," I said. "But you still haven't answered my question. What is your stupid plan?"

Victor began pacing slowly, like a tiger in its cage. "Our plan envisions an empire spanning the globe. There have been many empires throughout history, and all have eventually failed. Some—like Alexander the Great's Macedonian empire, or Genghis Khan's Mongol empire—did not survive much longer than their founders. Others, like the Roman Empire, slowly crumbled away under the stress of war, corruption, and mismanagement." He stopped pacing and looked out the window again. "My colleagues and I have learned much from studying the mistakes of the past. For an empire to survive, it must have strong, decisive leadership *always*."

"And let me guess who's going to provide that. You?"

Victor spun around to face me. "No, Daniel," he snapped. "You are not listening. Empires cannot be run by one man. Individuals die, become enfeebled, or at some stage simply lack proper judgment. In this new utopian world, we will sweep aside all existing forms of rule and instead create a new form of government—a chronocracy—with leadership from the time-jumping community." He walked over to his desk, reached into the top drawer, and pulled out a jump rod. "For countless centuries these devices have been passed down from generation to generation, a symbol of our training and dedication. We, the holders of these devices, are the chosen few, the protectors of humanity." He held up the jump rod triumphantly. "We have always worked in the shadows, selflessly giving our lives for the world's future. But what is the point of all this sacrifice? Why do we shed our blood to save the past while selfish, arrogant fools continue to squander our future? Do you think that is just?"

Every bit of me wanted to find something wrong with what he'd said, but I couldn't. "No. It kind of sucks how hard we fight to fix things in history, while everything in our time is a mess."

"Exactly! Now imagine a world where chrononauts ruled in perpetuity. We have proven ourselves to be selfless. We have proven ourselves to have only the ultimate goals of humanity at heart. We could lead humanity away from its corrupt descent and toward a new world of peace and prosperity." He reached his hand toward me, as if offering a gift. "And as holders of time-travel devices, I invite you and Ms. Cahill to be a part of all of this. You would rule along with us, and you could help ensure that the world proceeds down the correct path—instead of its current direction of greed and self-destruction." He clenched his hand tight. "Join me now, and no longer will you merely fix history—you will make it."

And there it was, the end of Victor's rambling sales pitch. The part where I was just supposed to forget he murdered my dad and enthusiastically leap to my feet, thankful that he considered me worthy to join him. How many others had heard this speech and said "I'm in" without bothering to dig deeper? What Victor was offering seemed incredible, but I had one advantage over all the others. Because of what my would-be assassin had told me in Anglo-Saxon times, I knew the price.

"So your plan is to have one big happy world ruled by time jumpers?" I asked. "And you think that's just going to happen if you get elected president?"

"Don't be absurd, Daniel," he chortled. "The grand changes I envision cannot be implemented by one person. I have amassed a body of followers and like-minded individuals from across the world, and together we will bring about a golden civilization where humanity can prosper." He smiled at me—a wide grin with perfectly white teeth—a politician's smile. "Imagine a world where all the boundaries that have separated us are eliminated. One nation. One language. No religion to cloud people's minds. Just people of all races living in harmony. Now tell me, Daniel, is this not a world you would like to be part of?"

"Yeah, it sounds awesome. If this entire rule-the-world thing doesn't work out for you, maybe you could go into sales. But when are you actually going to get to the part about how you're going to achieve all of this?"

Victor's eyes narrowed and he paused but said nothing. It was strange and slightly unnerving to actually see him quiet for once.

"Come on, Victor," I encouraged. "You've given me the flashy commercial, but what's the fine print?"

"Rest assured that the plan is infallible and that its culmination is fast approaching. You would be a fool to reject my more than generous offer."

"That's the best you're going to give me?" I snorted. "You can't expect me to even think about joining you without knowing *exactly* what I'm getting into. And I'm sure Sam would have the same response."

Victor turned to face his bodyguard standing in the corner. "Do you hear that, Drake?" Victor chuckled. "I believe young Daniel here has confused my tolerance of Ms. Cahill's transgressions as some sort of weakness he can use to pry more information out of me." Victor turned back toward me and all humor disappeared from his face. "Your feeble attempt at manipulation would be amusing if it were not so insulting," he said, his tone icy.

Okay, maybe the Sam card was kind of obvious. "If you're trying to hide the fact that you're messing up history," I said, shifting to a different tack, "you don't have to worry—I already know."

One of Victor's eyebrows raised by the slightest fraction. On anyone else, it would have meant nothing, but on Victor it meant that I'd actually surprised him. "Do you now?" Victor slowly stroked his chin for a few seconds, clearly pondering his response. "Tell me, Daniel," he finally said. "What do you know of how time flows?"

Definitely not the question I was expecting from him. "Well . . . uh . . . Sam told me that it's kind of like a river, constantly flowing. And sometimes that river accidentally changes direction, and then we have to jump back in time and fix things to get it back on its proper course."

"A serviceable explanation." He crossed the room to stand in front of a huge medieval tapestry hanging next to the door. It depicted a knight on horseback charging toward a castle on a hill. "Come here please, Daniel."

Warily I shifted to stand a few steps a way from him, closest to the door in case I had to make a run for it.

He swept his hand in a grand motion over the knight and castle. "I like to think of time as more like this tapestry. So many tiny strands, each reflecting a person's life. Some short. Some long. Some of vibrant color that catches the eye, and others just plain, almost invisible. And underneath all these strands are the long strands of the warp, around which all threads are woven, holding them together."

"River, tapestry, does it really make that much of a difference?"

"It does for what I am about to tell you." Carefully, he pinched the end of a tiny thread and plucked it out, then held it up in front of me. "Do you see this thread? I can remove it, and many others like it, yet not affect the design at all. The tapestry still hangs there, a marvel to observe, its integrity unbroken. So it is with our travels into the past. We are only concerned with fixing the long threads of the warp, the ones that run through the entire work and risk unraveling the whole design. If an inconsequential thread is unfortunately plucked out by our actions, the tapestry of history does not become visibly altered." He blew on his fingers and the thread fell away. "Surely you have noticed this?"

"Well . . . yeah. Sam did mention that history can fix itself from minor glitches."

"Exactly, Daniel! History has shown a remarkable tolerance for minor alterations. Now imagine what would happen if a large number of these minor, nonthreatening adjustments were made with almost surgical precision at exactly the right time and place in the past so that they all led to major changes in the present."

I could feel the blood drain from my face as my jaw hung open. "But . . . but . . . the jump devices only take you to glitches. How could you—"

Victor raised his hand, cutting off my question. "I am about to become the president of the most powerful nation on earth. Through my machinations, I have formed the mightiest organization the world will ever see, with world leaders, generals, and titans of business and industry completely obedient to my slightest whim. I did not get to this position of power by divulging the inner secrets of my organization to upstart teenagers who had only recently begun to travel through time. There are limits to our little information game, and this is one of them. Just know this." He pointed to the empty space to the right of the tapestry. "The future has not yet been woven, but mine is the hand that controls the loom."

No evil chuckle. No mad glint in his eye. Just a confidence that what he was saying would happen. Which made things a thousand times scarier.

He clenched his fist and raised it. "Everything my followers desire has become theirs. Wealth. Power. Privilege. Positions of leadership. Those loyal to me have become the elite of the world, and we are heading to a glorious future where chrononauts and their allies will rule." He held out his hand to me. "Pledge your loyalty to me, Daniel, and you will be rewarded. Do not suffer the same fate as those who have tried to go against me." He plucked another tiny thread from the tapestry, held it in front of my face for the briefest of moments, and then blew it off his fingers. "The choice is yours, Daniel."

I stared blankly at him for a few seconds as the enormity of his plot hit me like an avalanche. "But . . . but . . . if you and your followers already have all this power, why do you want to kill billions of people?"

Victor raised an eyebrow. "How do you know of this?"

"My father left me a letter in his will, warning me of the destruction to come. He told me to run as far away as possible."

"Perhaps he felt you needed a vacation. You do seem rather stressed."

"Cut the crap! I thought we agreed no lying!"

Victor's eyes narrowed. "Yes, your father knew of the collateral damage required to bring our plan to fruition. It is on this point that he and I disagreed most of all. He believed that with the current power wielded by my group, humanity could be encouraged to change without violence—but he was wrong." He skimmed his fingers over the tapestry, and a look that almost seemed like sadness crossed his face. "Even as president, I will not have the power I need to enact the changes necessary. I will be given a few short years to push the most popular items on my agenda, and these in turn will be subjected to endless months of politicized debate, and ultimately little will be done."

"But . . . but . . . couldn't you get at least some of your changes in without having to kill off so many people?"

"*Some* is not enough, Daniel," Victor sighed. "The only way to truly bring about the scale of change necessary is to create a worldwide catastrophe. The horrors of World War II broke the British Empire and allowed communism to sweep across half the globe. But even that much destruction was not enough. Governments and nations still stood." In a sudden blur of movement, Victor snatched the tapestry off the wall and threw it to the floor. "My grand vision demands war, plague, famine, and rebellion to be unleashed across all continents." His eyes sparkled with the same intensity that I'd seen in Temujin. "I need governments to topple, borders to shatter, and chaos to reign. Only then, when the last vestiges of modern civilization have been completely destroyed and the world has descended into anarchy, will its people be ready for what we have to offer. I and my allies will send our armies sweeping across the globe, erasing borders, uniting people, and bringing order and peace to a savage world."

I felt like I was going to throw up. His vision was far worse than anything I could have imagined. "You think people will just let you do this? As soon as your nutjob scheme starts, everyone's going to point their fingers at you."

"Your father clearly neglected to include modern history in your curriculum. Allow me to fix his oversight. When America is under attack, its people rally behind their president; to do otherwise is viewed as unpatriotic. Take Pearl Harbor or 9/11—both incidents allowed presidents to wage war with almost no checks on their actions." He waved toward the window and the view of Washington. "Imagine what powers the people of this country will give me when the devastation I envision occurs within our very borders."

I tried to find a flaw in his reasoning, some point that might wipe that irritating, self-satisfied smirk off his face. "People will find out the truth. They'll execute you for treason."

"Truth?" Victor scoffed. "Truth is just a few strokes on a keyboard. It will be whatever I want it to be. And anyone who disagrees will be silenced or branded a traitor."

With each of Victor's points, my spirits plunged a little lower.

He clapped his hands together. "So that is the plan, Daniel. Do you require any further clarifications?"

"No," I muttered. "It's all too clear."

"Good, then I believe it is my turn for a question. Please tell me about your charming friend Ms. Cahill. How has she been faring during your adventures?"

For a second, I didn't even register that he'd stopped talking, my mind was still reeling from the sheer scale of destruction he envisioned. Then Sam's name penetrated my muddled thoughts. "Leave her out of this!"

"Do not fear; I mean her no harm. I only inquire about her health. She is quite a rarity—a female time jumper. I hope you always take good care of her."

Was that some kind of threat? "She's fine."

Victor raised an eyebrow. "Shall I remind you again about me answering in kind?"

I let out a long sigh. "I've jumped with her only three times, but, from what I've seen, she kicks ass and definitely doesn't need me to take care of her. She's saved my life more times than I can count and probably hasn't suffered anything worse than a bruise."

Victor had this creepy look on his face, almost like a proud parent.

"Why do you even care about Sam?" I asked.

Victor gazed fondly at the photo on his desk. It was the only time I'd ever seen him look remotely human. "I promised a good friend I would look after his daughter, and I have kept my word as well as possible. Unfortunately, she insists on traveling into history and, without an experienced hand guiding her on those journeys, I worry. But Robert trained her well."

"You keep saying my dad was your friend, too, but you've been nothing but a pain in my ass. Why do you *really* care so much about what happens to her?"

Victor's head snapped up. "I am finished asking my questions," he said curtly. "And you have only one left. Do you really wish to waste it by inquiring about my interest in Ms. Cahill?"

No, I didn't. I had tons more questions. But the one image that kept leaping to mind was of him pulling threads out of the tapestry and casually discarding them. "You killed my father, broke into my house, stole my jump rod, and threatened me. Since I've met you, I've been living in constant fear of what you'll do to me next. So what's next?"

Victor calmly clasped his hands in front of him. "Nothing."

"Nothing?" I blinked in surprise.

"Yes, Daniel. Nothing. Although you did kill two of my men, I have recovered their time-travel devices and given them to others allied to the cause, so there is no net loss for me. More importantly, in the last few months, you have successfully resolved three time anomalies, which has saved chrononauts loyal to me from risking themselves in the past. So why would I even think of harming you? If anything, I will once again repeat my offer." He reached his hand out to me a second time. "Join me, Daniel. Together with Ms. Cahill, you could rule a continent someday. Everything you could possibly desire could be yours. Why fight against me when I have already won?"

I recoiled from the hand as if it held a live cobra. "I . . . I . . . I can't."

"I understand," Victor said. "I have given you a lot of information to digest and you no doubt still feel animosity toward me. But do not let your anger prevent you from accepting the opportunity of a lifetime. Think about my offer. Discuss it with Ms. Cahill as well. And when you two finally do decide to join me, do not hesitate to call me. But until then . . ." He walked over to the door and pulled it open for me.

"Good luck on your future travels, Daniel," he called as I hurried out of his office. "But be careful in the past. It is dangerous. And make sure to keep Ms. Cahill safe."

I stumbled for the elevator, my mind reeling. Everything about his twisted plan made me sick. Most horrifying of all was that it could actually work.

CHAPTER 26

After the tomblike quiet of Victor's office, the traffic noise on the street startled me out of my horrified daze. Victor needed to be stopped. But how could I, a measly teenager, stop this madman?

I need to call you, I texted Sam, hoping she was awake this early on a Saturday.

A few seconds later, a text appeared: Why?

I sighed and shook my head. Before Mongolia, Sam and I texted and video-chatted almost constantly—now I couldn't send a simple text message without having to justify it. I knew she wanted to keep her distance, but was this how things were going to be between us now?

Too long to explain over text, I replied, and then hit the call button. I didn't bother using video; seeing her right now would only make things a thousand times more painful for me.

It rang a few times before she picked up. "I told you, Dan," she said, sounding still half asleep. "No more personal stuff. We need—"

"Yeah, yeah, I know. I'm not calling about that. I just met with Victor in his office."

"WHAT? Have you lost your mind? Why would you—"

"Look. Can you skip the lecture and just *listen* for a second? Victor actually told me what he has in mind, and let me tell you, we're royally screwed."

"What happened?" The sleepiness was gone from her voice now and she seemed completely alert.

I sat down on the curb, in between two parked cars, and told her everything Victor had said, including the tapestry analogy. After I finished my story, Sam was silent. "You still there?" I asked.

"Yeah, sorry," Sam muttered. "I just woke up, and now you've sprung this on me. I'm just . . . kind of . . . freaked out. This is way worse than anything I imagined. I mean . . . how can he alter the past without creating glitches? And . . . how does he even do it?"

"I've been thinking about that since I left his office. If he's found out how to jump anywhere in time, and not just where glitches send him, then we're screwed—he's won. But I don't think that's true, or he wouldn't have been so secretive. I think they're stuck going to glitches just like we are, which only confuses me more. Like, if we were trying to alter the past, what could we have possibly done in Mongolia? Or Wales? I don't remember there being tons of opportunities to change history when I was enslaved by the Romans."

"There are more than just those few, though. Neither one of us has been jumping for very long. Victor and his guys have been plotting for twenty years—that's a lot of glitches to work with. They could have ended up anywhere in time. And don't forget all the glitches in African and Indian and Latin American history that we never even hear about."

I pinched the bridge of my nose to fight back the rising headache. "You're right. Who knows what they could have done if they landed in the '50s or the '60s?"

"Ugh. That tapestry thing is totally freaking me out. I'm used to looking over my shoulder constantly whenever I go out, eyeing every single person I meet with suspicion. It might seem paranoid, but it's kept me alive so far. But how do we protect ourselves from things that happened in our past?" An uncharacteristic note of fear entered Sam's voice. "I don't want to be another thread Victor just plucks out of his tapestry."

The same horrible thought had been eating at me ever since I left Victor's office. Despite his assurances that he had no plans to target me, I kept wondering if I could actually trust him. But no matter how hard I tried to find some fault in my logic, I kept coming to the same conclusion. "I don't think Victor's going to do anything to us. Or, more particularly, you."

"Me?" Sam snorted. "Besides that creepy moment at your dad's funeral, I've never seen him before. Why would he care about me?"

"That's what I'm trying to figure out. You should have seen him during our meeting. He had this weird look on his face when he talked about you. He even said 'she will never come to any harm from me,' and the very last thing he told me was to make sure you're safe. So he's clearly worried about you. And when I pressed him about it, he just said he was 'good friends' with your dad, and that he had promised to 'look after' you."

"What? That makes no sense. He was good friends with your dad and we saw how that worked out."

"Exactly! But there's got to be something. Think about it. He killed both our dads. He killed your brother. He's stolen jump rods from Dave, Brian, Professor Gervers, and countless other people. But other than a few threats, he hasn't actually done anything to you or me—even after I admitted that we killed two of his guys. Are you absolutely one hundred percent positive there is nothing linking you two?"

"Linking us? Like . . . what? You think I'm the secret love child of him and my mom? First of all . . . ewwww . . . and second of all, hell no! Should I remind you about my hair color, and that my mom and Victor both have black hair?"

"I know. But what then? Why is he protecting you?"

"Look. Instead of trying to figure out why he seems to be my biggest fan, why don't we accept it as fact and use it to our advantage?"

I sat up straighter on the curb. "Like, how?"

"Well, I haven't gotten that far yet." A note of irritation creeped into Sam's voice. "But there has to be something we can do. After all, we've still got our jump devices. If we can't stop him in the present, there must be some way to stop him in the past."

"Right . . . Because we've done *so* much against him in the past already. I'm sure he's just shivering in his shoes at the thought of us jumping again."

"Hey! Like I said, the plan is a work in progress. I'm sure by the time the next glitch happens, we'll think of something."

"I hope so. I'm not ready to jump again without a definite goal. You're right about me and the near-death experiences."

"Wait . . . you mean you *haven't* been trying to get yourself stabbed or enslaved by every joker with a pocketknife?"

"Ha, ha. Very funny. And this is coming from the woman who's suggesting that we jump to some random spot in the past, totally clueless, and hope we magically figure out how to stop Victor." I snorted. "Temujin would have a fit if he heard us talking like this."

"Well Temujin's not here now, is he? So we're stuck with whatever the two of us can think of. And right now, going into the past is all I got. It's not like the good guys are rushing to help us. Hell, you can barely get them to stop kidnapping you. But if you have a better plan, I'm willing to listen."

Sam's words made me think of Dave and Brian and their laptop. Decades of information, all available for the low-low price of one jump device. "You know what? I think I know what we need to do. Dave and Brian have the names of all jumpers who are allied with Victor, right? Plus the dates they traveled out, and where and when they landed in the past."

"Yeah, and? Knowing that stuff won't stop Victor, or they'd already have done it."

"But what if they weren't looking for the *right* way to stop Victor? They were only talking about flipping people against him. But what if we figured out how he's messing up history? It might be hidden there in all of Dave and Brian's information. I know it's kind of iffy, but what do you think?"

"Wow. That actually is a good idea. Just one minor problem: we don't have an extra jump device to trade."

"Yeah, *we* don't. But there were four other time travelers in Mongolia when we first landed. How many will we find the next time there's a glitch?"

Sam paused. "You know they're not going to just hand over their jump devices to us, right? We might have to do some *persuading*. Are you okay with that?"

I would never be free from the memory of the first man I killed. The way his eyes glazed over in shock. The sickly smell of his blood. "No. I'm not. But this is war."

CHAPTER 27

Around the corner, the familiar, prisonlike shape of my school came into view. After suffering the worst spring break ever, trudging back into this depressing place kind of summed up everything that was wrong with my life.

A few days ago, I'd been out on the Mongolian steppe, saving history. I had the sun on my face, wide open grassland ahead of me, and the thump of hooves in my ears. Now I was trapped in the sickly glow of fluorescent light bouncing off beige walls, with lockers banging and students shouting in my ears. The wide berth people had given me after my fight with Nick was gone. I was just a normal kid again, blurring into the background along with everyone else.

At the far end of the hall, I spotted Jenna by her locker and waved to her. She definitely saw me, but she turned her head away and slammed the locker shut, making a pointed display of turning her attention else-where. She'd been like that since the mall. I'd texted her at least a dozen times, and she'd ghosted me. Before my time jump, I'd had the ridiculous idea that I might have to choose between two girls. Now I couldn't figure out which one liked me less.

Everywhere I turned, kids were bragging about their spring breaks. Trips to sunny beaches. Hanging out with friends. Awesome parties. Spending time with family. After Victor had unleashed his plan, how many of them would still be alive?

My morning classes passed in a blur. The teachers blathered on about meaningless crap while I slouched in my chair at the back of the class, thinking only about Victor's plot. How had he managed to mess up history to his advantage? And would Sam and I be able to undo what he'd done? But so far I had come up with nothing, and it had only led to two sleepless nights.

The one glimmer of hope I had left was the fact that I was meeting up with Eric tonight. He had promised to teach me some new device settings; hopefully, he'd have at least one that would prove useful.

At lunch I sat at my regular table, facing Jenna's, hoping she might join me. But she stayed with her friends, her back turned toward me. Any time one of them caught me looking, they'd whisper to her, and she'd hunker down and pay extremely close attention to her lunch while the other girls glared at me.

On the far side of the cafeteria, Nick sat with his friends. His nose had healed since I'd broken it, although his face still looked puffier than I remembered. A cold wave of hate emanated from that little corner of the world toward me. All during lunch I felt his stare, promising revenge.

What am I even doing here?

Maybe I should just take the rest of March off. Maybe even the school year. I clearly wasn't going to learn anything, and there were much more important things to focus on.

At the end of the day, I went to my locker and picked up my backpack, then shuffled out with the rest of the herd. The sidewalks seemed more crowded than usual today. Even with my mind on my meet-up with Eric, I sensed something was up. This many people didn't stick around after school unless a fight was about to happen. I ignored the lingering pain in my calf and picked up my pace. The crowd moved with me.

Oh great . . .

I turned the corner to find Nick and his three friends blocking the sidewalk. Instantly a circle formed around us.

"You messed up my nose, Renfrew!" Nick said. "Now you're going to pay."

This again?

They couldn't beat me last time with four on one—what made them think they could do it today? My eyes swept over the crowd. Nick probably had more friends scattered around, waiting to jump me. Not much I could do about it, though. Even if the entire football team was lurking in wait, this fight was going to happen whether I wanted it to or not.

I clenched my fists until my knuckles cracked. A fight might be just what I needed to help me forget about Victor and my pathetic love life for a few minutes.

"You should pay *me*," I replied. "I improved your face."

"You caught me by surprise last time." He snapped his fingers and Amir, Devon, and Kyle separated themselves from the group to stand behind him. "But we'll see who's laughing after this."

The crowd fell silent. No shouts in support of Nick this time. I guess they finally realized what a loser he really was.

My eyes narrowed as Temujin's advice rang in my head: *Be ruthless and crush those who oppose you, so they never dare to challenge you again.* Clearly I'd been too easy on Nick and his pals in our first fight.

I dropped my backpack and shrugged out of my jacket, wincing as the movement tweaked the wound in my shoulder. "Bring it."

"That's it, Renfrew!" Nick spluttered. He began bouncing from side to side on the balls of his feet, fists raised. To a casual observer, it probably looked like a boxing stance. To me, it just looked like some bad dance moves. As for his three friends, they stood behind him—far behind him.

I snorted at Nick's pathetic display and held my hands loosely in front of me, ready for anything. A hard elbow could probably shatter his nose and cheekbone, while one good kick to the side of his knee would bring him crashing down and probably tear some ligaments too. I just needed him to get within striking distance.

"STOP!"

Nick looked around. Jenna rushed into the circle and stepped in front of me. She faced Nick and splayed her arms out to block him from coming any closer.

What is she doing?

Nick laughed. "What's the matter, Renfrew—you need your girlfriend to save you?"

Jenna's back stiffened. "I'm not saving him, you idiot—I'm saving you."

Nick stopped laughing. "You're crazy. He's going to get his ass kicked."

"Look at him, you moron," Jenna said. "Does he even look the slightest bit scared? He already broke your nose. What part of you is he going to break next?"

Jenna stood there with her hands on her hips and stared Nick down.

I bit my lip to stop myself from smiling. Jenna never ceased to surprise me.

Behind Nick, Kyle looked at me carefully and then shook his head. "You're on your own, bruh," he said to Nick as he backed away. Amir and Devon followed him.

"You guys suck!" Nick yelled after his retreating friends. He took one last look at me, then scowled and stormed off through the crowd, pushing people aside as he went.

Now that the entertainment was over, the crowd began to disperse, quickly leaving Jenna and me alone on the sidewalk.

She turned to me, her head slightly angled down, but her eyes raised. "Hi," she said tentatively, as if unsure how I'd react.

"Hi," I said back, just as tentatively. "What was that all about?"

She shrugged. "I didn't want you getting in trouble. You had a pretty wild look in your eye."

"Well . . . uh . . . thanks, I guess."

"You *guess*?"

"No. You're right. A fight was the last thing I needed. So, thanks." I picked up my coat and backpack from the ground. "What happens now?"

Her face softened as a faint smile emerged, reminding me of when I'd first met her. "Kinda seems like you should take me out for fries or something."

My ears perked up. "Out? As in you and me together in the same place?"

Her smile bloomed. "If you're lucky, I might even let you sit at the same table."

I chuckled and we started walking to the student parking lot. "Uh, not that I really want to talk about last week at the mall, but . . . I know I told you some crazy stuff, and . . . well, I don't have any idea how you feel about it."

Jenna stared at the sidewalk in front of her feet and avoided answering for a few seconds. "I believe you," she finally said.

I stopped walking. "You do? I barely believe it, and I'm living it."

She exhaled slowly. "You told me so many lies that I didn't know what to believe. So I had to look at the facts. Your apartment is a museum. You had genuine Mongolian arrows stuck in you. And you disappeared from right in front of me! So time travel is actually the only thing you've told me that makes sense." She put her hand in mine. "And that means you're pretty incredible."

I felt my cheeks going pink. "Really? So how come you've been avoiding me?"

"I needed time to think. It's not like I could ask anyone for advice."

"But the middle of a fight seemed like the right time to patch things up?"

Jenna laughed. "All right, that might not have been the best timing. I had to jump in, though. I knew you'd destroy him. But what if he got lucky? I'm not really interested in bandaging you up again."

At the burger place, we ordered, then sat down facing each other at a table in the corner. Jenna rested a hand on top of mine. "So, tell me about your spring break." She gave me an encouraging smile. "The real one."

I leaned back in my chair and stared at the ceiling. "You sure?"

"I'm here, aren't I?"

I met her earnest gaze with my own. "All right, you asked for it." And I launched into the whole story of Temujin and his quest to rescue Borte.

Jenna listened without interrupting. She just sat there casually munching from her box of fries, her eyes growing wider by the minute. At the end she blinked and shook her head as if trying to process what I had said. Then she nodded a few times. "So that's what the truth sounds like," she said breathlessly. "Honestly, I don't blame you for lying. If I hadn't seen you disappear, I wouldn't believe a word of it." She glanced at her phone. "Oh crap! We've been here for more than an hour! I have to get home."

She stood up to go and stopped herself. "Do you want to give me a ride?"

I smiled at her. "Absolutely."

As we walked back to my car and made the short drive to her house, she asked me tons of questions about time travel. Some I could answer; others were still mysteries to me. The more I told her, the more relaxed I felt, as if I was dumping a load of heavy books out of my backpack. Time-jumping was such a lonely world; it felt great to finally let someone else in.

After I pulled up in front of Jenna's house, she faced me and put her hands on my shoulders. "I have one more question for you." She peered into my eyes, as if searching for the truth. "What else haven't you told me?"

Oh boy . . . Sam's not a guy. The smiling congressman who's probably going to be the next president killed my dad and wants to wipe out a good chunk of the human race. And I like you way more than I should.

I exhaled slowly and locked eyes with her. "Jenna, I'm sorry. You're going to have to trust me when I tell you some things are safer for you *not* to know. I promise you, though, I've told you everything I can right now."

She kissed me on the cheek. "Okay." Her lips curved up in a mischievous smile. "It's like I'm dating a secret agent."

"Oh, so we're dating now?"

She grinned. "Someone has to protect you from Nick."

I leaned over and kissed her. For half a second I thought of Sam, but I pushed her from my mind. Jenna was here, in my arms. She knew what I was, and she wasn't running away. Which was a hell of a lot more than I could say for Sam.

"You want to stay for dinner?" Jenna asked.

"I can't. I have some more time-jumping stuff I have to do tonight."

Jenna's brow creased. "You're not going to get yourself stuck full of arrows again, are you?"

"No, I should be okay." At least I hoped so. Eric had seemed honest about wanting to meet up with me. But then, things were rarely as they seemed when it came to time jumpers.

CHAPTER 28

Even at eight p.m., the college campus was full of life. Students strolled around the common or just hung out; a group was playing flag football on the well-lit quad. I made sure to wave and make myself noticed by as many of them as possible. Eric seemed like an okay guy, but I'd be a fool to trust him completely. It was safer to have lots of witnesses to my arrival, just in case it turned into a disappearance.

I approached a guy reading on the steps of a nearby building. "Hey. Do you know where the medieval club meets?"

He peered up at me over his glasses as if I was some annoying insect. "Oh, the fantasy dress-up club?"

"Umm . . . yeah, I guess."

He went back to his reading and, without looking, pointed to a brick building across the green.

I hurried over to the building and stopped outside the main entrance. As I stood there, wondering if I had the right place, a girl with shoulder-length braids walked past me. She carried a large cooking pot and had a small piece of bright orange-and-blue-patterned cloth poking out of her backpack. Maybe it was a costume? "Excuse me," I said. "Do you know if this is where the medieval club meets?"

"Yeah." She stopped and looked me up and down. "Are you a member? I don't recognize you."

"Eric invited me. I'm his cousin, Dan."

"Oh yeah," she said, her face brightening. "He said you were coming." She balanced the pot on her hip and stuck out her hand. "I'm Adjoa—or, as I'm known inside the club, Queen Yaa Boakye of the Great Ashanti empire. Come with me." She used her student ID to buzz us through the door, and then she led me into a small lecture hall, where any concerns I had about this being a trap disappeared. About thirty people milled around, dressed as warriors and nobles in bright tunics, colorful cloaks, and flashy jewelry. Unsurprisingly, not a single person was dressed like a peasant.

I chuckled to myself. These people would be really bummed if they ever ended up back in the actual Middle Ages. Lots of peasants—not so many nobles.

Eric was off to one side, wearing the arms and armor of a Roman soldier. His costume looked authentic—probably something one of his dads had brought back from history. He saw me and began walking over. "Dan! Glad you could make it. Everybody, this is Dan. Dan, this is everybody."

A whirl of people said hi or introduced themselves properly, most of them using their character names. I shook hands with more royalty than a Buckingham Palace family reunion. A few did tell me their real names, but I forgot them instantly. Most of the people here seemed to be about Eric's age, but a few looked older, probably grad students.

"So when can we talk?" I asked Eric after all the introductions.

Eric patted the back pocket of his jeans. "I have the whole list of settings here. But you want to just hang out for a bit? You might actually enjoy it."

"I wasn't actually planning—"

Adjoa stood at the front of the room and clapped her hands loudly, cutting off my response. She had changed while I was being introduced to everyone, and now wore the orange-and-blue cloth wrapped around herself as a dress with one end draping over her left arm. Multiple beaded necklaces covered her neck, and her long braids were tucked under a headscarf. "Greetings and salutations, noble peers of the realm and travelers from far and wide!" she announced. "Let the merriment begin!" She placed the large pot on a table at the front of the room and the aroma of a hearty stew wafted through the air.

People began taking their places along the rows of seats in the lecture hall. Eric motioned to the first row. "Come on."

I hadn't really planned on sticking around and being part of his dress-up gang. But it was better than sitting home alone watching TV. I shrugged and sat down, placing at my feet my backpack containing a pair of rattan fighting sticks. Another little precaution in case Eric was planning something.

"Thank you, everyone," Adjoa began. The room quieted instantly. "I, Queen Yaa, will be talking to you today about barley, a wondrous grain used as a staple food in many cultures. And, as a special treat, I have brought this tasty and historically accurate barley stew for all of you to sample."

For the next twenty minutes, Adjoa went on about barley and farming and then explained how she'd made the soup. For most of the presentation my mind wandered, always winding around to Victor and his plot. Although I did pay a bit of attention when she passed around little paper tasting cups.

"So what do you think?" Eric asked when she had finished.

"Tastier than most food I've had in history."

Eric laughed. "No, I mean about the meeting so far."

How to answer that diplomatically? "I guess it's fun to play medieval prince or princess for a night."

Eric clapped his hand on my shoulder, which I considered an oddly friendly gesture from someone I had tried to blow up a few days ago. "Don't worry," he said. "It gets better."

"Could you maybe just give me the jump commands now?"

"Come on, Dan, just trust me. I want you to meet a few people."

"Fine." I slumped back into my chair.

Following Adjoa, a guy who called himself Achilles rambled on about ancient Greek poetry for a while. Then the lecture portion of the evening seemed to be over, and people got up to mingle.

Achilles headed straight to me. He reached out his hand. "Hi, we haven't met yet. I'm Achilles." He had light brown hair and a scruffy beard and wore a white robe draped over one shoulder in the fashion of ancient Greece.

I shook his hand. "Dan."

"Dan?" He laughed. "That won't do. We gotta get you a persona."

"Huh?"

"You know, someone you pretend to be when you come here. Outside this room, I'm Steve, but here I'm Achilles, a rich merchant from Athens." He then launched into the complete personal history of his made-up persona. I had no choice but to listen. Did he talk for ten minutes? Two hours? Just when I was wondering whether it was possible to die of boredom, Eric saved me. "Okay, everybody. It's time to go!" he announced.

Achilles stopped rambling and glanced at his phone. "Nine thirty already?" He looked back at me. "We usually grab some food after this. You wanna come with?"

"Sorry. I, uh—"

"Dan!" Eric called. "Can you stay for a few minutes? I need to get your club paperwork filled out."

I shrugged apologetically to Achilles. "Duty calls." I slid away from the wall and hurried over to Eric as the rest of the crew headed for the door.

Eric grinned. "I see you met Achilles."

"Is he always like that?" I whispered.

"Yup." Eric laughed and pulled a few folded-up sheets of paper from his back pocket and handed it to me. "Here you go. Every command that my dads taught me."

Finally! My hands trembled with anticipation as I unfolded the sheets.

The first page had a detailed pen drawing of the jump rod turned to a specific setting, a description of what the setting did, as well as the activation words. My excitement faded as I read the heading *Traveling to a Time Anomaly*—I already had that one. I flipped through the other pages.

Find Other Time Travel Devices. Had it.

Find Other Time Travelers. Had it.

Leaving a Time Anomaly. Had it.

I flipped to the second-to-last page: *Find Water.* I didn't have that one. It was better than nothing, but it was tough getting excited about. Fresh water was not going to stop Victor's plan.

The final page was titled *Detect Locals.* I studied the description. This setting would allow me to locate "normal" people in the time period I ended up in. It would have been great to have had this one in Mongolia; the Merkits never would have captured me. But other than that, it didn't sound too useful. I leafed through all the pages again, just in case I had missed one. Nope.

"Is that everything?" I asked.

Eric shrugged. "That's all I've learned. Do you know them all?"

"I know some of them. But there are some new ones. Thanks." I didn't want him to feel bad, but I didn't know if I could hide my overwhelming sense of disappointment. I'd been stupid to let myself believe that Eric could help me.

Most of the other club members had changed back into their street clothes and left. Along with Adjoa, Eric, and me, seven other stragglers were still in the room.

I folded the papers and put them away in my back pocket. "Thanks again, Eric," I muttered. "I guess I'll see you."

"Wait," Eric said. "There's one more thing."

Adjoa hurried over to the door and taped a piece of cardboard over its narrow glass pane. "They're gone," she said as she locked the door.

The thud of the deadbolt shocked me into survival mode. The barley soup and Greek poetry had lulled me into a false sense of security. Now I was trapped here with Eric and a bunch of strangers.

Without making it look obvious, I scanned the room for other exits or anyone with weapons. There was only the one way out. And the only weapon I remembered seeing was Eric's Roman sword, which wasn't currently visible, and was probably in his backpack. I edged toward the door, trying not to attract attention, but everyone was watching me.

Eric stepped in front of me and held his hands out to his sides. "Dan, I haven't told you everything about us. This is more than just a medieval club."

"Okay . . ." I casually unzipped my backpack and placed it on the floor at my feet, the pair of fighting sticks inside within easy reach if things got messy.

Eric shook his head. "You've met my dads. They had confidence and drive once, but now they're beaten men. They sit around collecting pictures of time jumpers like they're baseball cards, in the hopes that they'll somehow manage to stop Victor. But they won't." Eric waved a hand around the room. "So I decided to do something."

A tingle of anticipation ran through me. "Are you saying you want to fight Victor?"

"We all do," Adjoa said. "My dad was murdered five years ago during a break-in at our house. The thieves stole nothing but his time-travel device, so I know they were Victor's men. I want revenge."

Another woman stood up. "My father took his own life three weeks after Victor's men visited him and stole his time-navigation device. He chose death over what he considered a meaningless existence."

Each of the people in the room explained how someone they loved had been killed or had suffered because of Victor.

As the last woman told her story, Eric nodded in satisfaction. "So here we are—the orphans of the time community. Just like you, our fathers tried to stand up to Victor, and either died or were so broken in the process that they've become shells of what they used to be. It's taken a couple years, but with the help of some generous anonymous donors, I've pulled this group together from all across the world. We have only one goal—we want to make sure Victor doesn't succeed."

I took a step back, stunned. It had never even occurred to me that there'd be others like me and Sam. Suddenly a whole world of possibilities opened up. They had access to all the notes and knowledge of generations of time jumpers.

"And you want me to join you?" I asked, my voice rising a notch.

"No," Eric replied. "We want you to lead us."

Me? Lead?

I looked around the room. Adjoa and the others were watching me intently. They all looked so hopeful, like I was the sudden answer to their prayers. They'd be so disappointed when they found out I was basically making it up as I went. "I can't," I said. "You got the wrong guy."

"No. We need you," Eric insisted.

"Why? You're all older than me and you already know each other. You're in college; I'm still in high school. Why can't one of you be the leader?"

"Because *you've* jumped back in time," Eric said firmly, "and none of us have. And you've survived multiple meetings with Victor when even our fathers didn't. We need your experience. There's no one left to train us." Eric put a hand on my shoulder, and this time it didn't feel odd at all. "What do you say?"

How could I possibly do this? I was only seventeen—

I stopped myself. If I was back in Mongolia right now, Temujin wouldn't let me get away with whining. He'd look me in the eyes and challenge me to be more. He'd tell me how, at the age of seventeen, he had pulled himself out of slavery to lead an army. He'd say that leadership had nothing to do with age; it was all about knowing what needed doing, and then getting it done.

I already knew we needed to stop Victor. And so far it had been just me and Sam against all of Victor's forces. But here were nine people just begging to help me. Eric could end up being just like Jelme, an incredibly loyal and protective friend who would be with me always. Maybe somewhere in this crew there was my own Bo'orchu, a calming presence in stormiest times, and my own Khasar, a fearless warrior regardless of the odds. But I'd never find out unless I found the courage and pushed myself to become the warrior and leader Temujin had seen in me.

The stakes in this war against Victor were as high as stakes get: the future of humanity. If I couldn't step up to be the leader of a willing group of college kids, I had no chance against Victor and his minions.

I held my fists close to my sides to hide how much my hands were shaking. "All right, I'll try," I said. "But first, I think you need to know what we're really fighting against, and then you can decide if you still want to be part of it."

A silence fell over the Medieval Club as I began telling them about Victor's plans. By the time I was done, the hopeful mood of the room had been replaced with an aura of despair. Some people were visibly angry. Some just sat there, stunned. As a group, they already looked beaten, and we hadn't even started to fight.

It was at times like this that Temujin would start spouting all that mystical-destiny mumbo jumbo of his, about how he was the chosen one of the great blue heaven, and he was destined to bring glory to the Mongols. Well, I didn't believe in destiny, and I sure as hell wasn't the chosen one of the great blue heaven. But this group needed a pep talk, and there was one thing I did believe in.

"Yeah, the odds suck, and if Victor catches us, we're dead. But we're *it*." I thumped a fist against my chest. "We're the last hope this world has.

So you have a choice now. You can either roll over and give up, and hope that Victor decides to spare you, or you can stick with me and *fight*. Just know this: I don't want anyone sticking around who isn't fully committed. Some of us will probably die, and there's a good chance we will fail. All I can offer you is the opportunity to do something against Victor. Because if we don't, no one else will." I met each person's eyes in turn. "So now that you know what we're up against, are you still with me?"

Eric jumped first to his feet. "Hell yes!"

"I'm in too," Adjoa followed.

One by one the others chimed in.

I stood there at the front of the room like a general reviewing his troops. They weren't an invincible horde of Mongols, but I felt an unfamiliar flush of triumph, and my palms tingled with anticipation of our coming battle. The odds still sucked, but somehow just knowing that Sam and I weren't alone in our fight filled me with hope.

I raised my fist above my head so that my tattoo was visible to everyone. "Throughout history, this mark has been the symbol of humanity's protectors. Victor and his buddies want to turn it into the symbol of Earth's conquerors." I punched my fist into the air. "To Victor's defeat!" I shouted.

Nine fists punched the air. "To Victor's defeat!" my little army roared back.

It was almost midnight when I stepped through my front door. I tossed my backpack on the floor and headed over to my weapon wall. Temujin's deel hung in the center, a filthy reminder of the world's greatest conqueror. Gently, I pulled it off the wall and held it, the musty smell of sweat and horses emanating from it. The smell didn't make me gag anymore, though. It reminded me of the Mongolian steppe and of the man this shirt had belonged to.

He'd only been about my age when he'd started his conquest. But through willpower and cunning, he had made his mark on history. He had told me that four things were necessary to defeat any enemy: purpose, willpower, friends to help you, and knowledge of your enemy. At that point, I had been on the path to failure. Sam had abandoned me, I had no friends, and I knew pretty much nothing about Victor's plans or how to stop him.

A lot had changed in the last few days. Thanks to my meeting with Victor, I knew much more about my enemy. And, with Eric's group behind me, I had a whole crew of new friends to help me in my battles. But the most important change had happened in me. I had finally found the courage to step up and take charge.

Temujin's deel hung loosely in my hands, a reminder of the man who believed that anything was achievable as long as you had the will to do it.

I hope you're right, Temujin, because I'm facing the fight of my life. I'm either going to win or I'm going to die trying.

HISTORICAL NOTES

The events of Borte's rescue happened in 1179 CE. The Merkit army, warned of the approaching Mongols, fled their summers pastures, but left many of their people behind to be killed or enslaved. After the rescue, seventeen-year-old Temujin spent the next twenty-seven years in near-constant diplomacy and warfare as he struggled to unite the various tribes of Mongolia. This period of his life is filled with stories of great victories, crushing defeats, and betrayal. During this time, Temujin's two closest friends—Jamukha and To'oril—turned against him because they had grown fearful of his growing power and ambition. Both were defeated. To'oril was killed around 1203 as he was fleeing a battle. Jamukha, after losing many battles against Temujin, found his once-great influence decreasing to the point that he became a bandit. He was captured and executed by Temujin in 1205. With Jamukha's death, all Temujin's foes inside Mongolia had been defeated.

In 1206, at a *kuriltai*—or grand meeting of chiefs—Temujin, at age forty-four, achieved his dream of uniting all the tribes of Mongolia under one banner. He was voted leader of the united Mongolian federation, and he took the title Genghis Khan (or Chinggis Khan in Mongolian).

Historians still aren't sure exactly what Genghis Khan means. *Khan* means "ruler," but the exact translation for the word *Genghis* has been lost over time. Historians can only agree that it was supposed to mean something powerful and all-encompassing, such as "universal" or "all the land."

Once Temujin had the power of all the horse tribes under his command, he turned his attention to his neighbors. He attacked northern and western China, and also the areas now known as Iran, Afghanistan, Kazakhstan, and Russia. As a military leader, he is credited with being one of the most successful generals of all time. He showed great cunning and insight, managing to regularly surprise his enemies by forcing his own armies to travel long distances at great speed, and then seemingly appear out of nowhere.

In warfare, he believed in giving his foes the chance to surrender first. If the enemy chose to fight, Temujin showed little mercy to those he defeated. After he conquered the Tatars, the people who had murdered his father, he had all males taller than the axle of a cart executed. And when his troops captured Merv in modern-day Turkmenistan, it is estimated that over 700,000 people were killed while the rest were sent into slavery or forcibly conscripted into the Mongol army. Although it is difficult to make an accurate count of how many people died during his rule, it is estimated that the Mongols killed more people during their years of conquest than were killed in the whole of World War I.

The legacy Genghis Khan left behind is a very complex one. On one hand, the brutality unleashed by his armies has been unmatched by any army in history. But, despite this savagery, Genghis Khan is credited with being one of the most important men in all of history. By breaking down the borders between China, the Middle East, and Europe, he created a safe travel zone between east and west, allowing for the spread of ideas and trade among all the people living in his empire. As a ruler, he was fair and just to his subjects. He drafted a universal law code for his empire, believed in equality for women, and tolerated all religions. In addition, he believed that a person's nationality and family connections meant nothing, and all that mattered was their ability. For instance, Jebe, one of his four great generals, was a captured warrior who had shot the horse out from under Temujin during a battle. Jebe's skill at battle, as well as his courage, impressed Temujin so much that he made him a general.

As for Jelme, Khasar, Bo'orchu, and Belgutei, they became great figures under Temujin's lead. Belgutei became famous for his strength and his wrestling ability, while Khasar is credited with being one of the greatest archers among all Mongols. Bo'orchu was richly rewarded for his loyalty to Temujin and was given a high-ranking position within Temujin's empire. Jelme became one of Temujin's four great generals and helped spread Mongol conquests across Asia and the Middle East.

Temujin died in 1227, at the age of sixty-five, after having been thrown from his horse. He was buried in an unmarked grave somewhere in Mongolia, which has still not been found to this day. It is rumored to be near Burkhan Khaldun, the sacred mountain, which even to this day is a restricted area within Mongolia.

The Mongol empire did not survive long after Temujin's death. As long as there were competent generals like Jelme and his younger brother Subotai carrying on Temujin's dream, the empire continued to expand. Seventy years after Temujin's death, though, his empire had started to shrink, as Temujin's sons and grandsons spent more time drinking and womanizing than conquering. The empire eventually split, fragments of it ruled by great-grandsons and great-grand-nephews of Temujin.

Today the empire is all but gone. The Mongols did not build great buildings like the Romans, or write epic stories like the Greeks, so not much remains of what was the largest land empire in history. The most notable remnant of Temujin's conquests is in the DNA of people. Temujin conquered so many lands, and took so many women as his slaves and wives, that roughly one in every two hundred males alive today still carries Genghis Khan's DNA.

On a final note, this book is heavily indebted to *The Secret History of the Mongols*, an account of Temujin's life and conquests compiled by an anonymous follower of Temujin only a few years after his death. It is the only known book in existence that speaks about Temujin's life from a Mongolian perspective. Without this important work, the remarkable story of Temujin's early life would have been lost to time.

Names

Throughout the book, I tried to use the contemporary Mongolian names for people and terrain as per *The Secret History of the Mongols*. The only exception is that in many instances I changed *q* to *kh* for ease of pronunciation. So Qasar became Khasar, and Burqan Qaldun became Burkhan Khaldun.

Keluren River = Kherlen River

Tayichi'ut = Taichiud

Kereyit = Kerait

Onngirat = Khongirad

To'oril Khan = Toghrul Khan

Kilqo River = Chikoy River

ACKNOWLEDGMENTS

This book is heavily indebted to the many people who generously spent time and effort to help make it what it is. As always, I want to thank my wife, Pam, and my three kids, Leah, Arawn, and Calvin, for their many read-throughs of the book and recommendations on how to improve it. Pam especially has worked incredibly hard (sometimes battling with me) to provide countless suggestions about pacing, story, sensitivity issues, and so much more. More importantly, I want to thank them for their constant support and love. Writing means that I'm often hammering away at the computer, lost in research, or leaving papers and books lying everywhere, and all four of them graciously accept this part of me.

I would also like to acknowledge the brilliant team of professionals who helped bring this book to life. I'm incredibly fortunate to have two superb editors, Peter Lavery and Maya Myers, who suggested countless improvements to my text. Maya's feedback in particular pushed me to make significant changes to many sections for the sake of clarity or accuracy. In addition, Mark, Megan, and Michela at Imbrifex Books have been fantastic to work with, and have gone above and beyond to ensure the success of the series.

This book is also heavily indebted to the incredible teachers and storytellers who instilled in me a love of history. First off, I would like to thank my mom, who first sparked my interest at a very young age by telling me our own family history. To hear about the struggles she faced as a child growing up in Germany during World War II brought the personal impact of history home to me. And when she told me about our earlier family history, including our original Swedish ancestry and potential Viking heritage, it set a fire underneath me to learn more.

I'd also like to thank my dad for always having historical documentaries on TV during the weekends when I was young. Although I would have preferred to watch cartoons, I did enjoy watching all those shows about wars and famous battles with him. My dad also had his own personal experiences from World War II and the Hungarian Revolution that he would sometimes share, but only rarely.

I'd also like to thank my stepdad, an avid reader of history, who always has some sort of story to tell me that he dug up in one of his books. He is also one of my first readers and biggest supporters.

In the realm of education, four teachers really stood out for me and nurtured my love of history: Mr. Batten, my high school medieval history teacher, who basically gave me free rein to research and present anything; Professor Corbett, my Greek and Roman history professor who had a passion for the subject that was unmatched by any other teacher; Professor Patenall, my Old English professor who instilled in me a love for the Old English language (which inspired *The Last Saxon King*); and Professor Gervers, my medieval history professor who taught me so much about how to read history critically—to understand that just because the words are written in a thousand-year-old document does not mean they are true.

Finally, I would like to thank all past and current members of my critique group. I have learned so much from all who took the time to read my chapters and suggest countless ways to improve them. There have been many members over the years, but the core group of Tom Taylor, Gwen Tuinman, and Cryssa Bazos have been an endless source of support over the last decade.

ABOUT THE AUTHOR

E ver since his mother told him he was descended from Vikings, Andrew Varga has had a fascination for history. He's read hundreds of history books, watched countless historical movies, and earned a BA from the University of Toronto with a specialist in history and a major in English. Andrew has traveled extensively across Europe, where he toured famous castles, museums, and historical sites. During his travels he accumulated a collection of swords, shields, and other medieval weapons that now adorn his personal library. Andrew currently lives in the greater Toronto area with his wife Pam, their three children, and their mini-zoo of two dogs, two cats, a turtle, and some fish. It was his children's love of reading, particularly historical and fantasy stories, that inspired Andrew to write this series. In his spare time, when he isn't writing or editing, Andrew reads history books, jams on guitar, or plays beach volleyball.

Connect with the author online:
🌐 andrewvargaauthor.com
🅕 @AndrewVargaAuthor
📷 @ andrewvargaauthor

This is the third book in the JUMP IN TIME book series. **The Last Saxon King**, was published in March 2023. The second book, **The Celtic Deception** was published in August 2023. The fourth book, **The Spartan Sacrifice**, will be available in August 2025.